Of Gods & Men: Book I

The
Ignoble
Lie

MATTHEW
PETERS

For Susan

In loving memory of
Scott and Jennifer Duke-Sylvester

SUNDAY

1

Under a spring sunset, the pyramids of Giza stood like pointed stone islands in a timeless sea of desert sand. At the northeast corner of the plateau, several armed guards perched atop camels at the base of the Great Pyramid of Khufu. The leader of the security force nodded as three lean bearded men garbed in long, white robes and carrying cameras and other electronic equipment approached. The trio formed a loose line and then trudged up the massive beige limestone blocks to the main entrance on the north face of the pyramid.

When they stepped inside, the cool air moved slightly like a palm frond breeze fanned by ancient servants. The men could still hear the hum of the generator outside as they made their way down a long, sloping, cramped corridor in the pale glow of the electric lighting. Following the metal conduit from the generator, they began climbing a longer passage. Their stated job was simple: set up the cameras needed to film the contents of the recently discovered room behind the west wall of the King's Chamber, one of only two known chambers in the vast structure. Official filming by an international team would commence in the morning and the world would soon learn of the contents.

An hour later, one of the men burst out of the pyramid's entrance covered in blood. Sweat drenched his brow as he bent over, his hands on his knees, trying desperately to suck oxygen into his lungs. Fortunately, the guards were not in sight. After a few moments, he raised himself to a fully standing position and wiped blood from his hands onto his dove-colored djellaba. He looked up at the sky beseechingly. The setting sun was glorious: red, orange, bronze. The scene was somehow new and final: the first sunset and the last. The celestial canvas suddenly looked like an unfolding scroll and for one fleeting moment on that scroll he saw painted what he'd glimpsed in the hidden room.

A golden rectangular chest with two winged lions with human heads on a peaked, shiny lid. Four gold rings were set into the bottom four feet, through which golden poles were placed for carrying. It was—

No, it couldn't be...

Could it?

It was almost impossible to believe, but what if it *was*? After all, it looked exactly as it was described in the Torah, though that source couldn't entirely be trusted.

But if there was even a chance that it was, no matter how small...

At least, that's what they'd told him. And in the end, that was all that really mattered: what *they* had told him. Because the money that would go to his family was more than he could ever make in a whole lifetime.

With shaky hands, he fumbled for his cell phone and punched the #1 button.

"Yes?" a voice said after one ring.

"It's as you feared."

"Now is the time," the voice responded.

"Allahu Akbar," the man whispered and ended the call.

He took a deep breath, the kind a long jumper takes just before the approach, then punched the code on his phone.

He held his breath until the explosive detonated.

Then there was nothing but blackness that stretched into forever.

2

Sitting behind the Resolute Desk, looking over the morning briefing, President John Paul Jenkins couldn't figure how it had all come to this. As vice president he'd been thrust into office after President Quinn's assassination last August, and he'd only garnered a slim victory in November. But the flailing economy had rallied in the new year, and now the stock market was robust, credit loose, unemployment low. Of course, he couldn't take all the credit for the turnaround. He paused in his reverie and ran a hand over the plum-colored leather cover of the family Bible next to the phone. God oversaw everything, no matter how big or small. Yes. It'd be blasphemy to take all the credit.

Things had been going swimmingly until two weeks ago...

He still couldn't understand it. Executive Order 15721 was nothing more than a statement of the obvious: it declared the U.S. a Judeo-Christian nation, limited immigration from suspect countries, and put funding of religious education on a par with public secular education. The twin threat of Islamic extremism from abroad and secularism at home made it all necessary. But incredibly not everyone saw it that way, and last week he'd been impeached by the House. Now, all that was left before being unceremoniously booted from office was his trial in the Senate. And that started tomorrow.

"I need to see you in the Situation Room," Waverley Banner said coolly, breezing into the office. The chief of staff's lanky build, composed manner, and confident swagger was that of a frontier gunslinger.

Startled, Jenkins nodded, suddenly afraid his belief that things couldn't get worse was about to be disproven.

He was so wrapped in fear that his arrival in the Situation Room seemed to come about via teleporter. Despite the surgery-bright lighting he was only vaguely aware of the formidable table centerstage, guarded by government-black wheeled chairs, the plush seats against the 21st century whisper walls where flat-screen TVs hung, and the booths for private phone calls, complete with privacy glass windows that could frost at the touch of a button.

Banner handed him a security briefing and motioned him to sit. "I want to bring you up to speed, Mr. President, before the rest of the NSC joins us."

Jenkins sat ramrod straight, heart thumping. Assembling the NSC was just a formality; this tête-à-tête with Banner would dictate the official response to whatever crisis existed.

"At approximately 8:00 p.m. Cairo time there was a terrorist attack on the Great Pyramid."

The president stared at the thin-lipped mouth that uttered the words. "What do we know?" he managed. The words tasted bitter. That the attack happened on the Lord's Day was especially blasphemous.

"ISIS claimed responsibility. And there's something else." Here Banner paused and eyed the president closely and dispassionately, almost as if examining a tiny insect under a microscope. "They're planning more attacks, in Egypt and here. But if we handle the optics right, this could work to our advantage."

"How?"

Banner took a deep breath then spoke in the resolute

manner of a preacher. "Their threat to attack synagogues and churches shows that the gravest danger to our security comes from forces outside the Judeo-Christian tradition, that Islam is America's number one enemy. You're the most faith-based president this country has ever had. Who better than you to defend against such a threat? The more we cast things in such terms, the more people will insist you stay on. They'll demand it. Why would anyone want to switch leaders when the country is under attack by Islamic fascists?"

"You don't think Congress has any idea about our relationship with the—" Jenkins began.

"No, Mr. President. I'm certain it does not."

"Is there any way to prevent the attacks on our country? I mean what senator in his right mind would vote to remove me if my counterterrorist efforts saved American lives?"

Banner hesitated for a moment. "There may be a way. ISIS raised a quid pro quo. Here's what they want..."

3

The doorbell startled Scott Larson and caused Isabelle, his cat, to scurry off to hide. He wasn't expecting anyone. Other than Zady, Brynn, and Aleister, no one ever dropped by his house in the D.C. burbs for a social call. And those visits were always preceded by a text—his preferred method of communication. It didn't require talking to people, and just about anything was better than *that*. But when the doorbell rang a second time, he raced downstairs, worried it was bad news.

His trepidation grew when he peeked out the window. Zady and Brynn stood on either side of their uncle's wheelchair. Beyond them, the maroon Bentley was parked in the semi-circular driveway. Larson opened the door and ushered them inside, trying to read faces for any signs of trouble, not exactly his forte.

"News flash," Zady said as they headed to the parlor. The sisters sank on opposite ends of the sofa; Aleister parked near Zady. Larson pulled up a chair and braced himself.

But when Zady spoke, the words didn't register right away. *Terrorist attack. Great Pyramid. ISIS responsible. Possible attacks on*

U.S. churches and synagogues. He heard what she said but couldn't absorb it.

Aleister, by force of habit, began rummaging through the pockets of his safari jacket looking for a cigar, but stopped when Zady glared at him. "The terrorists have offered a quid pro quo," he said. "ISIS promises not to carry out more attacks if they get the nameplate by noon tomorrow. They also want the coordinates of the cave."

Everything else receded as Larson tried hard to process things. His eyes rested on a framed photo on the end table, of a young bride and groom. Dru Chesley—striking in her mermaid dress, yellow hair, and violet eyes—stood close to her big, muscular groom, who smiled at her with soft, tender fascination. Brent always adored Dru. But they were dead, victims of a mass shooting at last year's Fourth of July parade. They'd left Larson this house, one of several they'd owned, and enough money for a lifetime, especially for an ex-Jesuit. In Larson's efforts to preserve it, it had become a mausoleum to their memory.

Brent had dragged Larson into the case that had changed his life. More than a year ago, a senator, Patrick Walker, was murdered in a confessional in D.C. A scroll with religious connotations had been found among his possessions, and FBI Agent Brent Chesley had called on Larson, his old college pal, for insight. The senator's murder was never solved, but Larson's involvement in the case had nearly led to his own death, thanks to an attempt on his life by his own order, and the discovery of a book, in a cave in Afghanistan, filled with shocking revelations.

It was the book ISIS wanted now, a collection of testimony gospels, firsthand accounts of events in first-century Judea. The accounts alleged that after the death of John the Baptist, Jesus had concocted a plot to make it look like he was the long-awaited Messiah by fulfilling the Old Testament prophecies ascribed to him. He was aided in this endeavor by his blood brothers—James, Peter, Judas, and Joseph, a literal rendering of

Matthew 13:55. After the crucifixion, Jesus' brothers had removed his body from the tomb to make it look as if he'd risen from the dead and claimed that anyone who did what the brothers said, would be granted eternal life.

So shocked was Larson by what he'd read, and so afraid its disclosure would create pandemonium, that—much to Zady's chagrin—he'd left the book where he'd found it: in a small chamber in the cave, behind a portcullis. The portcullis could only be raised by inserting rocks with the names of the brothers on them (stone nameplates of a sort) that were embedded in the walls of the cave. There were six nameplates in all—John, Jesus, James, Peter, Judas, and Joseph, which had to be pried from the walls and placed in the right order in slots in the cave floor. Once this was accomplished, and by some unknown mechanism, the portcullis lifted, giving access to the small chamber and the book.

Larson had absconded with one of the nameplates necessary to access the book—the one marked Joseph—to prevent anyone else from getting it, had hidden it so that only he knew its location. He'd done it to protect Zady. This was what ISIS wanted, along with the coordinates of the cave. Just what they were planning to do with the book was anybody's guess, though blackmail cracked Larson's top-ten list of possibilities.

"And you want my opinion as to what we should do," Larson said, returning his focus to the present. "Well, it's quite simple, really. We should wait."

4

The Kennedy Caucus Room in the Russell Office Building served as the meeting place for the fifty-one Democratic senators. A dozen Corinthian columns flanked the room's long sides and French windows painted it with afternoon sun, infusing the rosettes and acanthus leaves on the ceiling with a golden glow. The lemony smell of furniture polish hung in the air, while at the head of a table draped in green damask, Majority Leader Madge Roberts sat alongside Fred Corrigan, the caucus chairman.

Corrigan brought the meeting to order with three brisk taps of his gavel. "Senators," he drawled in a thick Georgian accent, "I've called this meeting to give y'all a sense of what's gonna happen tomorrow. I've asked Senator Roberts to sit with me. She'll help answer your questions.

"The House has chosen five members to present the case against President Jenkins. Chairwoman of the House Judiciary Committee Ananya Chandler will serve as the chief prosecutor and will present us with the Articles of Impeachment. Then we'll adjourn and meet with our colleagues to try to agree on some procedural matters: a timeframe for the trial, if witnesses —including the president—will be called, whether rebuttals will be allowed, how questions will be handled, and so forth. Speaking of which, I'm sure you have some questions now."

A senator in the front row raised his hand.

Roberts' cell phone buzzed. She took her phone out of her jacket. A text from her chief of staff about an urgent call in her office down the hall.

She excused herself and left the room, trying to calm her stomach-flutters. It couldn't be good news—urgent phone calls never were. When she got to her office Carl Thompson was leaning his considerable bulk against her desk, arms folded across his chest.

"I thought you left," Roberts said.

"The phone rang as I was headin' out."

"Who is it?"

"Aleister Mabrey."

Mabrey was a private security contractor Roberts had worked closely with in the past, his company DoveCo. deploying forces, mostly peacekeepers, to various hotspots around the globe. Over time they developed a friendship. And since his intelligence-gathering capabilities and contacts inside the capital were almost unparalleled, Roberts had come to rely on him for security updates over the past few years, especially while the opposing party—secretive, and eschewing bipartisanship—occupied the Oval Office.

She picked up the receiver and started to push the button to take the call when she noticed Thompson staring at her. "Is there anything else, Carl?"

"No, ma'am. I just thought you might like it if I stuck around. In case you need anything."

Roberts suspected that whatever Mabrey was about to say was not something she should share, at least not right away. She might be able to tell Carl at some point, but she wanted to first hear the news alone.

"That won't be necessary."

"But—"

"Carl, I said that won't be necessary."

Thompson started to say something then stopped.

"Good afternoon, Carl."

"Good afternoon, ma'am." Thompson left and shut the door behind him.

Roberts put the receiver up to her ear and pushed the button. "What cha got for me, Aleister?"

Mabrey wasted no time on pleasantries. "There's been an attack on the Great Pyramid of Giza. Four dead. ISIS has claimed responsibility. More attacks are on the horizon, in Egypt and here."

"Good Lord," Roberts said. "I don't have to tell you the timing couldn't be worse. The trial starts tomorrow."

"I'm well aware." There was a pause. "I can't go into the details but try to stay focused on the trial."

"What about more attacks?"

Mabrey drew a deep breath. "There might be a way to prevent them," he said slowly.

"How?"

"I'd rather not say. I just ask that you trust me."

"I do trust you, Aleister."

"Thank you. I'll do everything in my power to prove your trust warranted. Stiff upper lip."

"Stiff upper lip," Roberts said then hung up.

Scanning her office, she took a minute to compose herself. She drew comfort from the familiar surroundings, the lace curtains, Berber carpeting, comfortable plush chairs. Her eyes gravitated to the painting above her desk. A couple of years ago, she'd replaced the canvas print of Monet's *Garden at Giverny* with a copy of Jacob Lawrence's *Daybreak—A Time to Rest*, part of a multi-paneled tribute to Harriet Tubman. In the print over her desk, Tubman lay face-up, a rifle across her chest, hiding in the reeds with a young couple and their baby. Tubman's feet were the centerpiece. Enormous. Grossly disproportioned. The toll of every long, arduous journey visible in the ridges, crevices, and muscles, which looked more like rock carvings than fleshy extremities. The painting always reminded Roberts that the price of freedom was eternal vigilance, the road long and hard. A person often grew dog tired along the way.

The walk back to the Kennedy room calmed her a bit. As she entered, the anxious eyes of her colleagues were upon her, their eager, upturned faces like meerkats. Corrigan paused mid-sentence until Roberts sat.

"What did I miss?" she whispered.

"Everything all right?" he asked from the corner of his mouth.

"Not exactly."

5

Underneath a car park at the Vatican Library, Pope Innocent XIV parted company with his security forces and proceeded deep into the shadowy recesses of the Apostolic Archives. At his side a tethered Bisschen, his mini dachshund, pumped his little legs furiously to keep up. The dog was a carbon copy of the pope's childhood pup, Hermann: mottled brown, ten inches long, the bold, confident swagger of a dog ten times his size. One of the first things Innocent did after becoming pope two years before was to lift the ban against pets in the papal apartments.

Innocent stopped when he came to two shelves, smooshed together, on his left. At the tug of the leash, Bisschen heeled and peered up at his human with sad round eyes. With some effort, the pope turned a crank. Slowly the shelves parted, revealing a metal door in a brick wall at the end of the aisle. Innocent coughed as he neared a pink infrared illuminator and switched the leash from his right to his left hand. He placed his right palm on the green touchscreen and looked straight ahead. A beep sounded. He entered the twelve-digit passcode. A lock popped. He twisted a metal knob, swung the door open, and went in, tugging

Bisschen along. After flipping the overhead light on, he turned around to shut the door.

When he did, he glimpsed Cardinal O'Rourke, the prefect of the papal household, plodding down the main aisle. The pope had forgotten to crank the shelves back into place! Horrified, he yanked the door closed and fell against it, shuddering, silently reprimanding himself for his memory lapse and his overall weakness. Here he was, the Supreme Pontiff, the sole legitimate heir of Saint Peter, the ultimate representative of Christ's power on Earth, and he was acting like a doddering old fool. What was wrong with him? *Yes, what indeed?*

Bisschen's bark interrupted his self-castigation. Innocent shushed him then closed his eyes tight, a vision of O'Rourke etched into his vision. A holdover from the pope's predecessor, the tall, slim, drooped, and bearded cardinal resembled an Old Testament prophet. More than once, when he and Innocent were alone, he'd say, in a slow, deep voice, and out of the clear blue sky, "'For the wages of sin is death.'"

And surely the passage wasn't coincidental. It could only refer to the measures Innocent had taken to secure the papacy.

On second thought, maybe it wasn't O'Rourke who'd passed by. Occasionally—increasingly more so—Innocent swore he saw him at times and in places he simply couldn't be. But the pope decided to brave his fears and check. As quietly as he could, he opened the door, tiptoed to the end of the stacks, and craned his neck around the shelves.

No sign of the cardinal.

After cranking the shelves back into place, Innocent returned to the primitive bunker, trying to push away his fear. He sat unceremoniously in the battered leather chair in front of the worn desk, convinced the meager furnishings were a not-so-subtle means of humbling him. Bisschen jumped in his lap, onto the desk, and curled beside the monitor. Innocent petted the tiny dog who responded with a warm, wet hand-lick. As the pope readied himself, blood pounded against the back of his throat and a shameful vulnerability, as if he'd been caught viewing porn, swept over him. He jiggled the mouse until the cursor appeared. The clock at the bottom right corner of the screen showed 10:00 p.m. Right on time. He took a deep breath then slowly typed the word he always used to start things off:

GREETINGS

His salutation was returned in a similar fashion.

Then he typed the question that had consumed him since ISIS' attack on the Great Pyramid:

WHAT CAN I DO TO HELP?

The reply was instant:

KEEP DOING WHAT YOU'RE DOING

He took this to mean that he should continue doing what he'd been told was *the* mission of his papacy: uniting the world's Christians—Catholics and Protestants—against Islam. But there was another question he had, one that concerned the impeached U.S. president and the start of his trial in the Senate tomorrow morning:

WHAT ABOUT JENKINS?

HOLD STEADY

Then a new message appeared:

WE NEED PETER'S PENCE

This was followed by specific instructions to deposit the money in a Swiss bank account in the next twenty-four hours.

Innocent's heart throbbed like a hummingbird. He gulped air, but it was like dry-swallowing a horse pill. Now they wanted his private slush fund, which amounted to several billion dollars.

"How dare they!" he exclaimed, pounding the table, which caused Bisschen to jump. Just as he was about to blast off a response, another message appeared:

SIGNING OFF

Innocent closed his eyes. What should he do? He couldn't turn over Peter's Pence. But if he didn't...

Well, he didn't even want to think of what could happen.

6

After making sure the door to the main corridor of the West Wing was completely shut, President Jenkins stepped behind his desk, sank into the leather chair, and picked up the receiver. He hadn't been surprised when Banner, who sat across from him in one of four chairs arranged in a permanent semicircle, had said the pope was on the line.

Jenkins coughed lightly into his hand then spoke. "Good afternoon, Your Holiness. Or should I say good evening?"

"Yes, Mr. President, it is late here. The Church is terribly saddened by the bombing in Giza and prays your country will be spared. May our Lord Jesus Christ wrap the world in His loving embrace, comfort the afflicted, and grant us His everlasting peace."

Jenkins was about to say "amen," but the pope rushed ahead:

"With regard to ISIS' quid pro quo—"

"As you know, Your Holiness," Jenkins interrupted, "America stands firm in its resolve to never negotiate with terrorists."

"Yes," the pope replied. "I understand your reluctance to

turn over the nameplate. I would like to propose an alternative. One that might benefit all parties involved."

"What kind of alternative?" Jenkins asked.

"I'm sure neither you nor anyone else wishes to see the death toll rise, especially at the cost of American lives. But instead of you handing over the nameplate, which admittedly risks tarnishing your administration, what if I did?"

"You?"

"Yes, Mr. President. If you retrieve the nameplate from Scott Larson, I'll make sure it's delivered into the right hands. That way the Church would incur the burden of dealing with ISIS and lives would be saved."

Jenkins asked Innocent to hold, rested the phone against his chest, and looked at his COS for guidance.

Banner extended an index finger. "First, getting the nameplate wouldn't be easy. Among other things, we've got the ever-meddling Mabrey to worry about. Second, there's no guarantee ISIS would keep its end of the bargain. Even if they get the nameplate, who's to say they won't carry out more attacks? Reject the offer."

"Your points are well taken," he told Banner.

"One more thing, Mr. President. To make sure the nameplate isn't turned over to ISIS, we need to watch Larson. If he leaves his house in the next twenty-four hours, we should follow him."

"Let's make it happen," Jenkins said then pushed a button on the console and held the phone up to his ear. "You still there, Your Holiness?"

"Yes, I'm *still* here," the pope replied.

"I'm afraid I must decline your generous offer. But I can't tell you how much I appreciate your willingness to help. I know that God—"

The pope mumbled something then the line went dead. Jenkins held the phone away from his ear and stared at it, perplexed. After a moment, he placed it on the receiver and shook his head.

Banner stared at him.

"I can't say for sure, but right before the call ended, I could've sworn the pope muttered something under his breath."

"Do you know what it was?"

Jenkins shook his head. "At first, I didn't. But now that I think about it, it sounded like 'Goddamn you to hell.'"

7

hortly after eleven p.m., Larson sat at his desk, playing solitaire on his computer. Though the Georgian house was spacious, he essentially lived in this one room. He placed a red eight below a black nine, thinking how the conversation with Zady had gone south after urging caution when it came to meeting ISIS' demands for the nameplate and coordinates to the cave in Afghanistan. The only way he'd been able to placate her was by saying he'd decide by midnight.

Zady...

He'd met her when he was teaching at Georgetown almost a year and a half ago. She'd come to a public lecture he was giving on the Dead Sea Scrolls and the Essene community that lived where the scrolls were found. She'd asked a question about the secret knowledge some said the Essenes and Gnostic groups like the Cathars and Knights Templar possessed. He'd dismissed it as conspiracy theory nonsense. That same night, Senator Patrick Walker was murdered. When, at Brent's request, he went to research the religious scroll found among the senator's possessions, he found Zady behind the reference desk at the Library of Congress, where she was doing an internship.

She'd asked him to coffee and went on to say that although she'd been told her parents had died in a car crash in France when she was a child, she'd become suspicious about the real cause of their deaths. She and her sister had been raised by her mom's brother, Aleister Mabrey, an Englishman, and owner of DoveCo., one of the largest private security companies in the world. Zady told him she'd recently come across her mom's journal. It was in pencil, which was a little odd, and in the last entry, her mom had erased a paragraph and wrote something over it. But she hadn't completely erased it. When Zady scrutinized it, it looked as if it said something about a search for secret Gnostic knowledge and mentioned Senator Walker. The entry, years old, fanned Zady's suspicions about the loss of her parents.

Shortly after their coffee klatch, Larson's Jesuit roommate had tried to kill him. Larson went on the lam, leaving his job and the Church. Zady had come to his aid and suggested they head to the south of France. Not only had her parents died there, but it was where the Cathars had made their last stand, at the fortress of Montségur in the Pyrenees. The night before they were massacred in 1244, four Cathars secreted a treasure off the mountain. Zady thought this might be the secret knowledge mentioned in her mom's journal, and which Walker might have been associated with. Her hunch proved correct. Among the fortress ruins, they'd found the first of many clues that led them on a journey from France to Italy, then on to Bulgaria, Armenia, and finally Afghanistan, where they'd found the controversial book about Jesus and his brothers.

Despite all that, Larson never discovered Walker's killer. Nor had Zady learned if her parents were murdered, as she suspected they were. But things had quieted down since they'd gotten back from Afghanistan over a year ago—a fact he attributed in no small part to his decision to leave the testimony gospels in the cave. And he didn't really feel like kicking

the hornet's nest in a way that might have unpleasant consequences, for instance, someone trying to kill him again.

Except...

No. He really didn't want to think about it like that. But...
Well, Dru and Brent were killed in a mass shooting at last year's
Fourth of July parade. Then President Quinn was assassinated
by a crazy young neo-fascist. And, of course, the pope had
died—

But no harm or even threat had come to Scott, Zady, or
Brynn. Of course, a lot of that was due to Mabrey. But getting
involved now, turning the nameplate over to ISIS, threatened to
end whatever ceasefire, however fragile, was in place.

A fluffy white ball materialized on the open windowsill next
to the desk. Isabelle stretched herself, settled into the sphinx-
pose then angled her head at him. Larson stroked the fur damp
from self-cleaning. Knowing that cats narrow their eyes when
showing affection, he took it as a good sign when she squinted
at him.

"What'll it be, Iz?" Larson asked, rubbing the cat's ears. It
was one of many times he wished she could talk.

But he knew the answer.

Larson cast one more look at Isabelle before grabbing his
cell off the desk. He pressed Zady's number and waited for her
to answer.

"Yeah," she said after the second ring.

"I'll give you the nameplate," was all he said.

MONDAY

8

"Hear ye! Hear ye!" the sergeant at arms declared from the center aisle of the Senate chamber at nine o'clock that morning. "All persons are ordered to keep silent, on pain of imprisonment, while the House of Representatives exhibits to the Senate the articles of impeachment against John Paul Jenkins, President of the United States."

Atop the chamber's rostrum, Madge Roberts stiffened in her chair. As president pro tempore, she would preside over the chamber until Chief Justice Timothy Buckner arrived. She looked up at the galleries packed with journalists, officials, and tourists. The cameras were hot; except for the deliberations before the final vote, the entire trial would be televised. Everyone watched as the handful of House prosecutors entered the chamber, with Representative Ananya Chandler leading the way.

From the well of the Senate, Chandler addressed Roberts in her soothing, dulcet tone. "Ms. President, the managers of the House of Representatives are ready to present the articles of impeachment. While president of the United States, John Paul Jenkins, in violation of his constitutional oath to faithfully execute the office of president of the United States and, to the best of his ability, preserve, protect, and defend the Constitution, and despite his constitutional duty to take care that the laws be faithfully executed, has willfully violated the United States Constitution by Executive Order 15721, which declares America a Judeo-Christian nation and orders all executive agencies to act accordingly. This order violates the Establishment Clause, the Free Speech Clause, the Free Exercise Clause, and the Equal Protection Clause. In this, John Paul Jenkins has broken the letter and the spirit of the Constitution, has failed to uphold the oath he took upon assuming the presidency, and has acted in a manner subversive of the rule of law and justice, to the manifest injury of the people of the United States."

When Chandler had finished, she and the rest of the House prosecutors seated themselves at a table in front of the Democratic senators. The four lawyers responsible for the president's defense sat at a table in front of the Republicans. Everyone stood as Chief Justice Buckner entered the chamber. He ascended the rostrum's steps and stood beside Roberts, whose duty it was to swear him in.

"Senators," Buckner said, "I attend the Senate in conformity with your notice, for the purpose of joining you for the trial of the president of the United States. I am now ready to take the oath." He raised his right hand and placed his left hand on the Bible.

As she swore him in, the irony of the situation—using the Bible to swear in the chief justice to preside over the trial of a president who'd violated the separation between church and state—wasn't lost on Roberts. Pondering the wisdom of the ban on all references to God in France's parliament, she stepped down from the rostrum and stood next to her desk on the aisle floor.

Buckner administered the oath to the senators, followed by a roll call attendance. The senators then approached the front of the room and signed the Oath Book with a black ink Parker Vector pen specially inscribed for the occasion. When everyone had signed and returned to their seats, Buckner asked everyone to stand and join in the Pledge of Allegiance.

When that was finished, he addressed those present. "Senators, ladies, and gentlemen, before you take your seats, I'd like to start things off with a prayer. Reverend Neville if you will." The judge stepped aside, so the reverend could take his place at the microphone.

Neville closed his eyes and bowed his head. Roberts, struck once again by the irony, watched most of the senators do the same. "Father in heaven, today we seek Your wisdom as we embark upon the task entrusted to the Senate by the Constitution of the United States. We ask that you guide each member of this chamber in determining President Jenkins' guilt or innocence. We also ask that the love and mercy of Your only begotten Son dwell in our hearts today and throughout these proceedings. We pray this in the Most Holy Name of Jesus Christ our Lord and Savior. Amen."

Roberts rolled her eyes. The battle between church and state was on.

9

Larson, Brynn, and Aleister were in their usual places in Larson's parlor at eleven o'clock that morning. Zady paced furiously before them.

"I don't know how all of you can be so calm," Zady said. "We've only got an hour."

But Larson was far from calm. While ISIS had taken credit for bombing the pyramid and given them until noon to turn over the nameplate, there'd been no follow-up communication telling them how to do so. The only thing to do was wait.

"Check your phone again," Zady told Larson. "Maybe they sent an email or a text. Aren't you glad I showed you how to link your email to your phone?"

"Very glad," he said. "But I just checked and there's nothing. Besides, I'd hear it."

"Unless the volume's too low. Or off."

"Give me a little credit," Larson said, fishing his phone out of his pocket. "You always assume the worst when it comes to —" He stopped when he saw that he'd accidentally turned off the sound.

"When it comes to what?" Zady asked.

"Never mind," he said, tapping the volume button.

"I swear, Scott, if your head wasn't—"

"Enough," Aleister said. "We have more important things to focus on. We need to decide what we'll do if we don't hear anything in the next few minutes."

"There's really not much we can do, right?" Brynn said. "We don't know where to take the nameplate."

Zady glowered. "I don't understand you, Brynn, or you," she said, brusquely nodding at Larson. "Is being passive a Catholic thing, because you two have cornered the market."

Larson looked at Brynn, who gave him an awkward smile. Until last year, Brynn had not only been a practicing Catholic, but a novitiate in the Sisters of Saint Joseph of Medaille—much to Zady's chagrin, and Aleister's, both of whom had a hatred of the Church that bordered on pathological. After Brynn learned of the attempt on Larson's life, she reconsidered her calling and left the order. Despite that, she maintained a level of faith that far outstripped Larson's.

Just then his and Zady's phones dinged.

"Well, that's weird," Zady said.

Larson looked at his phone. The text message consisted of three words:

JEFFERSON MEMORIAL NOON

The sender was unidentified.

"Great," he said. "You get anything more than 'Jefferson Memorial Noon' from an anonymous sender?"

"Nope," Zady replied. "And isn't it just a tiny bit odd that we both got the same message at the exact same time?"

"Should we try texting them back?" Larson said.

"We could," Aleister said. "But I don't think it would do any good. And we can't trace it because my guess is the sender used a burner."

Larson looked questioningly at him.

"Haven't you ever seen a spy movie or read a novel where

they use burner phones?" Zady asked. When Larson remained silent, she went on. "You can pick them up at any convenience store. You use them then throw them away. They're virtually untraceable."

"Great," Larson said. The day just kept getting better.

Zady shrugged. "The one good thing is we came in two cars."

"You and Scott go on ahead," Aleister said. "Brynn and I will meet you at the memorial. I'll arrange security."

"No time for that," Zady said. "C'mon, Scott." She dashed out into the rain that had just started to fall.

"See you guys there," Larson called over his shoulder. He raced to the white BMW parked in front of the maroon Bentley. Behind the wheel, Zady reached over and opened the door.

"What took you so long?" she asked.

Larson sank into the passenger's seat, rested the nameplate on his lap, and closed the door in one not-so-fluid motion.

"What happened to your Saab?" he said.

"Gone." She wrenched the car in gear and shot out of the driveway. The tires shrieked, the backend fishtailing before the car gained traction on the wet surface.

"Pretty flashy," he said.

"It's Uncle Al's. And no comments about my driving."

"So, is this thing equipped with any surprises?"

"One or two."

"How long will it take to get there?" he asked.

"Once we get on the Parkway, about forty-five minutes. It's going to be close, but we'll make it."

Larson took a deep breath then spoke as calmly as he could. "Let me just say this now. After we hand the nameplate off, I'm done. I'm doing this under protest."

"I'm kind of surprised at the drop-off location," Zady said, ignoring him.

"Why?"

"You think the way ISIS treats women it'd be something

more phallic. Like the Washington Monument. The Jefferson Memorial's so yonic."

"'Yonic'?"

"Opposite of phallic. From the Sanskrit word for vagina, 'yoni.'"

Larson felt his face flush. "Yes, that's, um, interesting. I didn't know there was an antonym for...for that."

Neither spoke as Zady turned left and then right onto Kensington Parkway. The rain, whipped by the wind, fell horizontally in huge sheets. The wipers swooshed quickly, rhythmically; the landscape sped past like a runny watercolor. The BMW still had that new car smell—Aleister must not have smoked in it yet—but the day's wetness seeped through, dampening the air inside.

Larson knew they were being followed before they reached the traffic circle, having noticed the black four-door sedan when they first turned onto the parkway. Now he watched in the sideview mirror as it followed them through the circle and onto Connecticut Avenue. From what he could tell through the rain, the driver was huge, barely fit behind the wheel, his hulking shoulders and bristly grayish hair like a silverback's.

Zady, casting quick furtive glances into the rearview mirror, switched lanes and the sedan followed as if it were hitched. Larson's stomach was hollow. He started to turn his head to get a better look.

"Don't!" Zady yelled. "Just pretend nothing's wrong."

"How worried should we be?"

She shrugged. "A little. But at least he's not trying to run us off—"

The sedan rammed their bumper. They jolted forward from the force.

"Fuck!" Zady exclaimed.

Larson grabbed the oh-shit handle and muttered something one-part prayer, two-parts swear. Despite the rain, Zady regained control of the car and sped up. The only saving grace was the lack of traffic on the three-laned one-way road. Staying in the middle lane gave them room to maneuver.

The BMW truly is the ultimate driving machine, Larson thought inanely. *And good for car chases in the nation's capital,* he added to the crazy commercial playing in his head.

The sedan rear-ended them again. Zady zig-zagged across lanes trying hard to avoid another crash. Despite the torrential rain, they only skidded slightly.

Six black SUVs approached, three on either side. The vehicles sped past, going at least ninety, then screeched to a halt a hundred yards ahead and began to align themselves across the lanes, bumper-to-bumper, forming a barrier across the road.

"We're gonna crash!" Larson yelled.

Instead of slamming on the brakes, Zady sped up, putting as much distance as she could between the BMW and the sedan right behind them.

Larson braced himself for impact. "We're going to—"

What happened next seemed to take place in slow motion. Right before they plowed into the SUVs, Zady flipped a switch on the dash. The BMW shot forward at such breathtaking speed Larson was sucked back in his seat. The car blew through a narrow gap between two SUVs just before the barrier across the road was complete.

As Zady struggled to regain control, there was a loud crash. Larson wrenched around to look. The sedan had hit the parked SUVs with such force it had knocked two of them over like bowling pins; the three vehicles lay on their roofs at odd angles in a tangled, twisted wreck. He didn't see any bodies—he didn't want to—but he knew they were there. Heart thumping wildly, adrenaline ricocheting through his veins, he was thankful there'd been no other traffic.

"Holy—" he began.

"Shit!" Zady finished.

"What the hell *was* that?"

"Just a little nitrous," Zady said. "Compliments of Uncle Al."

"Should we warn him about the wreck?" Larson asked.

Zady bit her lip. "No, it's too late. The road will be closed. Looks like we're on our own."

Larson gave a half-hearted thumbs up and smiled weakly, hoping they'd reach the memorial before he threw up or fainted.

10

Zady turned left then took a right onto Beach Drive. As the wind died down and the rain fell in a steady curtain, peering through the windshield on this wet, dark day was like standing in a cave behind a waterfall. Larson eyed the clock on the dash: twenty minutes till showtime. He worried about where they'd park and mentioned it to Zady.

"I'm going to head onto 17th and then Independence," she said. "There's a weird intersection that loops around the Ericsson Memorial. We should be able to park there. If we park too close to Jefferson, it'll raise a red flag."

"Do it," Larson said. Then after a moment: "Who do you think was chasing us?"

"I don't know. The government, the Church, Assassination Guy from some secret society, pick one."

They reached the circle around the memorial and Zady got off on Ohio Drive. They flew past a cricket field at warp speed and skidded to a stop opposite the tip of Franklin Park. It was 11:50 and the rain just kept coming.

Zady clicked off the ignition and looked at Larson. "Ready? It's a half mile to the memorial. We're going to have to run like the wind."

Larson nodded, glad that he'd been doing the elliptical a few times a week.

"One, two, three, go!" Zady grabbed her beat-up leather tote from the back seat, threw open the door, and sprinted through the rain.

It took Larson longer to work himself out of the car, but soon he was running hard through the downpour, cradling the nameplate in his arms like a football. He knew his way from here. As he sprinted over the bridge and crossed to the path on the other side of the street, the front of the memorial came into view. He took small strides on the slick pavement, making sure his footfalls landed directly beneath his hips, and darted around the few umbrellaed pedestrians braving the weather. Zady, now only a few feet ahead, bore left on the path closer to the Tidal Basin. He followed her lead. The gun-metal sky, the downpour, and the ticking clock lent the day an Armageddon feel, one that even the pleasant scent of the rain couldn't erase, for this rain didn't feel like a cleansing or a baptism; it felt like the Flood.

When the path split again Zady bore right, avoiding the washed-out trail on the left; Larson dutifully followed. The memorial was straight ahead now, no more than a few hundred yards. Steely rods of rain fell with no sign of slackening. Without a watch and his phone in the front pocket of his jeans, Larson couldn't stop to check the time, but he knew they were cutting it close—it had to be noon give or take a couple minutes.

They cut left at the end of the path, ran around the memorial to the entrance opposite the Tidal Basin, then raced up the marble steps two at a time. The pedestrian traffic was lighter than usual. Had to be the weather. Three people—two women hunkered beneath umbrellas and one young man who'd abandoned all hopes of staying dry and frolicked in the rain Gene Kelly-style—dashed down the steps. A few folks were scattered on the portico. The bronze statue of Jefferson loomed larger as

Larson homed in. There weren't many people inside, just a couple of stragglers waiting for the rain to slacken. Was that a blessing or a curse? It'd make it easy to identify the ISIS contact and there'd be fewer people in harm's way. But it'd also make him and Zady sitting ducks.

Before running between the portico columns, Larson glanced up at the sculpture on the pyramidal pediment showing The Committee of Five, the drafters of the Declaration of Independence—Jefferson, Adams, Franklin, Sherman, and Livingston—and wondered what the Founding Fathers would say about rendezvousing with terrorists.

Other than the blessed dryness of the shelter, the first thing he noticed when he pulled up in front of the statue next to Zady was the old couple. He bent over and pulled out his cell.

"It's two minutes past noon," he panted at Zady.

"Shit!" She wrung out her hair and approached the elderly couple, who'd started to walk away.

Larson tucked the nameplate under his arm, clutched his knees, and scanned the place, trying to figure out the best move. Was it better to wait and see if anyone showed up? Or should they check the area outside the memorial for a suspicious-looking person lurking about? But what did a suspicious person look like? And Larson and Zady *were* late, only by a couple minutes, but who knew if it was too much? There was no etiquette for dealing with terrorists. Maybe they'd missed the handoff. If so, there'd be more attacks and Zady would blame him. Sure, he'd hesitated to turn over the nameplate, but he was here now, ready to do his part to prevent more bloodshed.

He couldn't hear everything Zady was saying to the old couple, but she was probably trying to determine, as subtly as possible, if they were as innocent as they looked. In these circumstances, no one could be trusted. Just because they were elderly didn't mean they were—

A thunderous bang and a glaring flash of light.

He found himself on the floor, unable to see. Smoke filled

his lungs. He choked and coughed, but no sound came out. His mouth was as dry as sandpaper, had a salty metallic taste like he'd come from the dentist. After a few seconds, his sight returned, first in rippling waves then in a foggy stream. But all he could make out was thick, purple smoke. He still couldn't hear, and the absence of sound echoed in his head like a noise-less requiem. He raised himself to his hands and knees, cough-ing, spitting, gulping at the thick air. As the smoke dissipated, the silence turned into an intense ringing.

Zady and the elderly couple rushed toward him from a vaporish, far distance. Staggering to his feet, he hugged Zady then looked at a spot on the floor a few feet away, able to see clearly now. A grenade with cutout holes in the casing lay on the marble floor. Near it was a canister that looked like a shaving cream can.

But what *wasn't* there, or anywhere else on the floor, star-tled him: the nameplate was gone.

11

A wet, stringy-haired Zady stopped her toing and froing for a moment and stared at Larson so intently he could feel it.

"You're positive you can't remember anything else?" she asked.

Slumping in a very expensive leather chair in Aleister's immense living room, Larson folded his arms across his chest and shook his head. He still felt muzzy.

"How many more times do we have to go over this?" he asked, rubbing his forehead.

"He's told you everything he remembers," Brynn offered from the sofa. "You were there, too, Zee."

Zady glared at her sister.

Nearly two hours had gone by since the incident at the memorial. Aleister and Brynn hadn't been able to get there, because of the pile-up on Connecticut Avenue. But after discovering the nameplate was gone, Zady had coordinated with her uncle to meet back home at their palatial townhouse, just steps away from the Supreme Court and the Capitol.

Every time he here, Larson felt like he was in a museum. The room's reticulated red walls and spacious

Venetian fireplace were punctuated with a high wedding-cake ceiling and sparkling chandelier. Exquisitely designed dove-white furniture filled the space and shone as brightly as the Pharisees' sepulchers in the gospels.

"Look," Larson said, "I didn't want to bring this up, but—"

Zady's eyes flashed. "God, help me, Scott, if you say, 'I told you so!'"

He kept his mouth shut. But it was true, he hadn't wanted to get involved in this, didn't think it was a good idea *at all*, and if he had to do it over, he wouldn't have given Zady the name-plate. Rubbing his temples, he was trying to think of a way to placate her when a loud whoop sounded and the elevator in the hallway hummed into action. Must be Aleister coming up from the garage, Larson thought. Not only did he have computer equipment down there that rivaled the Bat Cave, but it was the only place he could smoke—a rule Zady enforced with the zeal of a martyr.

The elevator door opened, and Aleister, dressed in safari-style trousers, shirt, and khaki sleeveless jacket, rolled into the room. A brown explorer hat and Merrell hiking boots completed the ensemble—though Larson wasn't sure why he needed them: it wasn't like he could walk, let alone hike. But the zany Brits were all about keeping up appearances. Muttering to himself, Aleister parked between the sofa and Larson's chair.

"I'm afraid I don't have anything helpful to report," Aleister told them. "The security camera in the memorial just caught a glimpse of the perpetrator, his jeans, and sneakers to be precise —I presume it was a man. In any event, he carried a large black brolly that hid everything else."

"A big black what?" Larson asked.

"Umbrella," Zady said. "You should really learn to speak Brit."

"After the smoke bomb," Aleister resumed, "we couldn't see anything. Although the blast brought the police and set security in motion, escape wouldn't have been difficult, most likely through the Tidal Basin and Potomac. Given the downpour, he wouldn't have stood out if he were wet."

"Anything special about the grenade and smoke bomb?" Zady asked.

Aleister shook his head.

"Any news on the nameplate?" Larson asked.

"I'm afraid not," Aleister said.

"Great," said Zady. "Where do we go from here?"

"I'm not sure there's a good option," Aleister replied. "I'll continue to monitor things to see if something definite emerges, but other than that..."

Zady threw up her hands. "So, we're just supposed to wait and see if there're more attacks? That's not a plan!"

"Maybe there'll be another text message, letting us know if ISIS got the nameplate," Brynn suggested.

"I hate to add another complication—" Larson began.

"Then don't," Zady snapped.

"Please, my dear," Aleister reprimanded. "Let Scott speak. We need every insight we can get—even his."

"Thanks...I think. What I was going to say is we don't even know ISIS sent the text. You said it probably came from a burner phone, right?"

Aleister nodded. "But even with the new cell phone project, it's impossible to say where it came from, or who sent it."

"New cell phone project?" Larson asked.

Zady nodded. "I just finished writing the code. It basically syncs all cell phones on the planet. So, theoretically, you could send a message to everyone at once. It'd come in handy during a crisis."

Larson couldn't imagine how such technology worked, so instead he settled for "Impressive," and left it at that.

"Not really," Zady replied. "It's easy once you get the hang of it."

"But the point is," Larson said, returning to the subject, "there's so much info we're missing. We don't know who has the nameplate. And even if ISIS has it, we don't know there won't be more attacks."

"Let me guess where all this is leading," Zady said, standing in front of Larson, hands on her hips. "The best thing to do is nothing."

Brynn said, "I don't think that's what he's saying, Zee. Uncle Al will continue to monitor things, and we'll all keep our eyes out for messages."

Zady had turned around to look at her sister as she spoke. Now she shook her head and forked her fingers at Larson and Brynn. "I swear, if you guys were a duo, you'd be called The Do-Nothings."

"I don't think that's fair," Larson said, though he was glad for Brynn's support. And, if he thought about it, was brutally honest, these days doing nothing *was* sort of his go-to move. "I'm not sure there's anything else we can do."

"I think they're right, my dear," Aleister said gently.

Zady blew a raspberry and then plunked her body on the sofa next to Brynn. "Fine. We'll just sit here and wait. That's what everyone around here is best at."

12

Pope Innocent froze.

In the dim subterranean lighting of the archives, he was sure he detected movement up ahead. The hair on the back of his neck prickled. Bisschen barked, but a tug of the leash silenced him; he heeled at his human's feet.

It couldn't be security.

Innocent was sure he'd eluded the guards when he rushed out of the Apostolic Palace. And there were no shouts of "The dove is loose! The dove is loose!"—the code used by security whenever the pontiff wasn't in sight—when he'd crossed the Belvedere Courtyard under the skull-white moon. Normally he didn't mind the guards tagging behind him like younger siblings, even on his trips here, so long as they parted company at the entrance, so he could continue, unobserved, to the secret bunker.

But tonight. Tonight was different. Tonight, he had to make the entire trip alone. Because at this point, no one could be trusted. At all.

"It's okay, Bisschen. We're all right." He spoke the words to calm the dog, but they were more for his benefit. A shiver ran up his spine as he stood stock-still in the aisle, eyes wide with fright. Despite the ermine-lined velvet cape draped over his cassock, a chill penetrated his bones. It was as if he were about to encounter a ghost right here in the sacerdotal stillness of the stacks...

Or rather, encounter a ghost *again*.

For just a few hours ago, he'd seen a ghost. As he trembled in the aisle, pondering what might lie in wait for him in the darkness, his mind flitted back to his horrific experience earlier that day.

After ushering out the small audience of cardinals seeking clarification of an encyclical, Innocent had sought solace in the loggia of the Chiaramonti Museum, the long narrow gallery that connected the little Palace of the Belvedere to the Vatican Palaces. It was one of his favorite places to visit. The very essence of the Roman Empire's power and glory shimmered from the many sculptures, paintings, and pieces of architecture on display. A small tour was in progress and much to the dismay of his security guards, he'd insisted on passing through to get to his destination.

Once he passed the tourists without incident, he stood, hands behind his back, observing one of a trio of women from the Roman relief, the only one whose profile was fully preserved. She was depicted in graceful midstride, gently lifting her long, flowing stola, left foot planted firmly in front, right foot behind, heel raised, only her toes touching the ground. A veil-like covering wrapped around her hair and cascaded to her shoulders. The woman's name—Gradiva—was a variant of the Roman god striding into war.

Reflecting on the quiet dignity of her face, Innocent was suddenly distracted by the unnerving feeling of being watched. He turned to the group he'd just passed, thinking it the source of his discomfort, and saw something so terrifying he was changed, altered in a way he knew right then would last forever.

He knew the old woman hadn't been there when he'd passed the group. But now, there she stood, apart, left profile facing him, draped in a long black dress hitched up to reveal four-inch black stilettos, hideously mocking Gradiva's pose, right foot firmly in front, left raised so that only the tip of her shoe touched the floor. She reminded him of a fourteenth century painting on the walls of the Camposanto, of death as an old woman with wild eyes and streaming hair, wielding a scythe.

When she saw him staring, the elderly woman made a slow, full circle around her lips with a pointy tongue, winked, then smiled evilly, revealing a set of jagged black teeth. That was hideous enough, but the worst part was that she—her size, build, and features, especially her wild eyes—was a shriveled version of his mother. And the dress. The dress was a replica of the dress his mother had worn the night she—

"Mein Sohn," the mother-thing croaked in a muffled voice that sounded like it came from the grave.

He'd wanted to scream. Instead, he turned his back on the woman—or demon, apparition, whatever the hell it was—and scooted back down the loggia. His heart raced and sweat poured out of him as he made his escape. He couldn't recall the last time he'd moved that fast and didn't look behind him until he reached the door to his apartment. Only then did he risk a furtive glance over his shoulder before he yanked open the door then slammed it shut behind him.

A shudder brought him back to the present.

What if that *thing* lurked in the darkness ahead?

Bisschen sat obediently at his feet, looking calm, which was more than he could say for himself—he could hear his heart pound in his temples and willed it to quiet, lest whoever or whatever was in the stacks heard it too.

He listened again. He thought, but couldn't be sure, the movement had stopped. Swallowing hard, he called in a wavering voice:

"Is anybody there?"

He cocked his head awaiting a reply, every nerve stretched

taut, half-expecting a sinister voice to respond. He waited a full minute, but the silence continued. Slowly, his heart rate steadied, and the muscles in his neck and shoulders loosened to the point they no longer felt like twisted metal bands.

"Well, my friend, should we continue?" he whispered to Bisschen.

The mini dachshund barked and wagged his stumpy tail.

Peering ahead one last time and not seeing anything, Innocent went on. It was almost ten o'clock; he had no time to lose. The deadline to turn over Peter's Pence, his multi-billion-dollar private slush fund, was upon him. He'd decided to contact the Council tonight, at their usual time, and act as if the last message he'd received the night before was to proceed as usual —that is, as if he hadn't received their request—no, it was a demand—to turn over Peter's Pence. If pressed, he'd say he'd had computer problems right after he'd been told to proceed as usual and sincerely hoped they hadn't sent any more messages. At best, it'd buy him some time to come up with a better plan. Worst-case scenario...well, he wouldn't think about that right now.

But something else weighed on him. Things had gone wrong in the States earlier that day, and he had no idea what had happened to the nameplate. What *was* certain was none of it boded well for him.

Arriving at the spot, he ordered Bisschen to sit and raised an index finger to his lips to keep him quiet. He turned the crank to part the shelves then stopped. The shadows had come alive. It was as if they breathed and pulsated. The feeling he was being watched, the feeling he'd had in the loggia when he'd seen that repulsive creature, returned, not as intensely, but enough to make him jittery.

When the feeling subsided a little, he turned the crank with a watchful eye over his shoulder. If he could reach the bunker, he'd be safe. He'd close the door, stay locked inside until the danger passed. He was looking fearfully over his shoulder as he traveled down the aisle that dead-ended in the entrance to the bunker.

And then he saw it—

Or didn't see it.

For instead of the scanning equipment and a door there was only a solid brick wall. He dropped Bisschen's leash and felt the bricks with both hands, examining them for any signs that the work was recent, but the bricks and mortar matched perfectly. It was as if there'd never been a door there.

And for the second time that day, Innocent felt like screaming.

13

President John Paul Jenkins felt the best thing to do after the first day of the trial was to have a quiet early dinner with the First Lady. So just shy of six o'clock they sat at the round table under the elegant chandelier in the President's Dining Room, enjoying a medium-rare filet, mashed potatoes, and asparagus. It should've been cozy. But Jenkins couldn't see his way through the mental fog that surrounded him like swamp gas.

He gazed across the table at Anne. Like a dutiful 1950s housewife, her thin frame was draped in a navy-blue dress with a modest neckline. She wore red lipstick, her heart-shaped mouth affixed with the permanent smile of the relentlessly cheerful. A casual onlooker would've seen happiness and devotion in her face. But like the sky before a sun-shower, beneath the bright surface of the perfectly coiffed golden hair and periwinkle eyes, Jenkins knew there lurked a vale of tears. Like Job, the first couple had given everything they could to the Lord, and He, in His infinite wisdom, had punished them.

Jenkins reached across the table to touch his wife's hand. He was about to tell her how sorry he was for everything. Before he could, a loud knock sounded on the double doors. An electronic device monitored his every move, so it was no secret to his aides where he was. But to interrupt him during dinner after the first day of the trial was a step too far.

"I wonder who—" Anne started.

Jenkins leaped from his seat and threw open the doors, intent on confronting whoever the hell it was that had the audacity to disturb him. But his anger drained from him like an unplugged tub when he found himself looking into the eyes of his chief of staff.

Banner's calm steady demeanor belied the urgency of the words that came out of his mouth and filled Jenkins with absolute terror:

"Mr. President, it's my duty to inform you that we are under attack."

14

It was half-past six when Senators Madge Roberts and Fred Corrigan, along with three Democratic colleagues and the five House prosecutors, entered Bullfeathers, the popular D.C. restaurant on First Street named for one of Teddy Roosevelt's many euphemisms for "bullshit." Yesterday Roberts had suggested getting together after the first day of the trial had finished and now that the Senate had voted on procedures, Roberts wanted to bring the House managers up to speed on what had been decided.

The maître d' ordered a busboy to shove three tables together. Everyone sank into their chairs and Roberts toed off her pumps and eyed the menu, thinking how good the bacon-Swiss burger and an ice-cold beer sounded. The server took their orders, promised the drinks and food would be out shortly, and headed for the back.

"So, how did it go?" Ananya Chandler asked, retrieving a pad and pen from her purse.

"We agreed on more than I thought," Roberts said. "The Republicans also see the need to avoid a long, drawn-out trial. The country is too divided; we need to come together as quickly as possible. And the more time we spend on the trial the longer it keeps us from dealing with other important stuff. It's ambitious, but we're gonna try to wrap things up by the end of the week—the presentation by both sides, closing arguments, questions. If all goes well, we'll go into deliberations over the weekend."

"Sounds speedy," one of the senators said.

"It is," Roberts admitted. "But it's in nobody's interest to drag things out. Our side thinks it's a clear-cut violation of the Constitution, while the Republicans feel they've got the numbers to acquit. And in this case, Jenkins' crimes are wideout in the open, so there's not a whole lot of behind-the-scenes investigating to do. When it comes to witnesses, we've agreed to cross that bridge if we come to it. At this point, neither side feels the need for any. We also decided the president can't be compelled to testify. Andrew Johnson wasn't. Clinton wasn't. There's no need to depart from precedent."

"How are questions from us going to be handled?" another colleague asked.

Corrigan cleared his throat. "Y'all will submit your questions in writing to Chief Justice Buckner. He'll alternate between parties, allow the prosecution and defense five minutes to answer."

"Is that five minutes each or five minutes for both?" the colleague pressed.

"Five minutes each," Corrigan replied.

"That's right," Roberts said. "Oh, and another thing. I think—"

Someone cried for everyone to hush. Roberts swiveled in her chair to watch the TV that blared in the silence blanketing the restaurant. CNN must be summing up the first day of the impeachment trial, Roberts thought. The management and clientele recognized us, knew we'd want to hear. But the "special report" chyron at the bottom of the screen caused her to freeze. Maybe it was about the incident at the Jefferson Memorial earlier that afternoon when someone had set off a stun grenade and a smoke bomb. Thankfully, no one was seriously injured, but the Capitol had been placed on lockdown for a brief period, the senators barricaded inside the Old Chamber until the all-clear signal sounded.

"We're getting reports that a synagogue in Hackensack, New Jersey, and a Catholic church in Bridgeport, Connecticut, have been bombed," the harried newscaster said.

Roberts watched in horror as the flustered newsman was bombarded with updates. He relayed info on attacks in Kansas, California, and Texas, while images of burning buildings, wounded people, adrenaline-driven first responders, and panicked folks searching for loved ones flashed across the screen. The quiet in the restaurant gave way to loud raucous shouts. Hateful expletives filled the air.

Roberts' stomach felt like it'd been scoured with Brillo. Never had she felt so helpless. She thought of the flight or fight response to danger, and how the third option—freeze—got too little airtime. Because that's all she could do right now. With tremendous effort, she turned her attention from the news to her colleagues. A couple of them seemed unable to move, their faces frozen in horror; the rest made phone calls, checking on the whereabouts of family and friends. She knew they were looking to her for comfort and answers, but she struggled to find words. It was all she could do to absorb what had just happened.

She wasn't sure how much time had passed when the sound of Jenkins' voice drew her attention back to the TV. Addressing the nation from the Franklin Room, the president sat surrounded by his national security team, his normally ruddy cheeks pale. The only thing familiar about him was the sandy comb-over that maintained steady vigilance over his scalp like a wave frozen at the start of the Ice Age.

"My fellow Americans," Jenkins said woodenly, as if somebody held a gun to his back, which in the current political environment couldn't be ruled out. "It's with tremendous sadness that I inform you of details of the attacks that occurred at 5:45 p.m. Eastern Standard Time. Bombs were detonated at five places of worship across this great nation: Temple Beth-El in Hackensack, New Jersey; Saint Andrew's Church in Bridgeport, Connecticut; Temple Sinai in Lawrence, Kansas; the Rock Church in San Diego, California; and All Saints' Episcopal Church in Austin, Texas. ISIS has taken responsibility for these cowardly attacks. The number is still being confirmed, but so far fifty-nine people are dead and more than a hundred wounded. My prayers go out to all the victims and their families and friends.

"At this time, I'm declaring a national state of emergency, effective immediately, as we can't be certain if the attacks are over. I ask for the full cooperation of the military, law enforcement, and every citizen. I also request that the Senate delay its impeachment trial. All our country's resources, all of its attention, need to be focused on responding to this crisis, above all, having a commander-in-chief firmly in charge of our great military. These attacks are despicable and evil. And make no mistake about it: the perpetrators will be brought to justice. I say to them now, 'There is no place you can hide. We will spare no expense in seeing that you're held accountable for these atrocious acts.' May God be with us all as we cope with this tragedy."

Business in the restaurant slowly resumed. A server approached Roberts' group with drinks. But the only thing she could do was stare at her beer sweating coldly in its icy mug. The thought of alcohol seemed inappropriate. The eyes of her colleagues turned to her. At first, she was unable to speak, but then four words rose slowly, grindingly from her throat, and were barely audible in the restaurant's din when they finally escaped her lips:

"God help us all."

15

At the Brobdingnagian table in Aleister's stately dining room, Larson's partially digested dinner rose to his throat. He swallowed hard then pushed aside his plate of toad-in-the-hole prepared by the English cook, Mrs. Paxton, a thick haughty woman seemingly unaware of the fall of the British Empire. Moments ago, Aleister's cell had rung, interrupting dinner, and he'd rolled into the living room to take it. Returning to the table, he'd conveyed what he knew about the terrorist attacks.

Now Zady peppered him with questions in the aggressive tone of a prosecutor cross-examining a hostile witness, while Brynn sat silently, a horrified look on her face.

"You said three churches and two synagogues?"

"I'm afraid so," Aleister replied. "In all parts of the country, from California to New Jersey. Over sixty dead, and nearly twice as many wounded."

"These were coordinated attacks?" Zady asked.

Aleister nodded. "The explosions occurred at 5:45 Eastern Standard Time." He paused then added, "ISIS has claimed responsibility."

Zady pounded the table with such force the plates rose a

couple of inches before crashing down. "Those cowardly bastards!"

"My God," Larson finally managed. "Well, either ISIS got the nameplate and still carried out the attacks, or they carried them out because they didn't get the nameplate."

"Thanks, genius," Zady snapped. She looked at her uncle. "Any progress on finding out whether they have the nameplate?"

Aleister shook his head.

"We need a plan right now," Zady said.

Larson scoffed. "Yes, but what? Until we know more about what's going on it's hard to know what to do."

Zady glared at him. Aleister took her hand. "I believe the most we can do, is keep trying to find out who has the nameplate. At least that will tell us if ISIS kept its word."

Larson bit his tongue. *Yes, because we all know how good terrorists are at keeping their promises.* The I-told-you-so urge was strong, but he knew he risked Armageddon with Zady if he opened his mouth.

"Are we sure the attacks are over?" Brynn asked.

"They appear to be for now," Aleister said. "ISIS hasn't said anything about more attacks, but we can't be certain." He looked at Zady who stared blankly ahead as if peering into another dimension. "One thing we might do is try to determine if there's a pattern to the attacks."

"Pattern?" Zady asked, her curiosity aroused.

Aleister nodded. "For one thing they were spread across the country, each in a different state. None in the capital. At first glance, the targets seem random, but maybe they're not. One also wonders why there weren't more attacks in Egypt, like ISIS said there'd be."

Larson stood and excused himself, planning on heading into the living room and turning on the television. But the liquid sadness in Brynn's eyes changed his mind. He remembered how it felt to be cloistered from society. Of the four of them, she was the most innocent and certainly the least deserving of pain. He sank down and reached for his cell for a more private look at the news when his phone—and Zady's—pinged with a text message.

Zady had been clutching her phone for the past several hours, ever since they got back from the Jefferson Memorial. "What does yours say?" she asked Larson.

"'Find the treasure.'"

"Same here," she said. "What kind of dumbass message is that? Could it be any vaguer?"

"I'm not sure," Larson said, staring at the message as if it were a Zen koan. Like the one they'd received that morning, it came from an unknown source. "Unless..."

"Unless *what*?" Zady urged.

"Maybe the testimony gospels, what we thought of as the Cathar treasure, isn't what this is all about."

"But if that's the case, what *is* it all about?" Zady asked. "And why did they ask for the nameplate in the first place?"

Larson shrugged. "I wish I knew. You think we should text them back and ask what treasure they're talking about?"

"It wouldn't do any good," Aleister said. "If they wanted to give us more information they would have. It seems they want us to play their game."

"Here's a thought," Brynn said. "Let's assume for just a moment that whoever sent the message is referring to a religious treasure. What could it be, what religious treasures are out there? There's the Ark of the Covenant, the Holy Grail, the cross, the crown of thorns. Maybe it's one of those."

"Yes," Aleister said. "Maybe if we look at things that way the nature of the treasure might become clearer."

"How so?" Zady asked. "I mean, 'Find the treasure'? Really? And all those things you just mentioned, people have been looking for them forever."

Aleister stared into the distance as he spoke. "The Ark of the Covenant is mentioned in the Book of Exodus, one of the five books of the Pentateuch central to Judaism. The grail, the cross, the crown of thorns have to do with Jesus, in the New Testament, the foundation of Christianity. What if the treasure the text refers to has to do with Islam?"

"Maybe," Zady said. "Especially if ISIS sent the text, which I'm almost positive they did. I guess we should see if there's a treasure mentioned in the Quran."

"Now I hate to be the pessimist here, but I think we're grasping at straws," Larson said.

"Scott, unless you can come up with a better idea, be quiet." Zady looked at Aleister and Brynn. "Anything else?"

They shook their heads.

"Okay," Zady said, going to the counter to grab her tote bag. "I'm going to drive you home, Scott."

"Do you think it's safe for him to be alone?" Brynn asked.

"Yes, Brynn, I think it's safe for him to be alone," Zady mocked.

"I was asking Uncle Al."

"I'll be all right," Larson said. "Whoever was chasing us today is dead. And whoever set up the roadblock doesn't seem to be after us now. Besides, we don't have the nameplate anymore. Even if it's not in ISIS' hands, it's out of mine."

"Nevertheless," Aleister said, "I'll have Sterling assign a couple of men to keep an eye on you, even if they just stay parked by your house."

Larson nodded and looked at Zady. "What are you going to do after you drop me off?"

"Dig around the library, see if I can figure out what the treasure is."

"What should I do?" Larson asked.

"Whatever you want," she said, heading for the door.

TUESDAY

16

Innocent tossed and turned for hours, but try as he might, sleep wouldn't come. First it was too warm. Then it was too cold. Then the satin sheets were too slippery. Curled on the pillow next to him, Bisschen snored, making matters worse. But Innocent's thoughts were the real culprit. Yesterday's events played over and over in his mind like scenes from a horror movie in an infinite loop, and he couldn't interpret them in a way that calmed him.

First, there was the ghost of his mother, or at least an ancient, obscene version of it, if his mother had lived to the fossilized age of the hideous thing he'd seen. Of course, she hadn't, she'd died relatively young, but that was another story...

Or was it?

Then there was the crazy vanishing bunker act in the archives, where his only means of communicating with the omnipotent Council had simply disappeared.

Were these events somehow connected? But that would mean—

He didn't really want to think about what it would mean. And yet he couldn't stop his mental movie projector from replaying scenes from his past, a past that might form a link between his mother's ghost and the disappearance of the bunker. Despite his best efforts, he remembered—no, he *saw*, in vivid detail, all the ghoulishness of that dark morning so long ago.

Wilhelm Rittenhaus was sixteen at the time. One morning, just past three—he remembered the time because he'd looked at the clock when his eyes opened—he was awakened by a sharp poke in the ribs. It took him a moment to realize that the source was his mother's finger, and though his eyes registered the fact, his brain had a hard time processing it. Why would Mother wake him at such an ungodly hour, and in such a boorish fashion? And why was she clad in a black dress he'd never seen?

But he didn't have time to ask questions, because she grabbed him roughly by the ear and dragged him around the back of the house—a one-story affair, with heavy timber accents and rough-sawn woodwork, built right into the mountainside of the Bavarian Alps—and to the shed.

He recalled the obsidian beauty of that spring morning. Enormous spruce and beech trees towered cathedral-high in the moonlight. The scent of mountain tassel flowers and woodrush perfumed the air. The dew of the grass on his bare feet was delicious. A strange glow radiated beneath the shed's locked door. Mother retrieved a key from the pocket of her black dress and inserted it in the large metal lock. Wilhelm stood frozen, scarcely able to believe he was finally about to see the secrets the shed held; for it was always locked, seemingly possessed of magical properties, and entering it was *verboten*. In the winter, when he was younger, it was the dwelling place of Krampus, the half-goat, half-demon creature that punished bad children. As he'd entered his teens, the shed had transformed into a sacred dwelling, an image reinforced by the statues of saints and other religious icons his mother removed from the home and brought to the shed in the middle of the night. But Wilhelm still hadn't been allowed entry.

Until tonight...

This night...

This unholy night...

Nothing could have prepared him for the scene that met his eyes when his mother threw open the door. Not even Krampus, in its half-goat, half-demon hideousness could've been more menacing.

At first, it was like looking into a church. At the far end a table covered with a white cloth rested upon a knee-high platform. A candelabra set in the center of the table was the only lighting, the flames of the candles flickering slightly in the breeze from the open door. A wooden chalice stood on either side of the candelabra and at one corner of the table a gold-painted monstrance held something dark and oddly shaped. In the dim lighting he couldn't make out what it was, but it didn't look like the Eucharist. Religious statues were arranged throughout. A giant crucifix leaned against the far wall behind the raised table. The cross had been crudely fashioned from two heavy beams, sloppily sawn to fit together, a rope tied around the point of intersection for reinforcement, a small wooden footrest nailed into place near the bottom of the vertical beam. Something like the smell of paint thinner and cinnamon hung in the air.

But it wasn't until Mother closed the door and shoved him up on the platform in front of the table that his gnawing discomfort turned to fear. From his new vantage point, he saw that the object in the center of the monstrance was a large, candied nut covered in sugar and cinnamon, a treat normally saved for Weihnachten and the arrival of the Christkind.

What could be the meaning of such blasphemy?

The candlelight revealed something else. The stations of the cross hung on the long walls of the shed. But they were unlike the stations in the little white church in the village that his mother forced him to attend daily after her husband left. These were crude caricatures made of twigs and twine, like the renderings of a demented druid. And as Mother pulled him down and pushed him in front of the giant crucifix, Wilhelm knew, with mounting terror, that the cross was meant for him.

During what followed, Frau Rittenhaus' eerie silence rivaled nature in its mute, deadly potential. After shoving him off the platform, she spun him around until his back faced the cross. Wilhelm watched, stupefied, as she motioned him to stand on the footrest and place his arms across the horizontal beam. He'd always been obedient, so he dutifully lifted his right foot and felt behind him with his bare toes until they found the little platform, then stood on it, arms outstretched. Surely this ritual was of vital importance to Mother, and if he could do anything to lessen her pain at his father's desertion, he'd do it, for he loved her. Terrified, he continued to go along as she reached under the table on the altar, removed three pieces of rope, and secured his hands and feet to the crucifix. He watched, wide-eyed, as she made her way to a darkened corner of the shed and turned on a battery-operated radio. Soon the shed was filled with the apocalyptic strains of Fauré's Pavane. She returned to the cross, stared up at him, and, for the first time in a long while, smiled.

But her smile was wrong.

And her eyes.

My God, her eyes...

She took a cloth from her frock and stuffed it into his mouth. Then she reached under the table a second time and pulled out a leather bag, set it at the foot of the cross, and pulled his pajama bottoms down, leaving him naked below the waist. Oddly, he couldn't recall any shame at this exposure but watched remotely, frozen in place, as Mother withdrew a kitchen knife from the bag, stepped onto the platform, and held the blade over the flickering candlelight. She returned to the foot of the cross, dropped to her knees, and castrated him.

He couldn't remember any pain, and upon examining himself later, discovered the procedure, including the suturing, was done with clinical precision. The last thing he remembered was her replacing the Bavarian nut in the center of the monstrance with one of his testicles.

Mother and son never spoke of that night. She sent him to the seminary shortly after and, in his final year, he'd received word she'd hanged herself in the shed, directly over the altar-table. The news of her death left him numb—or, rather, the numbness he'd felt after the sacrifice of that night continued. He concluded that the woman who'd birthed him had suffered a psychotic break after his father left.

All this brought him full circle to recent events. Was he, too, mentally ill? He knew genetic predisposition played a role; such illnesses often ran in families. Maybe his father had been sick as well. Wilhelm had no siblings, and he didn't recall any uncles, aunts, cousins, or grandparents, so he couldn't trace the family history for mental illness. Now he wondered if seeing the demon, the day before, and the disappearance of the bunker were part and parcel of a sickness he'd carried with him throughout his life. Perhaps, now that he thought about it, the Council was a product of a mental defect. The idea of a dozen people exercising such enormous power was rather preposterous. But if he *had* imagined it, what did that say about his sanity? From now on, he'd stay vigilant for more signs of mental deterioration.

But what if things got worse?

Sensing his human's discomfort, Bisschen roused himself from the pillow and licked Innocent's face. Wishing the little dog could talk, the pope patted his head and stared at the ceiling until the sun came up.

17

Larson emerged from the gray shadowy stages of sleep courtesy of a ringing and banging that wouldn't go away. Unable to stop the racket of what he thought was an annoying dream, he slowly realized that someone was at the door. And whoever it was, wasn't going away. He withdrew his head from under the covers to see Isabelle staring at him from her regal recline on the pillow next to him. She hated company as much as him and maintained a disgusted and alert I-can-be-gone-in-an-instant posture as she monitored his reaction to this rude summoning. Wondering who the hell it was at what the digital clock showed to be 1:19, he swung his legs over the side of the bed and slammed his feet into slippers.

"I'm coming, I'm coming!" he yelled.

At the sound of his shout, Isabelle tore off the bed.

"Sorry, Iz," he said, stumbling toward the stairs.

Larson was more annoyed than afraid: if someone were out to harm him, he doubted they'd pound on the door and ring the bell. Plus, Lance Sterling, Aleister's security chief, had stationed two men outside the house. Still, he was relieved when halfway down the stairs he recognized Zady's voice boring through the door. Once he realized it was her, he raced the rest of the way down and threw open the door.

"Christ, Scott. What took you so long? Nice jammies."

Larson looked at his racing car-covered pajamas. He'd found them in Brent's drawer and though they were too big, he'd cinched the waist tight enough to stay up.

"Um, it's a little late, or early depending on—"

She dragged him to the parlor, pushed him into the club chair then plopped herself on the sofa. Before he could say anything, she yanked her cell phone from her satchel and began talking as her thumbs navigated the tiny keyboard.

"Okay, so this is what I found...or didn't find."

"About?" he asked.

"Hello? About what the treasure might be. I just came from the LOC."

He stared at her stupidly.

"Library of Congress, Scott. C'mon. Get with the program."

Larson yawned then rubbed his eyes. Now that there was no immediate threat to his person his sleepiness had returned with a vengeance. "I knew what you meant. Didn't they close hours ago?"

"Yeah, but I have permission to stay if I need to. Uncle Al."

"Right."

"Anyway," she went on, "I checked into what he suggested —you know, that it might refer to something Islamic. Now, there's a reference to treasure in the Hadith—the record of Mohammed's actions and words. Translated from Arabic, it reads, 'I was a hidden treasure; I loved to be known. Hence, I created the world so I would be known.' It's one of the Hadith's greatest hits; it's cited *a lot*. But..."

"But what?"

"I don't know, it seems vague. The quote refers to Allah as the 'hidden treasure.' It's not something concrete, something you can dig up, like an ark or a grail. It sounds more like Jesus' claim that the kingdom of heaven is within, that you should store up your treasure in your heart, you know, that sort of thing. It doesn't sound like something we can find and turn over to ISIS."

"So, not a good fit."

"I guess not. But then I thought of something else." She looked at him expectantly.

"If you're pausing for dramatic effect, you better move on. It's late and I'm tired."

"The first time we were looking for treasure or secret knowledge it had something to do with Jesus. What if this treasure also has to do with him, maybe something in the New Testament that we haven't thought of?"

"Well, other than the grail, the cross, the crown of thorns, or his bones there's not much else that could serve as a physical artifact. And in terms of actual treasure, there's nothing in the New Testament about any riches, of Jesus or the Apostles. Just the opposite: Jesus condemns material wealth, says it separates people from God, that it's easier for a camel to go through the eye of a needle than a rich man to enter heaven, etcetera."

"Okay, so maybe we're not looking for something in the New Testament."

"I don't know how many times I have to say this," Larson told her, "but I don't think getting more involved is a good idea. It sounds like a ridiculous wild goose chase. I really don't know why you're so hell-bent on all this."

Zady set down her phone, covered her face with her hands, and growled. When she dropped her hands, her face was rouged, but there was a hint of sadness in her voice when she spoke. "Scott, why are you blocking me? I mean, what if this has something to do with the deaths of my parents? You went with me to find the Cathar treasure, what's so different this time?"

"People were out to kill me then."

"Oh, and that car chase yesterday was a Sunday drive? Hello! We almost died. So, some people have already tried to kill you. My guess is more will follow. C'mon, Scott. There's got to be more to it. I know you're not a coward."

"Okay. If you really want to do this." He took a deep breath. "In the past fifteen months, I've come to see peace and quiet as good things. I'm not cut out for a life of death-defying thrills. Besides, I don't want anything to happen to you."

"Me?"

"Yeah. If we were to go gallivanting about, looking for another treasure, and you got hurt or killed, I couldn't live with that. Besides..."

"What?" she said sharply. Just then her cell phone buzzed. "Hold that thought. It's Uncle Al."

Her face paled as she listened to Aleister's words. "I'll head home right now," she said woodenly. She ended the call and stared blankly at the wall.

"What is it?" Larson asked.

"Brynn's gone."

"What do you mean 'gone'?"

She spoke in a monotone that did more to reveal her shock than if she'd screamed. "There's a balcony off her bedroom. She must've stepped out to get some air—you know how much the whole house can stink of cigars. Aleister found a rope on the railing. She's, she's gone."

"You think her disappearance is connected to the nameplate and treasure?"

"It's one *hell* of a coincidence if it's not."

Out of all of them, Brynn was the least culpable. He could understand if someone kidnapped him, or Zady, or even Aleister. But to make Brynn the sacrificial lamb, when the only thing she'd wanted was to love and serve God, was a step too far. She was the last person in the world who deserved this.

The familiar furniture, Isabelle's bed in the corner, everything he needed in the universe, was here, right inside this house. Even the last remnants of his faith seemed embedded in its very walls. He silently said goodbye to all of it, trying as best he could to make peace with his decision. He didn't know if what he was about to say—and what he would have to do after he said it—were right, but he'd made up his mind, did what Zady had urged him to do, taken a stand. He suddenly felt vulnerable, awkward, like he was wearing a new suit. He swallowed hard. Shame, regret, and anger coursed through him.

"I'll do whatever it takes to get her back," he said firmly.

18

Larson smelled cigar smoke as soon as Zady inserted her key and opened the front door. Aleister slumped in front of the fireplace in a nightshirt, puffing violently on a cigar, streaming bluish smoke into the stale air. When they came in, he threw the stub into the fire and turned his chair around to face them. Zady ran over and hugged him while Larson stood alone, feeling like an outsider. A lump in his throat made it hard to swallow.

Zady pulled away and cleared her throat. "I'm not even going to yell at you for smoking in here. But shame on you."

Aleister chuckled weakly. The result was a violent hacking cough. Larson was taken aback by how old he looked.

"Now that that's over with, let's figure out what we're going to do," Zady said, pacing the length of the large room.

Larson deposited himself in a chair, grateful the strength in Zady's voice had returned. "I assume there wasn't anything special about the rope you found on the balcony?" he asked.

Aleister blew his nose into a tissue produced from the sleeve of his nightshirt. "Nothing at all, I'm afraid. Sterling is still scouring the upstairs, but so far, he's found nothing. I've given this much thought, and I'm afraid that Brynn's disappearance is connected to the nameplate and the text about finding the treasure."

"They've got to be," Zady said. "I mean, what are the odds they're not?"

Aleister looked at Larson. "Scott?"

"The timing makes it hard to believe it's a coincidence," Larson said. "But I still think we should consider all the possibilities," he said slowly.

"Okay, let's consider them," Zady said, proceeding to count on her fingers. "First, there's the possibility ISIS has Brynn. Second, there's the possibility ISIS has Brynn. Third, there's the possibility ISIS has Brynn. Unless we want to consider alien abduction, it's pretty clear ISIS has Brynn. The only thing to do is to figure out what the treasure is, find it, and hope we can trade it for her life."

"There's at least one other possibility," Larson said. "Besides ISIS, who has an interest in the nameplate?"

When Zady and Aleister just stared at him, he answered his own question. "The Church."

"You think the Church kidnapped Brynn?" Zady asked.

"I'm saying that at this point we just don't know," Larson replied. "Maybe the Church kidnapped Brynn because we tried to turn over the nameplate to Islamic terrorists, giving ISIS access to the damaging info about Jesus and his brothers. If that's the case, we should focus on finding out where the nameplate is and get it back so we can give it to the Church in exchange for Brynn. So, the question is, do we look for the treasure or do we look for the nameplate?"

"Shit!" Zady exclaimed. "This is a mess! But I'm glad to hear you say 'we,' Scott."

"How about this?" Aleister said. "Why don't you and Scott try to figure out what the treasure is, while I try to find out who has the nameplate. Hopefully, we'll get another text that clarifies things."

"Well," Zady said, "given the circumstances, I suppose that makes sense. I just wish we had a better plan."

"I do, too, my dear. Have you made any progress in figuring out what the treasure could be?"

"Not much. But I feel more optimistic now that he's on board," Zady said, jerking a thumb at Larson.

"There's something else I want to mention," Aleister said. "It might be nothing, but it could be worth checking into. As you both know, last year I helped relocate the Mandaeans from southern Iraq to Switzerland. They were persecuted by Saddam Hussein in the past and then faced extinction by ISIS."

"Yes," Larson said.

Aleister nodded. "An interesting group. Some call them the last Gnostics. They're considered Christians, but they revere John the Baptist instead of Jesus. There's even some Mandaean hostility to Jesus, some of whom call him a deceiver. The Mandaeans, like many Gnostics, are said to possess secret knowledge that accounts for their beliefs, which is said to be recorded in what's called *The Book of Hagu*. Of course, there's no guarantee that it's the treasure the text refers to, but I thought it worth mentioning. It might deserve a closer look."

Zady looked at Larson. "Why don't we head over to the library and start digging around?"

"Sounds good," he replied, feeling for the first time since they arrived that he really belonged.

19

Since it was just a few blocks, Larson and Zady went on foot to the Library of Congress. But as they walked along, the night felt like a black curtain from behind which a threat might emerge at any moment. The streetlights hung over the road like gallows. Larson felt as if he were on the way to his execution. Though they didn't speak, Zady must've felt the same, for when they got within a few hundred yards of the library, she grabbed Larson's hand and started jogging. Shadowy shapes materialized in the darkness as they ran.

At the back of the Thomas Jefferson Building, they stopped at a heavy-looking door, what looked like an employee entrance. Zady fished her card-swipe from her tote bag and opened it. Larson followed her up two flights of stairs. They went down a number of long expansive hallways, and through several doors, then down some stairs, and finally through a narrow gallery until they reached a door that Zady opened with a key. Inside was a small office, a desk, table, and two chairs.

Larson took a seat at the table and watched Zady remove a paper-thin laptop from her bag.

"So, what now, Sherlock?" she asked.

"I thought of something on the way over," Larson said. "*The*

Book of Hagu is mentioned in the Dead Sea Scrolls. Maybe there's something in them that'll give a clue to where the book is."

"What do the scrolls say about it?"

"I don't remember off the top of my head," Larson said.

"*You* don't remember something in the Dead Sea Scrolls? I thought you wrote a book about them."

"I did. Not exactly popular with the Church. The Vatican has dominated the translation of the scrolls since they were found. Some of the contents of the ones we know about still haven't been released. And there's a good chance other scrolls were found that were never disclosed to the public."

"Why don't we pull them up and see what they say about the book?" Zady said, typing on her laptop.

"You can't really access them online," Larson said. "Not in a way that's convenient. Besides, I can't read off a computer. I need to hold a book in my hands. I'm old-fashioned that way."

"I guess it's a good thing we're at the library then, huh?"

"Yeah. See if you can pull up the version translated by Vermes," he told her.

Her fingers dashed over the keyboard. "Got the call number."

"Good. But the stacks are locked. How are we going to get it?"

Zady stared at him as if he were stupid. "I have the keys," she said, reaching inside her tote bag. "And we're right near the African and Middle Eastern Reading Room. Let's go get it."

20

Heavy, oppressive darkness.

Am I dead? Wrapped in a winding sheet?

Shades of gray emerging through closed eyelids.

God, I have to pee. My head. It's like a block of cement. Must've been drugged. Come on eyes, open. You can do it. Please help me, God. I don't have the strength to—And who put a caterpillar in my mouth? Open, eyes, open. Who's that?

A man stood at the foot of the bed where she found herself. Scraggly beard. Long white-yellowish shirt. Tan trousers ending mid-calf. Young, probably mid-twenties. Middle Eastern. ISIS? Thinness of an ascetic. His skin glowed with the fervor of a zealot. Brynn couldn't remember ever seeing eyes so sharp; they pierced her with their stare.

What does he want? Did he—No, he didn't. There's no pain down there, thank God. But I'm in different clothes. Sweatpants and a sweatshirt, socks. He must have changed my clothes. But who is he? What am I doing on this bed in a room that looks like it's made from Lincoln Logs dirty and worn from too much play? And what's around my ankle? A shackle and chain. A chain—

Adrenaline evaporated the rest of her lethargy. She lifted her head from the pillow and raised herself on her elbows. Her eyes darted about the room. A bolt on the floor to her left. A chain puddled around it that ran to the shackle on her left ankle. A window covered with dark thick fabric nailed into the log wall. A closed door across from her. Another closed door on her right. A chipped drinking glass filled with clear liquid on a bedside table.

She needed a drink; her throat was so parched she could barely swallow. But was that just water in the glass? Or was something mixed in, whatever drug she'd been given, or something worse? But even if she was willing to risk it, could she reach it, and, if so, would her captor let her drink?

A staring contest ensued. Her every sense heightened, she heard the man breathing, smelled the moist unpleasant odor that permeated the room, sensed the tightness of the chain around her ankle that chafed at her slightest move. But for the first time she realized her hands were free. She didn't know whether to speak, or even if she could, her mouth was so dry. Her chin and lips trembled.

Despite her faith, or because of it, she was terrified. Trying desperately to calm herself with thoughts of God, her mind raced until it rested on St. Augustine's plea: "Lord, our hearts are restless until they rest in you." But the words felt inadequate, empty. She wasn't restless. She was in danger of losing her mind from fear.

She stiffened at the man's approach. Fists at his sides, he gazed at her with otherworldly fascination. Was he going to hit her? Rape her? Kill her? She knew then, with a clarity that surprised her that she'd rather be killed than raped. This was the cruel civilian world Scott had warned her about, her first real, ugly encounter with it since leaving the sanctuary of the order.

Brynn watched as the man extended his right arm at impossibly slow speed. She closed her eyes for a moment, not wanting to see where his hand was going, praying this would all just go away, that perhaps, despite her growing clarity, that it was all part of some incredibly vivid nightmare. But she knew it wasn't. When she didn't feel anything—he hadn't touched her—she peeked through scrunched eyes.

He'd taken the glass from the bedside table and raised it toward her, motioning her to drink.

She didn't know what to do. But she was so thirsty, she didn't feel she'd last another minute without liquid, though it'd only add to the fullness of her bladder.

The man cocked his head. He nodded and took three sips from the glass, then offered it to her again.

This time she didn't hesitate. She took the cup, raised it to her lips, poured a little liquid into her mouth, then forced it down. It was like rain falling on cracked, baked earth. The thought that if the man wanted to kill her, he would've done so, calmed her, and she took another sip then another until after a few greedy gulps the glass was empty. She set it on the little table and stared at her captor. She felt she could speak now, but didn't know if she should, or if he'd even understand her.

"You must drink," he said in a thick accent.

Brynn found the words and the fact that they were in English almost comforting but immediately reproached herself. She shouldn't take too much solace from them. The man could do anything he wanted to her. There was nothing she could do to stop him.

"You speak English," she said, trying to steady her voice.

"Yes. Does it surprise you?" His huge dark eyes flamed as he spoke. Brynn almost worried his face would catch fire.

She cleared her throat. "I'm grateful we can communicate."

"The chain will let you use the toilet, through there," he said, pointing at the door to her right.

Oh, thank God. Now she could finally use the bathroom. She struggled to sit up and was just about to lift herself off the bed when the man's next words froze her.

"Go while you are still able."

21

"Okay, I'm pretty sure *The Book of Hagu* that Aleister was talking about is mentioned in the Damascus Document," Larson said after he and Zady had retrieved the copy of the Dead Sea Scrolls and returned to the small office in the LOC. "Um, yeah, here it is, section ten: it says the judges of the Essene community at Qumran 'shall be learned in the Book of Meditation and in the constitutions of the Covenant—'"

"So, where does it mention *The Book of Hagu?*"

"Right there," he said, not looking up from the book. "Sometimes it's called *The Book of Meditation* or *The Book of Hagi.*"

"Gotcha."

"Here it is again. Same document, section thirteen. Members of the community shall be formed in groups of ten, 'And where the ten are, there shall never be lacking a Priest learned in *The Book of Meditation*; they shall all be ruled by him.' The next section says the priest of the congregation should be 'learned in *The Book of Meditation* and in all the judgments of the Law so as to pronounce them correctly.' And, if I'm right, it's mentioned in another Dead Sea Scroll...Oh, what the hell is it? I think it's the Messianic Rule." He flipped pages. "Here! In the first section. It's talking about the 'last days' and it says that during this time, the youth shall be instructed in *The Book of Meditation*."

"Great. But do we have any idea what *The Book of Hagu* slash *Hagi* slash *The Book of Meditation* is and where it might be?"

"Some people think it's another Dead Sea Scroll, the Temple Scroll to be specific."

"I don't think I'm going out on a limb by assuming the Temple Scroll is about the Temple in Jerusalem."

"Right, the building, the furniture, sacrifices at the altar, other laws. But there's not much secretive about the Temple Scroll—it's pretty cut and dry. Whatever's in *The Book of Hagu* is supposed to be secret. New members of the Essene community were required to take vows, mostly about piety, observing the rules of the community, etcetera, but one of them was to safeguard the secret books."

"But that begs the question of what the secret books are and where we can find them."

"I just thought of something else," Larson said. "In the Damascus Document there's mention of the 'Midrash Sefer Moshe.' It's in some of the other Dead Sea Scrolls, too. While experts disagree over whether it's the same as *The Book of Hagu*, there's agreement on one thing: both date to the time of Moses —'Moshe' is Hebrew for 'Moses'—and his successor, Joshua."

"Hold up. If *The Book of Hagu* dates to the time of Moses, centuries before Jesus, how can it have info on Jesus and John the Baptist that the Mandaeans are so concerned about?"

"Good point," Larson said.

"Shit, Scott, what are we going to do? We've got nothing. Time's ticking away, and we have no idea where Brynn is, if she's okay, or what the hell the treasure is. I hate to sound like you, but I feel like we're grasping at straws, wasting time trying to find answers when we just don't have enough to go on."

"Look, I've hesitated to mention this because it seems like a ridiculous longshot, but one of the Dead Sea Scrolls, the Copper

Scroll, written in the first century AD, mentions a treasure. The thing is, the amount doesn't make sense. It's simply too large an amount."

"Too large for what?"

"The scroll mentions twenty tons of silver, twice that of gold, some mixed precious metals, altogether ninety tons. But such a huge amount doesn't square with the facts. In the early 1990s, NATO held a conference on prehistoric gold and estimated that a treasure that size would've made up more than a quarter of all the gold and silver in the world at the time. How could anyone, let alone a small poor religious community like the Essenes, get their hands on that kind of wealth?"

"Okay, first, I can't believe you didn't mention this until now," Zady said. "Second, it's weird that a military alliance would hold a conference like that. But third, and most importantly, if there really was such a treasure someone would've found it by now."

"Exactly," Larson said. "No one's ever found anything. When I was working on the book about the Scrolls, I spent a long time researching it. But I couldn't find anything solid, and if we go down that path, we risk losing time, time that we need to save Brynn."

"Then why did you mention it?"

Larson shook his head. "I don't know. Maybe I just needed to say it so I can affirm it's a dead end."

Zady blew a frustrated raspberry. "Look, why don't we check with Uncle Al to find out where in Switzerland he resettled the Mandaeans. Maybe somebody there knows more about the book. It isn't much, but it's all I can come up with right now."

"If that's what you think is best," Larson said, "then let's do it."

22

The cameras were rolling in the packed Senate gallery. Madge Roberts had been too focused the day before to pay attention to them, but she was aware of their presence today, and thought about the millions of people across the world watching these events unfold. She felt like a lab specimen under a microscope. It wasn't just the president on trial; it was democracy itself. Especially after yesterday's attacks, and Jenkins' request to delay the trial, differences of opinion cleaved the air, threatening to tear the tattered fabric that barely held the nation together.

At nine o'clock sharp, Chief Justice Timothy Buckner brought the Senate to order. Immediately, Minority Leader Peter Bell asked to be recognized.

"Your Honor," he began, "in light of the ignominious attacks yesterday and per the president's request, I move that we postpone this trial until a more appropriate time." A murmur rippled through the floor and the galleries.

"Order, order," Buckner said, pounding his gavel. When silence returned, the chief justice removed his bifocals and rubbed his eyes. He considered things for a long moment then cleared his throat and said, hoarsely, "As the presiding officer, it falls within my purview to rule on this matter. I'm going to grant the motion to postpone. We'll reconvene one week from now, at nine o'clock Tuesday morning, to determine when the trial will recommence."

Before he could bring the gavel down, Roberts sprang to her feet. "Your Honor, while you do have the power to rule on this matter, it can be overturned by a simple majority. I move for a roll call vote on postponement. I also move that, prior to the vote, arguments for and against the motion be allowed."

"I'm going to have to consult with the parliamentarian," Buckner replied. "Mr. Sykes, would you approach?" A giraffe of a man sitting at a tiny desk in the well stood and climbed to the justice's side. In the minutes that passed before Sykes returned to his seat, a good deal of head shaking occurred.

"That motion is in order," Buckner said quietly, looking at Roberts. "I'll recognize a speaker for and against postponement, each with a ten-minute time limit. Then we'll take a vote. We'll recess for now to allow each side to prepare. We'll reconvene at one o'clock." He banged his gavel.

Roberts told her colleagues to meet in the Old Senate Chamber. "If that's how they want to play it," she muttered, gathering her things. It was definitely going to be an uphill battle. She thought again of the Harriet Tubman painting in her office. Yes, the price of freedom was eternal vigilance, the road long and hard. It was only the second day of the trial, but already she felt dog-tired. "Stay with me Harriet," she whispered exiting the chamber.

23

Brynn stood shakily before the fabric-covered window clutching an edition of *The New York Times* as her captor clicked a photo with a cell phone. The paper probably meant they were still in the States, but she couldn't be sure. She assumed it was Tuesday, the day on the paper, but she didn't know the time, or even if it was day or night, so completely was the room shrouded. The only light came from a rickety lamp on the bedside table; another artificial source glowed in the next room. The chain attached to her ankle hurt, but she could move about and was able to use the bathroom.

She limped back to the bed and massaged her ankle as best she could. The man watched her carefully, a predator studying his prey, then ducked into the other room and returned with a chair. He placed it at the foot of the bed, sat, and continued to observe her.

She was still scared, incredibly so, but her heart no longer felt like it would slash through her ribcage. Stark terror could be maintained only for so long. Much to her surprise, she was famished, her stomach felt like it was eating itself, and in the heavy silence it growled. Still, she didn't dare ask for anything to quell her hunger. The last thing she wanted was to provoke her captor in any way. Besides, her sanity, her survival, rested on transcending her physical and mental anguish. If she were to get through this, she must find comfort in God. It was to Him she must direct all her faculties. Though she'd been praying silently for hours, she knew she hadn't completely turned herself over to Him in the way she needed to.

Her mind raced through scriptural explanations for suffering, explanations she'd used when trying to help other souls in pain. But most of them—suffering as purification, as mystery, as expiation for sin—seemed glib. She eventually settled on a reason that felt truer: suffering to experience God in new ways, to participate in the life of Christ. She threw herself into prayer with complete abandon, forced herself to feel the passion: the Last Supper, the Garden of Gethsemane, the arrest, betrayal, and crucifixion. She remembered Saint Loyola's plea to consider what Christ our Lord suffers, or desires to suffer, so He can be with us in our own.

At some point in her reveries, her captor leaped from his seat with the speed of an ejected pilot and ran out of the room.

Brynn stiffened. She couldn't breathe. Where had he gone? And what would he do when he got back?

After a few seconds, he came in holding a book, plonked down in the chair, and thrust the book in front of him as if he were warding off a demon. The title was in Arabic, so Brynn couldn't read it, but the cover showed a man in front of a deformed Statue of Liberty. Lady Liberty stood on a pile of skulls, her tablet transformed into a short-fused bomb, her torch reshaped into an explosive device.

"It's all in here!" the man screamed, his eyes rollicking.

"I'm sorry," Brynn said, "I don't understand."

"Of course not," he scoffed. "You're American. This is Sayyid Qutb's *The America I Have Seen*." He pointed to the book as if no further explanation were needed.

Brynn stared at him, awaiting further illumination, but

none followed. After a moment, he set the book in his lap and stared off into the distance.

"I-I'm not familiar with the author...or the book," Brynn said, rubbing her stomach to ease its growl.

"Of course not," he repeated. "Your society is rotten and ill, just as Qutb says. You are technologically advanced, but primitive in other ways—your senses, your feelings, your behaviors. Spiritually and morally bankrupt. Your science and technology have no heart, no soul. They are divorced from religion. And your religion is confined. Americans go to church more than any other people in the West, but your religion stays in the church, which has become a social club. It is the individual, not Allah, that is at the center of your society. You have all become little gods, a herd of golden calves."

In the silence that followed, Brynn's stomach rumbled louder than before.

"Your stomach speaks of hunger," the man said. He rose to his feet and left the room.

Soon Brynn heard the whir of a can opener, the splash of the can's contents poured into a vessel, the hum of the microwave followed by a ding. The man returned carrying a tray with a bowl, napkin, and spoon. When he set the tray on her lap, she confirmed with her eyes what her nose already knew: he'd fixed her a bowl of chicken noodle soup. Hunger took over and she gulped down the soup. Though unevenly heated, it was like manna from heaven. Food had never tasted so good.

The man watched her eat for a moment then sat down and pulled out a cell phone from his pocket. He spent the next couple of minutes typing. When he was done, he set it on the floor and crushed it with his foot.

"There," he said, satisfied. "I sent the picture to your sister and priest. If I don't get the nameplate in the next three days, you will be with Allah."

24

Gazing out the window of the Learjet, Larson wished he could flip his feelings off. Flying over water always set off his hydrophobia. But he didn't have the time or the emotional energy to deal with that. He had to focus on getting to Switzerland and finding the Mandaean leader Aleister—who seemed very pleased with their decision to go to Bern—had told them about. Maybe he'd know where to look for *The Book of Hagu*—if that *were* the treasure the text referred to. He had to do everything he could to try to save Brynn.

Zady sat across the aisle. Clad in riding boots, indigo jeans, gray top, and tan scarf, she leaned against the window, typing furiously on her laptop. Despite her worry and fatigue, she looked beautiful. When she caught Larson staring, he averted his eyes and tried to focus on the surroundings.

The cabin of Aleister's plane was a flying living room: plush seats with built-in surround-sound, an enormous flat-screen TV, thick brocade carpeting, and a refrigerator stuffed with gourmet foods and drinks. In the back were two double beds, more comfortable than anything he'd ever slept on. And God only knew what kind of special technology the plane was equipped with. Aleister always was full of surprises.

"Did you hear me?" Zady asked.

"Yup," he said, though he hadn't. He'd been too lost in his thoughts for her words to register.

"What did I say?"

He hadn't much experience with women, but he knew he was in trouble. "I'd repeat it, but I'd rather hear you say it again," he said weakly.

"Nice try, Scott."

"You think Isabelle will be alright?" he asked.

"Yes, Mr. Non-Sequitur. Uncle Al will take good care of her. He was pretty insistent we go to Switzerland."

"Yeah, I noticed that. What did you say before?" he asked.

"Is this a retroactive conversation? If so, I look forward to hearing what you've already said. 'Let's play religious jeopardy,' is what I said earlier. It's something you should be good at."

He shrugged his shoulders and nodded. At least engaging his intellect was better than wallowing in emotional turmoil. Anything was better than that.

"Gautama Buddha, Dionysus, Quirinus, Attis, Indra, Adonis, Krishna, Zoroaster, and Mithra," Zady said.

"What are gods born of virgins?"

"Ding, ding, ding, we have a winner."

Zady was putting on a brave face, but it was forced, like smiling at a funeral. Larson saw her pain, felt it fill the cabin. Combined with his, it made it hard to breathe.

"Here's another one," she said. "Osiris, Attis, Tammuz, Adonis, and Dionysus were all born on this day."

"What is December 25th?"

"You're good at this, Scott. The Egyptian god Osiris even died on a Friday and was resurrected three days later. Sound familiar? Also, people who celebrated Dionysus' mysteries ingested him by eating bread and drinking wine. And Tammuz was not only born of a virgin on December 25th, but died with a wound in his side, rose from the tomb after three days, and left it empty. Okay, how about this one?"

Their phones dinged. Zady, whose phone was on the seat, drew first. Larson wormed his hand in his pocket to pull his out.

"Shit!" Zady exclaimed.

"What is it?" Larson gave up trying to get his cell and leaned across the aisle so he could see the phone in Zady's outstretched hand. It was a picture of Brynn holding a copy of *The New York Times*. She looked terrified. The text accompanying the picture was more alarming:

> You have 72 hours or she dies.

25

Chief Justice Buckner reconvened the impeachment trial at one o'clock. The Democrats chose Roberts to make their case. The Republicans, to her surprise, stuck with Senator Bell, who asked to be recognized. One row up and directly across the aisle, Roberts turned to watch her elderly Republican colleague draw himself up to his full height and cough once into his large hand.

"Thank you, your Honor," he said. "Distinguished colleagues, ladies, and gentlemen, I needn't remind anyone here that we are under attack by the forces of evil. For this reason, I urge that the trial against President John Paul Jenkins be delayed. We all saw what happened yesterday, how places of worship across this great nation were targeted and attacked by the cowardly forces of ISIS. Seventy people dead, one-hundred-and-twenty-nine wounded. It's the highest casualty toll we've suffered from Islamic terrorists since nine-eleven. The fact of the matter is we don't know when more attacks will occur. That's right; I said 'when,' not 'if.'"

Bell uttered the last word a little too forcefully, for he paused a moment, and furtively tried to adjust his dentures with his tongue. When he resumed speaking, his panic-stricken look coupled with the moment it took for his mouth to sync with his words, made Roberts think of a poorly dubbed Godzilla movie.

"That's why the president has declared a national emergency," he continued. "At this point, it is crucial he remains firmly at the helm. This tragedy reminds us that Islamic extremism is the gravest threat we face. And there is no greater vindication of the president's official recognition of the Judeo-Christian foundation of our great country. We must not only rally 'round the flag, but around the faith, faith in the one, true God. That is our only hope of triumphing in this war on terror. I ask you to take this to heart in your vote. Thank you." With that, Bell took his seat.

Roberts stood and eyed her Democratic colleagues then the Republicans. "Impeachment trials are hard," she began. "They're about removing a sitting, elected president from office, something that's never happened in our nation's history. That's an important responsibility. It's one the framers of the Constitution didn't take lightly. Nor should we. But the Constitution makes it clear that it's our duty, as senators, to take up this matter, to conduct a trial to determine whether the president should be convicted of the charges brought against him. Each of us should feel the weight that this tremendous responsibility places on us—not only as senators, but as citizens of this country.

"Now, I'll be the first to condemn yesterday's attacks. I, along with all of you, was appalled at the violence. I sat stunned, horrified, watching the news reports come in. These cowardly acts are beyond the pale and the perpetrators must be punished to the full extent of the law. When I look at the list of the dead and wounded, I'm reminded that Jews and Christians were killed, men and women, young and old, rich and poor. And in this diverse group of victims I'm reminded of one of the greatest things about America, something so fundamental to who we are as a nation that it's inscribed on our currency: '*E pluribus unum*': 'Out of many, one.' And we stand as one in opposing these attacks. Security has been tightened, our military remains on alert, and I think I can say that all of us are preparing ourselves physically, emotionally, spiritually for whatever comes next. We're all doing what we can, what we must, in the aftermath of yesterday's tragedy.

"But the threat of terrorism is unlike other threats to our national security. It's not an enemy we face out in the open on a designated battlefield, until one side is beaten or surrenders. Terrorists lurk among us, in our midst. Unfortunately, and despite our best efforts, this threat will persist into the foreseeable future. Yes, this country has done what it can to prepare. We hope for the best and prepare for the worst and we will continue to do so regardless of who occupies the Oval Office.

"But let me ask you this: if now is not the time for this trial, then when? And given his flagrant disregard of the Constitution, if not Jenkins, then who? If we don't act now, impeachment risks becoming a paper tiger, serving no use whatsoever. Now, there's never a 'good' time for impeachment. Andrew Johnson's trial took place after the Civil War, when our country was struggling to rebuild itself into a nation better than it'd been. Impeachment proceedings were launched against Richard Nixon during Vietnam. In each case, senators were prepared to undertake their constitutionally prescribed duty to determine the president's guilt or innocence, and whether he should be removed from office. Today we *must* forge ahead, heavy as the burden might be. Is it the perfect time for this trial? No. But that's the point: there never is a perfect time for such proceedings. Come what may the government of this country must continue to function. It did so during the First and Second World Wars, and during all the conflicts before and after. We must not let terrorists dictate our agenda, nor the pace of our politics. Thank you." Roberts took her seat.

"Thank you, senators," Buckner said. "Now we'll proceed to a roll call vote. When the clerk calls your name, please stand by your desk, and say 'yea' or 'nay' regarding the motion to post-pone the trial."

The clerk called the senators alphabetically; each stood to cast his or her vote. Roberts knew it was going to be close, but only a simple majority was needed. Her stomach clenched as the votes came in and were recorded and tallied:

Forty-nine in favor of postponement, fifty-one opposed, perfectly partisan. The trial would continue the next day.

26

Z ady had forwarded the picture of Brynn and the text to
Aleister and now had him on speakerphone. "What
now?" she asked. "We still don't know if whoever has
her wants the nameplate or the treasure. And even if we find
one or the other or both how are we going to let whoever has
Brynn know?"

The desperation in her voice moved Larson. Seldom in his
life had he felt so alone, so helpless, so completely out of ideas;
he couldn't even imagine how Zady felt.

"I think you and Scott should continue on to Switzerland to
see if you can find out anything about the book, while I stay
here and try to determine who has the nameplate." Given the
circumstances, Aleister's voice sounded surprisingly calm.

"I don't know," Zady replied. "A huge part of me feels like I
should be closer to home. I have a feeling Brynn never left the
States. Plus, she's holding a copy of *The New York Times*. I know
you can get it internationally, but it just seems to confirm what
my gut is telling me. Going to Bern seems more and more like a
wild goose chase."

"I think you should stay the course," Aleister said.

Zady screwed up her face and looked at Larson. "Scott, what do you think?"

Before he could answer, their cell phones dinged. He read the message:

> Find Moses' treasure

Zady read hers at the same time. "We just got another message, Uncle Al," she told him. "It says 'find Moses' treasure.'"

"Well, at least it's a little more guidance," Aleister said tentatively.

"Is it really?" Zady asked. "Shit, I don't know. I'm going to talk to Scott and see what we can come up with. Call me the second you find anything out." She ended the call and stared at Larson. "You're up, genius."

"Other than the Ark of the Covenant, I have no idea what Moses' treasure could be," he said, silently berating himself for his inability to think of anything else.

"Great. Now what the hell are we gonna do?"

"We need more info," he said. "Maybe there's something we're missing."

"No shit, Sherlock!"

"I'll tell you one thing," he said. "I don't think the answer's in Switzerland."

Zady blew a frustrated sigh through her lips. "I agree. But I don't think telling the pilot *not* to head to Switzerland is a game plan."

"Point taken. But whatever Moses' treasure is, it has to be in the Middle East. Moses spent his life there—in Egypt, and then in the desert, looking for the promised land. If we're going to figure out what the message means, we're going to need more sources. I say we head to Jerusalem. There's a good religious library there, the École Biblique, I've used it lots of times. And that way, once we figure out what we're looking for, we'll already be in the right neighborhood."

"I'll tell the pilot and let Aleister know the change of plans," Zady said. "But Scott," she said, gentling her voice, "we have to be quick. We've got to find her."

"We will," Larson replied, sounding more confident than he felt.

27

Brynn wished she could retract her question because as soon as she said it, she knew it sounded facile. But there was no way to take it back. The man rose to his feet quietly and calmly, which scared her more than if he'd leaped up, screaming. But his eyes glowed and the blood rushed to his face. For a moment, she feared he'd hit her. Or worse. Instead, he curled his hands into fists and spoke in the quiet, calm tone of a sociopath.

"The question isn't why *we* hate *you*," he said, "but why *you* hate *us*."

"I don't," Brynn said meekly.

"Yes, you do. You only say that to trick me. All women are seductive temptresses."

"Not all of us."

"Yes, you are." The man considered her for a moment. "Your country is making war against Muslims everywhere, all under the guise of fighting terrorism. America wants to control the Middle East just like the French and British in the last century."

Brynn was about to disagree, but the man pressed ahead.

"The declaration of war on Afghanistan and the invasion and occupation of Iraq were not about 9/11. They were the start of World War Three, pitting the Christian West against the Islamic East. What Jenkins has done now, declaring the U.S. a Judeo-Christian nation, is a logical consequence of everything that came before."

"But not all of us agree," Brynn said. "Isn't lumping all Americans together, saying we all want to destroy Islam, the same thing as labeling all Muslims terrorists?"

"You are right," the man said. "There is a difference between America's government and its people. Just as Americans are fooled into thinking they control the government, they were fooled into war against Iraq. And not all terrorist acts are the work of 'Islamic extremists,' as your president says. Some of them are the work of the enemy within."

"You mean domestic terrorists?" Brynn asked.

Her captor smiled, but it didn't reach his eyes.

WEDNESDAY

28

ind Moses' treasure.

The words had been burned into Larson's mind since he and Zady had received the text. Though they'd been on their way to Switzerland to talk with the Mandaean leader about *The Book of Hagu* the text had changed their destination to Jerusalem, and the École Biblique, where they now sat at a small table surrounded by piles of books. They'd been researching for hours, and dawn was approaching.

Larson knew the time to save Brynn was dwindling. After checking into the King David Hotel, they'd slipped into this library courtesy of the punch code Larson remembered from his time spent researching the Dead Sea Scrolls. But ever since his break with the Church, he was a persona non grata, and didn't feel entirely safe here—it was, after all, a Catholic institution. Of course, given the hour, they were the only patrons. In the short time he'd had to research, he'd come up with several ideas. Only time would tell if they were any good. He closed the book he'd been scanning and set it on top of the pile.

"What've you come up with?" Zady asked. "The sun will be up soon. Then three days becomes two."

"Maybe something," he said.

"Not liking the sound of that."

"I know. Well, first, there's always the Ark of the Covenant."

"Isn't that a little too cliché?" Zady said.

"I didn't say it was a sure thing, but—"

"People have been looking for it forever. The most anyone's come up with is that a group of Ethiopians have it."

"The Ethiopian Jews, also known as the Beta Israel," he said.

"Yeah, them. Trust me, it's not the Ark. But why is ISIS, or whoever's sending the messages, being so vague? 'Find the treasure.' Then 'Find Moses' treasure.' I mean, hello! Why are they making it so damn hard?"

"Keep your voice down. We can't be sure we're the only ones here." Ignoring the snarky, lip-curled face she made he said, "But what if it *is* the Ark and—?"

"What if nothing."

He sighed, but knew it wasn't worth pursuing. Zady had already made up her mind. "Truthfully, I have my doubts it's the Ark—"

"Because it's not."

"So, I came up with a couple other ideas."

"Shoot," Zady said.

"Moses died before the Hebrews reached Israel. There's a first-century Jewish work called *The Assumption of Moses* that contains secret prophecies he revealed to his successor, Joshua. In it, Moses refers to secret books and talks about a mysterious figure named TAXO. Now, using the Atbash cipher developed by Hugh Schonfield, it—"

"Using the what developed by who?"

"The Atbash cipher developed by Doctor Hugh Schonfield."

"Yeah, Scott. Not helping."

"It's a simple substitution code. There're twenty-two letters in the Hebrew alphabet. The cipher exchanges the first eleven letters for the last eleven in reverse order. To take the English alphabet for example, Z would become A, Y would become B, X would become C, and so on. Using it, the name TAXO is rendered Asaph. Who knows? Maybe Asaph is the mysterious Teacher of Righteousness mentioned in the Dead Sea Scrolls."

Larson was flipping through a book as he explained but raised his eyes when he heard Zady pretend-snore. "What's the matter?"

"Sorry, I dozed off. I don't think ISIS could care less about the Teacher of Righteousness, and, in terms of finding secret books mentioned by Moses in a first-century work only two people have ever heard of—that would be you and the person who wrote them—I think it's a dead end."

"All right. Then how about this? Reference is made—in the Apocrypha, Midrash, and Old Testament—to Moses having detailed plans of the Temple. That would've been long before Solomon built the First Temple in Jerusalem. Maybe that's what Moses' treasure refers to."

"When did Moses live?"

"Some say the fourteenth century, others the thirteenth century B.C. But there's no historical proof."

"What do you mean 'no historical proof'?"

"There's no historical evidence to support anything in the Old Testament prior to 900 B.C., some would even say prior to 300 B.C."

"So, you're saying there's no evidence for most of the people in the Old Testament—Abraham, Noah, Moses?"

"That's right. Some scholars think people in the Bible are at best only based on real, historical people, or represent them, like allegories."

"So, religion is essentially make-believe, like I've known all along. Great. When did Solomon supposedly live, according to the myth?"

"Three or four hundred years after Moses."

Zady chewed her lip. "So, that would mean Moses had plans of the Temple three or four hundred years before Solomon built it? Where would he have gotten them?"

"That's the $64,000 question. Nowhere does it say he

received them atop Mount Sinai, along with the command-ments. It's also odd that many of the Dead Sea Scrolls refer to priests being appointed to 'the Temple' in the time of Jacob. Because Jacob, whose sons were the leaders of the twelve tribes of Israel, came *before* Moses."

"So, where was the Temple then?"

"Where, indeed?"

Zady shook her head. "It's interesting, but I'm not sure how it relates to Moses' treasure. Why would plans for a temple, supposing Moses had them, matter to ISIS, anyway? No. The more I think about it, the more I think Moses' treasure is just that: treasure—silver and gold and whatnot."

"Why?" Larson asked.

"Because ISIS' back is against the wall. It needs money. It's faced some big setbacks over the past few years. I would think it wants to get its hands on something it can use to buy guns and bombs and shit."

Larson thought for a moment. "But if that's the case, then what's the treasure?"

"I'm not sure," Zady replied, typing on her laptop. "But I have an idea."

He stood up, about to return to the stacks for more sources, when she held up an index finger.

"What?" He fought to keep the annoyance out of his voice.

"According to these passages in Exodus, Moses left Egypt with a shitload of treasure."

"Can you be a little more specific?" he asked.

"Okay, remember when God tells Moses to use silver and gold to make the tabernacle, Ark, table, lampstand, altar, and priestly garments, after he fled Egypt? Well, this says Moses used over a ton of gold and three and three-quarters of a ton of silver to do it. It's all here in Exodus 38:24-25. Like I said, a shit-load of treasure."

"That makes more sense than the amount in the Copper Scroll. I mean, it's still a huge portion of the gold and silver in the world at the time, but Egypt *was* the dominant civilization then, so it adds up."

"How come you didn't remember this, Scott?"

"After a while you start to take certain passages for granted," he said more defensively than he'd intended. "To the point they don't register anymore. The golden calf and making all those objects out of silver and gold are like that."

"I'll tell you another reason," Zady said. "You get too wrapped up in the details and can't see the bigger picture. The whole forest-for-the-trees thing."

Larson's thoughts turned to the biblical account of Moses. There was something about the Ten Commandments that niggled at the back of his brain whenever he thought about them. He almost had it.... Yes, that was it.

"I just remembered something," he said, trying to keep his voice down. "It might be nothing, but then again—"

"Just spit it out," Zady told him.

"You know how the commandments were inscribed on stone tablets Moses carried down Mount Sinai?"

"Yeah, so?"

"They couldn't have been in Hebrew. Written Hebrew didn't exist at the time Moses allegedly lived, not until hundreds of years later in fact. They had to be written in hieroglyphics, which Moses, being raised in Egypt, would've understood."

29

"How many times do I have to say this? The treasure *isn't* the Ark of the Covenant," Zady said, following Larson into his third-floor room of the King David Hotel. "It's the treasure in Exodus, the one Moses schlepped out of Egypt. And why is your room so much bigger than mine? We're right next to each other."

"I'm not saying you're wrong," Larson said, ignoring her last question and laying a stack of books on the dresser across from the queen-sized bed. "I'm just saying it could be something else."

"Yeah, something like the Ark of the Covenant," Zady said, sinking into one of two chairs at the round table in the corner. "Even your window's nicer. I like the arch at the top."

After opening the drapes, Larson joined her. "Well, it could be the Secret Books of Moses mentioned in *The Assumption of Moses*." He was so tired he couldn't see straight. "Or the plans for the Temple, or even *The Book of Hagu*, if it goes back that far."

"You make me so mad," Zady said, yanking her phone from her bag with one hand and shielding her eyes from the sun with the other. "I'm gonna call Aleister and see what he thinks." She got up and closed the drapes then pushed a number on speed dial. "Seriously, Scott. You need to buy a vowel and solve the puzzle. You're such a—Hi, Uncle Al. Any news?" She listened to the response. "Okay, well keep trying...Yes, I know. Me, too. Listen, Scott and I need your help." She relayed the last text and ideas for what Moses' treasure might be. "Yes, they all sound good. Right. But isn't one of them best? Say, for instance, the gold and silver Moses took out of Egypt when he fled from Pharaoh?... All right, but we're running out of time... I know. Okay, bye."

Larson raised an eyebrow.

"He said he's following a couple of leads on Brynn, which is good, but..."

"What did he say about Moses' treasure?"

"He said he's not convinced any of the ideas are best. But I think he knows in his heart which one it is."

"And that would be *yours*," Larson said.

"Damn it, Scott, I don't know. Every minute that goes by is wasted if it doesn't bring us closer to Brynn. I don't know what the hell to do. I'm so tired I can barely keep my eyes open, but we have to keep going."

"I don't think we're going to be much use to Brynn unless we get some rest." Zady started to protest, but he went on. "Not for long, maybe just a power nap. But, honestly, at this point, I can barely form a coherent thought."

Zady considered for a moment. He could see the battle waging inside her. "I guess you're right, but not a long rest."

30

Larson woke to a buzz. It was his phone in his pants pocket.

Another text. Was it Zady? Did it have to do with Brynn, or Moses' treasure?

He yanked out the phone, looked fuzzily at the screen. The first thing he saw was the time: It was almost noon. He'd slept for hours. Then he read the message, again from an unknown source:

> Ag + Au

The pounding at the door made him jump. Fully awake, he sprang from the bed and peeked through the hole in the door. It was Zady. He threw open the door and she stormed in, thrusting her phone in front of her.

"Shit! Shit! Shit! I can't believe we slept so long! Did you get it?"

"I got it," he said.

"So, it looks like I was right. Ag and Au, the chemical symbols for silver and gold. I knew we were dealing with a real treasure. It must be the gold and silver Moses took out of Egypt. But there's one thing that bothers me."

"I'm glad there's only one thing," Larson said.

"If Moses didn't really exist, is his treasure make-believe, too?"

Larson rubbed his chin. "Fair point. Well, I suppose one way to approach it is to tie the treasure to someone we know existed around the same time. That way, we can at least figure out whose treasure it could've been. A real historical personage."

"So, the fourteenth, or thirteenth, century B.C.? That's kinda broad. Is there any way to narrow it down? We're running out of time here."

"Wait," Larson said. "Last night, or early this morning, I ran across something that might help. I didn't think much of it at the time, but some of the Dead Sea Scrolls mention great events, important things, that happened at the end of 490-year blocks, starting from the creation of the world. According to the Essenes, the most important event in human history took place at the end of the seventh block. The tenth block marked what they considered the end days, around 115 or 120 A.D. So, if we start there, let's say the year 120, and count backwards, by three 490-year blocks, we get an approximate date of 1350 B.C."

"Which means? C'mon, Scott, you're making my head hurt."

"So, according to the Essenes, the most important event in human history happened circa 1350. While we don't know if or when Moses existed, if the treasure refers to the silver and gold he took out of Egypt, then that year should tell us."

"But what? *What* should it tell us?"

"Which pharaoh ruled Egypt at the time, which we do have historical data on. The Book of Exodus doesn't name the pharaoh."

"I'll check who it was." Zady thumb-pumped her phone. "Amenhotep IV, a.k.a. Akhenaten, became pharaoh in 1350 B.C." She sucked her teeth. "I don't know. It seems like a stretch. And even if it's true, why would the Essenes consider the rise of an Egyptian pharaoh the most important event ever?"

"I don't know, but it's all I can come up with right now. I say we try to learn all we can, as fast as we can, about Akhenaten's wealth."

"I guess it's some sort of plan," she admitted.

Just then their cell phones dinged. Zady was still holding her phone. She looked at it then read the text aloud:

"'Sixty hours before she dies.'"

31

Larson stood in front of the hotel bathroom mirror wielding a disposable razor, doing what he could to remove the bluish stubble on his face and neck. Shaving hadn't been a priority over the past couple days. Zady had gone back to her room to splash some water on her face and grab her tote bag. The plan was for her to come right back and strategize. Another call to Aleister was on the horizon. And then they would—

Zady threw open the door to the room—he'd left it unlocked—and stormed inside. Larson dashed out of the bathroom, half his face and neck covered in shaving cream. Without a word, she grabbed him by the arm and tugged him to a chair at the table. He plonked in the seat and noticed the envelope clutched in her hand for the first time.

"What's that?" he asked.

Silently, she handed it to him. It was a small white envelope. No address. No postal marks. He turned it over and saw it was sealed with a small blob of red wax. He tore it open and pulled out a piece of paper. There was printed English on both sides, so small and neat it looked like the work of a calligrapher.

"Have you read it?" he asked.

"Skimmed," Zady replied. It was the first thing she'd said since returning. Larson was glad to hear her speak, even just the one word; her uncharacteristic silence was unnerving.

"I'll just read it aloud," he said.

Zady nodded.

"'Consider mankind as the flocks of God. He made the sky for the enjoyment of their hearts, he repelled the greed of the waters, he created the breath of life for their noses. His images are they, the products of his flesh. He rises in the sky for their hearts' desire, for them he has made the plants, animals, birds, and fish—all for their delight.' Underneath that it says, 'Pyramid Texts'."

Zady stared at him, waiting for an explanation.

"The Pyramid Texts are the oldest known ancient Egyptian texts. From what I remember, they date back to the third millennium B.C."

"So, this is from a book?"

"Not exactly," Larson said. "The Pyramid Texts are inscriptions carved into the walls and sarcophagi of royal tombs."

"What you read sounds a lot like the creation story in Genesis."

"Yes, it does. But this was written long before that."

"What's on the other side?"

He turned the paper over and read the five lines of text. "'I have done no falsehood. I have not robbed. I have not stolen. I have not killed men. I have not told lies.' Below that are the words 'Book of the Dead,' another ancient Egyptian text."

"And those sound like some of the commandments," Zady said, thumbing her phone. "According to this, the commandment-sounding passages come from Spell 125 of the Book of the Dead, which dates to the mid-sixteenth century B.C. Isn't that at least a couple of centuries before Moses is supposed to have lived, if he really did?"

"It is," Larson said.

"The real question is who put this in my room?"

Before he could answer, Zady pushed a button on her phone.

"Yes, my dear." It was Aleister.

"Hey. I'm going to put you on speaker." She set her phone on the table and relayed the last texts: the one that seemed to confirm that the treasure they were looking for was gold and silver, and the sixty hours Brynn had left.

"Oh, no," Aleister exclaimed.

"Wait, there's more," She told him about the envelope she'd found in her room and summarized what it said. "It looks like someone's pointing us in the direction of Egypt, but I don't know what to do. I feel like we should just come home and help you find Brynn. Something tells me she's not in Egypt, that she's a lot closer to the Potomac than the Nile."

"No, no, don't do that," Aleister said.

Zady furrowed her brows then cocked her head at Larson.

"O-kay, it sounds like you don't want us with you."

"It's not that. It's just that I, too, have a feeling. That I'm close to finding Brynn."

"But how would our coming back change that?" Zady asked.

"I can't say for sure," Aleister said quietly, "but I think it's better to have more irons in the fire."

"*Can't* say or *won't* say?" she pressed.

"Even if the messages about the treasure are coming from a different source, I'm sure they both have something to do with Brynn. You and Scott should keep looking for it. It sounds like the clues are leading you to Egypt. You could go to the library at Alexandria—we have contacts there—if you need to research the Egyptian creation story or Spell 125 in the Book of the Dead."

Zady's eyes widened. Then she let out an exasperated sigh. "Well, if you think you've got a good lead on Brynn—"

"I do, Zady. I really do."

She looked at Larson and shrugged. "All right, then. Scott and I'll head to Alexandria."

"I think it's for the best," Aleister told her. "Let's touch base soon."

"Yes, let's." She ended the call and stared out the window.

"Looks like we're headed to Egypt," Larson said.

"Yup," she replied distractedly, not looking at him.

"What's the matter?"

Zady shook her head as if to reset her brain then set her eyes on his. "Did you notice anything odd about that conversation?"

"Well, there's plenty of odd to go around," Larson said. "Do you mean how it sounded like he didn't want us to go back home to help him find Brynn?"

"That and when I told him about the commandment-sounding passages from the Book of the Dead. I never said anything about them coming from Spell 125. But he already knew. What's going on, Scott?"

"I wish I knew."

32

Aleister Mabrey tried his best to muster his wits, but with Brynn missing he found it all he could do to "hold it together," as the Yanks would say, though he was glad Zady and Larson would be out of the country, and, hopefully, out of danger, as he did everything he could to find her. That was his intention.

Though he couldn't tell Brynn's location from the picture Zady forwarded, it'd given him an idea; he'd blown up the image and at its edges, around the black curtain, the rough-hewn wooden logs indicated a cabin. And that idea had led him here, to his spartan office at DoveCo. headquarters in Reston, Virginia.

He was about to pursue his lead on his computer when, out of the corner of his eye, he caught a glimpse of the photo on his desk of him and his two nieces in Fira, on Santorini, outside a seafood restaurant on the red, white, and black sand. He recalled the tall, steep cliffs in the volcanic caldera of the Greek archipelago surrounded by an azure lagoon on three sides. Cotton-white homes, their windows alive with red geraniums, straddled the cliffs in precarious splendor. A blue-domed church, near where they stood in the photo, yielded a spectacular view. Curvy, pristine yachts sailed in the lagoon alongside the wooden vessels used in the waters for millennia. The crystalline air there was clement, the breeze divine.

He swallowed hard and blinked fast. Crying was un-British. But Brynn was gone, and as hard as he tried, he couldn't quite process it. The possibility of becoming a weepy old man disgusted him and stiffened his resolve. He sat up as straight as he could in his wheelchair to focus. It'd been a long time since he'd accessed the database, but he was confident he could still do it. Taking a deep breath, he dredged his memory. There was only one way to get in. Of that, he was certain. But the ultra-secret nature of the data made any record of accessing it dangerous. Lethal. And he needed to stay alive, for now at least, until he rescued Brynn...and finished the letter to his nieces. Because he could never tell them the truth while he lived.

But for some reason, knowing they'd discover the truth once he was gone made the thought of dying easier. Because he wanted them to know, needed them to know, didn't want them to continue wandering in darkness for the rest of their lives. He couldn't stand to break their hearts much longer, and now given everything that was going on, he knew he had to finish the letter soon.

One by one he navigated the complicated security screens in a seemingly endless stream of digital hurdles. Along the way, he hit a few walls but racked his brain till he remembered the right commands, knowing a failed attempt to pull up data would be investigated immediately. After more than an hour, he found what he wanted. He committed the coordinates to memory then turned off the computer and called Lance Sterling into his office.

Sterling stepped into the room a moment later, his composed manner providing much-needed comfort. Mabrey motioned for him to sit in the chair at the side of his desk.

"You wanted to see me?" Sterling said, lowering himself into the seat with military rigidity.

Mabrey looked into the sparkling gray eyes he'd trusted ever since coming from across the pond and establishing his mercenary company. "I need you to do something for me," he said. "Ready your top guys. We're going to get Brynn back, no matter the cost, no matter the danger."

"Of course," Sterling said. "Will that be all?"

"Yes."

Sterling got up to leave and was halfway out the door when Mabrey stopped him. "Oh, and Lance?"

"Yes, sir?"

There was so much Mabrey wanted to say, how getting Brynn back was the most important mission they'd ever undertaken, that he, Sterling, and any or all of the other men, might not come through.

"Never mind," Mabrey said.

Sterling nodded and shut the door behind him. Mabrey removed the key from around his neck and opened the desk drawer. He took out the unfinished letter, reread it, then picked up a pen and began to write, blinking back tears as his hand moved slowly across the page.

33

At nine o'clock that morning, lead prosecutor Ananya Chandler stood before the Senate to begin her argument for Jenkins' conviction. Roberts was impressed with the way Chandler carried herself, tall and lithe, the very embodiment of grace. Her lovely mocha-colored skin and piercing green eyes mesmerized, and the Bindi in the center of her forehead was like a smudged crimson beauty mark, a stamp of approval from the gods.

"No issue divides Americans more than religion's proper role in the public sector," Chandler began in her dulcet tone. "As stated in the First Amendment, 'Congress shall make no law respecting an establishment of religion or prohibiting the free exercise thereof.' The Founding Fathers were very clear on this point. They had to be. Their ancestors had fled from religious persecution, and they, in their wisdom, sought to firmly establish tolerance in the New World. But surely, one might argue, the founders were Christian and wouldn't object to calling America a Christian nation.

"But most of the founders weren't Christian. They believed in one, true God, for sure, but for the most part they were Deists and Unitarians. Their view of God was one of a clockmaker, one who'd set the universe in motion then left it to run its course, according to the notion of free will to which the men subscribed. This conception of God left little room for divine interference in human affairs, or of personal salvation through Jesus Christ. There is no mention of God, let alone Christ, in the Constitution. The Treaty of Tripoli in 1796 went as far as to state in Article II that 'the Government of the United States of America is not, in any sense, founded on the Christian religion.'

"But let's put these things aside for a moment," Chandler continued. "Let's give Christians their due. Let's see what Jesus himself says on the proper role of church and state." She opened a Bible she produced to a marked place and pointed with a finger. "In Matthew 22:21 Jesus says, 'Render to Caesar the things that are Caesar's; and to God the things that are God's.'"

She raised her eyes to look at her colleagues then flipped to another marked page in the book. "In the same gospel Jesus also says that 'when you pray, do not be like the hypocrites, for they love to pray standing in the synagogues and on the street corners to be seen by men. I tell you the truth, they have received their reward in full. But when you pray, go into your room, close the door, and pray to your Father, who is unseen. Then your Father, who sees what is done in secret will reward you.'"

She paused. "Whenever religion and politics become entangled both are worse off. History shows how the blending of political and religious authority has been used for oppression: the Pharaohs in ancient Egypt, Caesar in imperial Rome, divine rule in the Middle Ages—all led to the corruption of politics and religion.

"The Founding Fathers, better students of history than are we, knew this. So much did they worry about the potential for corruption if politics and religion were mixed that Article VI of the Constitution states that 'no religious Test shall ever be required as a Qualification to any Office or public Trust under the United States.' This shows an inherent belief that God isn't partisan, that no one person or institution can claim to act in God's name unless they wish to lay claim to the thorny crown of self-righteousness. For if you claim to act in God's name, what prevents anyone else from doing the same? Is one person's religious belief more valid than another's? If so, why? What criteria can we use to determine whose belief should prevail?

"There's irony here, too. For if we allow religion to dictate our politics, we become like the Islamic theocracies this president and his administration have deemed the gravest threat to our security.

"And beyond that is something overlooked on both sides of the debate. Government involvement in religion risks the sanctity and inviolability of religion itself. The Founding Fathers worried that the government might prevent people from practicing their religion just as much as they worried that one faith would dominate and force its views on the rest. This, they feared, would force people, through taxation, to support a faith they didn't believe in. Keeping government out of religion lets religion flourish and lets each person follow their faith. It also lets those who choose not to follow a religion or believe in God to live without persecution. For freedom *of* religion also means freedom *from* religion."

As Roberts nodded from her seat her phone vibrated in her jacket pocket. *Who in the hell would be calling or texting me now?* Everyone knew where she was. She pulled out her cell as discreetly as she could and held it under her desk. It was a text from her chief of staff:

> There's a manila envelope sitting on your desk marked confidential. Thought you'd want to know.

Why was that damned fool bothering her about the mail?

She shook her head, pocketed her phone, and tried to turn her attention back to Chandler's opening salvo. But now she was distracted. What was in the envelope? Who sent it? Did it have anything to do with the trial? *Thanks a lot, Carl.* She'd give him a piece of her mind the next time she saw him. Of that, he could be sure.

34

At Ben Gurion Airport in Lod, Israel, Zady yanked Larson back around the corner of Terminal 1.

He looked questioningly at her.

She shook her head.

Though he'd rounded the corner first, she'd spotted something. With his back hugging the wall, he craned his neck to look. A few private planes on the tarmac were loading and unloading passengers in the bright afternoon sun. Ground crew-driven luggage trains piled high with black bags taxied about. One morbidly obese woman drove a motorized cart at reckless speed, dodging obstacles left and right, nearly running over an old man who flipped her the bird as she raced past.

Then to his far right he saw it: Aleister's Learjet surrounded by armored vehicles and a group of soldiers with assault rifles. The sun glinted off the weapons and dark glasses of the soldiers, temporarily blinding him. He rubbed his eyes, hoping it was a hallucination of some sort, a trick of the sun, but when his vision refocused, the vehicles and soldiers were still there. A sickening dread filled his stomach and threatened to launch from his throat.

He pulled his head back. "Do you think they saw us?" he yelled over the roar of arriving and departing planes.

Zady said something.

"What?" Larson screamed.

With the speed of a magician, she produced her phone from her tote bag and began typing. When she finished, she pointed the phone at him. He shielded his eyes so he could read it:

> We're going to have to come up with another plan.

Larson tugged his phone out of his pocket and typed:

> What's going on?

Zady read the words then shrugged her shoulders. She held up a finger then typed some more.

Larson typed on his phone:

> Pilot?

She nodded.

They waited a moment, but there was no response from the pilot. Larson watched as Zady pulled up Google then navigated through several screens before she typed a message and showed it to him:

> We need to get to Terminal 3.

Larson nodded then pumped his arms up and down as if he were jogging.

Zady shook her head then typed:

> It's two miles. Let's take the shuttle.

Once onboard Zady took Larson's cell from him and disabled the tracking device on it then did the same to her own phone. Just before the shuttle reached the terminal, she quietly transferred a paper sack from her tote to Larson's overnight bag.

After passing through the terminal's automated glass doors, Zady pointed to the restrooms. When she entered the women's room, Larson went into the men's. Finding an unoccupied stall, he closed the door, put a tissue cover over the seat, and plunked down. He took out the paper sack Zady had stuck in his bag and opened it. Inside was a passport, several hundred shekels, a wig of flowing hair—darker than his, and a fake beard and moustache. The passport had a photo of him with long, dark locks and facial hair, with the name Lester Baumgarten, an Israeli citizen born two years after Larson.

He'd never worn a disguise in his life. Who was he: James Bond trying to shake the Russians? But they did need to get out of Dodge and the Learjet was surrounded. This is what he got for getting mixed up in all this. He donned the disguise and left the stall feeling ridiculous, less like Bond than Maxwell Smart, trying to evade the evil clutches of KAOS.

When Zady came out of the bathroom, he barely recognized her. The blonde wig and hazel contacts, the way she carried herself, everything about her was different. Obviously, she'd done this before.

"*Obtenez le prochain vol vers Le Caire. Air Sinai,*" she said in perfect French.

"*Oui,*" he replied.

Then she was off.

There were so many airlines at the front counter it took him a moment to find the line for Air Sinai so he could buy a ticket to Cairo. The cavernous lobby was fresh out of a Kafka novel. Names were being called over the intercom, as were flight arrivals and departures. Passengers stood in line, fidgeting, talking on their phones. A young mother with a little dark-haired daughter stood in front of him, the mother urging the child in hushed Hebrew to never mind her doll, it was already packed. Larson smiled at the girl who smiled back, but the mother tugged her arm and stared suspiciously at him. The air smelled of coffee mixed with perfume and bad breath.

Nearing the counter, he tried switching his thoughts to Hebrew. But he was so anxious he could only think in English. So many questions plagued him. What if someone had seen him enter the terminal sans long hair and beard then emerge from the restroom like a hirsute Superman? Why did Zady insist on heading to Cairo instead of Alexandria, like they'd told Aleister? And where was she? He switched his overnight bag from one shoulder to the other in nervous anticipation.

After what felt like both an eternity and a flash, he reached the counter and asked for a ticket to Cairo, rather proud of his fluid Hebrew. The skinny attendant stifled a yawn and asked for Larson's passport. After Larson handed it to him, he took it with tobacco-stained fingers and scrutinized it with jeweler-like intent, peering back and forth from the photo to Larson. Finally, he handed it back, printed the ticket, and told him the flight left in an hour.

When Larson turned away from the counter, he spotted Zady at the end of the queue. Even when they made eye contact, her face remained impassive. He gazed at her longer than he should have, and when he realized it, chastised himself and stared at the floor, preparing himself for what he knew would be the toughest hurdle so far—Israeli airport security.

The line wasn't long, despite the grilling each passenger received, and by the time he reached the guard, his stomach was somersaulting; his mouth felt like sandpaper. He still had his passport out, so he handed it to the guard and tried to force a smile, convinced he looked like the village idiot.

The cartoonishly muscled man glared at the passport then at Larson and let loose a barrage of questions, leaving him no chance of an answer before the next one. Where would he stay in Cairo? Why was he going? How long would he be there? The guard stared at him with eyes like sharpened stakes.

Heart throbbing so loudly he was sure the guard heard it, Larson said he was staying at the Hilton—God, please let there be a Hilton there—and was going to take in some sites: the Egyptian Museum, the Citadel, the Mosque of Ibn Tulun. He wasn't sure how long he'd stay, which is why he hadn't booked a return. He threw in some nods as he spoke, trying desperately to keep his voice steady.

The gimlet-eyed guard's stare was more violating than a cavity search. "Don't you think Egypt is an odd destination right now?" he asked.

Larson fumbled for a reply. His lips and tongue felt disconnected from his thoughts, as if they were striking out on their own into unchartered and hostile territory. Worse, since the interrogation was in Hebrew and his thoughts were in English, his false starts and hesitations came out in a bilingual hodge-podge that only ended when the guard barked the words he dreaded most:

"Step out of line."

35

Hurtling through space not in a vehicle of any sort but without feeling the coldness of the vast illimitable darkness. Emptiness, mostly. But straight up ahead there's a galaxy, shining incandescently like spilled glitter on a black velvet curtain. And another. And another. Planets come into view, or at least planet-like bodies, half the size of galaxies, purple, green, red ochre. A splash of celestial yellow from some distant star. Atomic explosions. The universe. The multiverse. An infinity of multiverses.

This was ALL.

This was EVERYTHING.

And it became clear to Brynn in one magnificent, glorious dawning, radiant as the First Morning, that this was all the material matter that had ever existed, existed now, and would exist forever—and the word "forever" she saw as pages falling from a calendar, without beginning or end, a self-contained, God-created whole where all the pieces were stardust and ONE, all things were ONE. And God was in ALL things.

And above, with the clarity of a hallucination, the words, not of Christ, or a saint, but then again, yes, they were the words of a saint, for everyone was of God, the words of a Romantic visionary: "You can't pick a flower without a star trembling."

Then dryness.

The kind that sucks every ounce of moisture from your body and makes it feel like your blood is made of dirt.

Barren desert.

Wind.

On her knees, bent over like a sapling in a storm or a woman trying to cross the deck of a ship in a hurricane. Before her, a rough-hewn, squarish block stuck in the sand. If you touched it, you'd get a splinter, and Mom would get out the tweezers but first she'd soak your hand in a beige enamel basin filled with water and Epsom salts and your skin would pucker.

When she saw the small wooden platform and feet and spikes and blood she knew. Slowly her eyes followed the calves, the thighs. Each inch that her gaze traveled up was met with a light so glaring it almost blinded her.

Cloth-covered waist, stomach, chest, neck. Then up and up and GLORY.

In place of a face was the light of a thousand suns so bright she couldn't look at it directly, it was like sun on snow, glaring, piercing. She cast her eyes at the gritty sand that burned through her bone-white wedding gown and set her knees on fire. Her head was much too heavy to lift, burdened with fear, shame, and a sense of majesty that weakened her, made her tremble like tissue paper.

The words floated down, dripped, like sweet, sweet honey, from above, from the light, that incredible brightness, from the mouth of the Godman. She tasted the words' sweetness before she understood. They resounded through her body like an amplified bass, reverberated off each bone, emptied her, filled her. It took some time, eons, before she realized the words were a question, one she must answer:

Do you wish to follow Me?

The words were reddish-purple. Green. Blue. Flashing, all colors of the rainbow. They smelled like roses. Once, a long time ago, a saint claimed the rosary and flowers had fallen from her lips in a moment of ecstasy. But she'd been a saint; Brynn was nothing.

How was she worthy of answering the question? Why would

INFINITE GLORY care if she followed HIM? She kept her eyes down. Tons of weight on her back and shoulders, mountains, oceans, continents. Incapable of a verbal response, she managed a nod, a slight upping and downing of the head, almost imperceptible, would be imperceptible to anyone except He Who had asked it.

Then take up my cross and—

The tomb was empty and smelled of vinegar and olive oil. And bleach? Though dark, the inside of the cave was illuminated by a light that burned inside her. Let your light shine before men...The space was clean, white-washed. It had been filled; now it was empty. She'd been empty; now she was filled. With hope. Love. Peace. She glowed, radiated, the warmth spreading from her core to her limbs, hands, and feet. He had been here and now He wasn't.

And His absence was everything.

This nothingness was the ultimate something, everything. The boldest I AM. And if Christ has not been raised, our preaching is useless and so is your faith...

And so is your faith...

Your faith...

Was she speaking or had the words come out of the stillness that surrounded her?

If you love Me, keep My commandments...

Obey...

And in that obedience is comfort. In that obedience is reliance. On God. Rely on God. Rely on—

Brynn opened her eyes and stared at her captor as if for the first time.

36

Waiting for more security goons to arrive, Larson thought his face would burst into flames. He glanced at Zady who stood in line completely composed, waiting her turn. He saw three men—they were so big, astronauts could see them from space—approach long before they reached him.

What should he do? Continue the Lester Baumgarten charade or just come clean?

Before he could come up with a plan, the biggest of the trio hulked in front of him, shouting commands in Hebrew.

"Stay where you are!"

He stayed. Getting around them would be like circumnavigating the globe.

"Set your bag on the floor!"

He set it down.

Lead guy was talking into a headset to his two companions and to Larson all at once, making it hard to sort out, especially since his racing mind wasn't processing Hebrew at top speed. He tried remembering if his real passport was in his pocket or in his bag but didn't find either possibility comforting. Then he remembered: It was at the bottom of his bag. The head behemoth was frisking him, while the other two knelt and began rummaging through his bag. Just as the guy groped Larson' genitals, a walkie-talkie on his belt squawked.

He stopped mid-grope, yanked the device to his mouth, and said, "Go ahead."

The three words that came out of the box confused Larson. Maybe because they were in Hebrew, and it took a minute for him to mentally translate them. Or maybe because he was so caught up in worrying about Zady, and that they'd never be able to save Brynn. But then their meaning crystallized, reinforced by Mr. Glad Hands giving up the assault on Larson's genitals and ordering his colleagues to stop searching his bag.

The words were: "Let him go."

"We're sorry," the guard said, sounding about as apologetic as if he'd told Larson to go screw himself.

Stifling a shudder, Larson nodded and picked up his bag. The guard led him to the front of the line and told him to set his bag on the conveyor belt and go through the scanner, which he did, feeling like he was sleepwalking or running a high fever. He didn't dare risk a glance behind him at Zady. He simply picked up his bag on the other side of the x-ray machine and kept on walking—through security, and down a long, immense corridor, one that felt as if it would never end, like in a dream where you see a door at the end of a hallway that you can never quite reach. Eventually the corridor did end, in a circular area filled with places to eat and shop, the kiosks set among huge standing columns like ancient temples. He looked up to find his gate, all of which fed out of the central area like spokes, and continued till he reached the sitting area filled with orange plastic chairs.

It wasn't until he collapsed in a seat that he realized just how shaken he was; the adrenaline must've carried him to the gate. His arms and legs trembled, and he was overcome by an exhaustion that had to resemble death. Tears blurred his vision, and he willed them not to leak onto his cheeks. He closed his eyes and breathed deeply assuming, hoping, praying Zady would make it through security without a blip, or at least with the aid of the same miraculous intervention that had allowed him to pass.

How had he gotten through? Was it Aleister? Yeah, had to be. Who else could it have been?

He opened his eyes and watched Zady come to the gate. He looked away as soon as he saw her, not wanting to take any chances. They'd come this far, but there was no guarantee they'd be allowed to continue. He risked another glance. She'd taken a seat at the far end of the waiting area and was casually flipping through a magazine.

How could she be so calm after what had just happened?

The voice over the intercom announced the plane to Cairo was boarding. He waited for his row to be called wondering all along if when the time came his legs would work. Fortunately, they did. He grabbed his bag, rose from his seat with surprising ease, and without glancing in Zady's direction, showed his ticket to the attendant then walked up the ramp to the plane.

37

A few hours into the flight, Zady wiggled into the empty window seat next to Larson. He wasn't sure it was a good idea for them to be seen together, but she must've thought it was safe enough and he trusted her completely. Besides, they had to figure out their next move. Talking face-to-face was probably no more dangerous than using the phone.

When she turned to speak to him, he was taken aback by how beautiful she looked. There was something about her that made each time he saw her new, as if she'd just emerged from behind a curtain. It wasn't just her disguise.

"Hey, Lester," she said flatly.

"Hi, um, whatever-your-name-is."

"Dominique," she said. "Dominique Ansel."

"Nice. A lot better than mine."

"Yeah, I know. Sorry about that. It was the best I could do at the time."

"How and when did you get the fake—?"

She waved him off.

"Do you think it was Aleister who called off the attack dogs?" Larson asked.

She bit her lip and stared into the distance. "Maybe."

"If not, who was it? Are you having doubts about him?"

"I don't know, to both questions. I mean, I still wonder how he knew the spell number on the letter."

"Maybe he had someone put the letter in your room," Larson suggested.

"Yeah, but why? And if so, why didn't he just tell us it was him?"

"Wait a minute. You don't think he had anything to do with Brynn's kidnapping?"

A softness entered Zady's eyes, a vulnerability that lasted just a moment. But in that time, Larson glimpsed what she'd looked like as a child, when Aleister told her that her parents had died in a car crash, an explanation she still found unconvincing. It was at this moment when he realized that it wasn't only finding Brynn that drove her on, it was also discovering the truth about her parents' deaths.

"I'm just saying I don't know who to trust. At this point, it seems like you're the only one I can." She stood up, took her bag out of the overhead compartment, and pulled out her phone. Seated, she started thumb-pumping.

"I guess we should figure out our next move," Larson suggested.

"We'll figure it out when we land. I don't want to give anyone a chance to know what we're going to do until right before we do it."

Larson turned his head toward the narrow, carpeted aisle. They were in economy, mid-plane, near an emergency exit. He craned his neck to look around. It was almost seven p.m., so the cabin lights were on. Some of the passengers had children with them, which he found reassuring. And it was a mix of people. None appeared suspicious. But how could you tell? He tried concentrating on the steady hum of the engine to calm him. A young man wearing too much cologne full-bladder-boogied past him on his way to the bathroom. Up ahead a flight atten-dant asked a woman if she needed anything.

"That's interesting," Zady said after some time had passed. She was still typing on her phone.

"What?" Larson asked.

"The whole go-to-Egypt-to-look-for-Moses'-treasure thing got me thinking. Maybe there's something in the Bible that could point us in the right direction. I haven't found anything yet, but there's a ton of references to Egypt. Listen to this: 'On that day the Lord made a covenant with Abram and said, "To your descendants I give this land, from the river of Egypt to the great river the Euphrates."' That's from Genesis. In a prophecy from Isaiah, chapter nineteen, there's mention of an 'altar to the Lord in the heart of Egypt.' And 'The Lord Almighty will bless them, saying, "Blessed be Egypt my people."' In Hosea, God says '"Out of Egypt I have called my son,"' which is echoed in Matthew's gospel. Seems strange. I always thought Egypt was the enemy."

"It's a little odd," Larson admitted. "But when you think about it, it's a love-hate relationship. Although Moses fled Egypt, others went there for refuge: Abraham and Sarah, Jacob, Joseph and his brothers, Jeroboam, Jeremiah, Baruch. Joseph even brought young Jesus there after he and Mary fled from Herod. Anyway, you look tired. Why don't you try to get some rest? There's not much we can do right now."

"I feel guilty sleeping," Zady said.

"Don't. We're going to need all our resources to save Brynn. Getting some sleep will only help."

"Maybe you're right," Zady said, leaning her chin on her fist and her head against the window. "But what if we get another message?"

"I'll stay awake and if we get anything, I'll wake you."

"Okay, but don't let me sleep too long."

"I won't."

A few minutes later Zady was snoring lightly. Larson

decided to tend to his full bladder. He stood up as quietly as he could and made his way to the back of the plane. Fortunately, the bathroom was free, so he went in and relieved himself.

When he returned, there was an envelope on his seat. He picked it up and turned it over. It was sealed with red wax, just like the one left in Zady's hotel room. Someone on the plane had left it.

38

Brynn couldn't be sure if it'd been a dream or a vision. She couldn't even rule out the possibility that the water she'd been drinking was drugged. But it had to be more than that. Because she had changed. She quickly reached the conclusion that she'd had a spiritual experience. It was the only explanation that fit.

On the one hand, everything looked the same: the man's bedraggled clothes, the yellowish light from the lamp, the rough-hewn log walls, the thick curtain that blocked natural light, making it impossible to tell day from night, and the chain that chafed her ankle at the slightest movement.

But everything felt different.

For one thing, she no longer felt like a prisoner.

She was free, a freedom that came to her—no, was gifted to her, because she knew, in a way truer and more fundamental than a physical law of the universe, or a mathematical proof, how completely reliant she was on God. Captivity had brought freedom. It was a paradox, but that was the way God worked. It was only when a person was lost that she was found. Damnation was a necessary precursor to salvation. A person had to be empty before God could fill her up, with faith, hope, grace, love.

Her self, *her* will, didn't matter; God's will did. God's will was *all* that mattered. It was all there was. It made no difference if she were held captive or lounged at home. As long as she surrendered her will to God, things would be all right.

And things would be all right because she was seeing things for what they really were. This transient, material world, with all its pain and suffering, was just a stopping point along the way to eternal union with God. To see things as they truly were, their temporality, their impermanence, *that* was reality. Her belief in TRUTH as an acronym for The Reality Underlying Total Honesty came back to her, crashed into her, collided with her will, destroyed any remnants of self she had left. She remembered her order's mission, the concern for souls, the heartfelt desire—the need—to serve God, to see Him in all things, to see everything as one indivisible whole. No, she didn't belong to the order anymore, but she would always belong to God, because she'd been given the ultimate gift, the gift of faith. And it was faith that would see her through.

But this was no rosy-eyed Pollyannaism. She wasn't closing her eyes to the harsh realities of life, refusing to see the evil in the hearts of so many people, glossing over the hunger, wars, and diseases that ravaged the world. No. This was recognizing that despite all human failings, there was still good, for God in His infinite mercy had kept people from destroying each other and the planet and as long as humanity existed it still had a chance. The question wasn't how a loving God could allow so much evil to exist, but how, despite ourselves, our base nature, there was still so much kindness and love in the world.

That was the question.

She'd journeyed through the long, dark night of the soul and reached the other side, which, in a physical sense, was where she'd started: chained to the floor in some unknown location, guarded by a man who might kill her. But she could never go back to the person she'd been before her spiritual experience. And for that she was grateful. Because now she knew what she must do. She knew it made no difference to the man sitting in the chair at the foot of the bed whether she lived or died. And in an important way, he was *right*: It didn't matter. What mattered was that she did God's will. That might mean the end of her life, but it also meant the beginning of her union with Him.... And maybe, just maybe, the start of the life of her captor. This was an opportunity to serve God by caring for the soul of the man who watched over her with contempt and despised everything he thought she was and stood for.

She made a commitment to God and to herself—which was actually one and the same—that from this moment on she would do all she could to tend to the man's spiritual needs. And that began by trying as hard as she could to feel what it was like to live his life. So, she looked at him as if for the first time, stared into the deeply set eyes hollowed with suffering, as dark as any she'd ever seen. And she saw something in them she hadn't seen before: the potential that God's light could enter and ease his burden.

39

"What do you think it means?" Zady asked.

"I'm not sure," Larson replied. The single sheet of paper inside the envelope he'd found on his seat after returning from the bathroom contained two lines of text, in the same fancy script as the one before:

Ezekiel 40-48
The Temple Scroll

"What are the chapters in Ezekiel about?" Zady said, typing on her phone. Without waiting for an answer, she blurted, "It looks like they deal with a vision he had of a temple. What about the Temple Scroll?"

"It's one of the Dead Sea Scrolls found at Qumran."

"O-kay, but what does Ezekiel's vision of a temple and a Dead Sea Scroll have to do with Moses' treasure or rescuing Brynn?"

"I wish I could say," he admitted.

He stared off into the distance, deep in thought. "Years ago,

I was at a conference, in Jerusalem. I think it was the fiftieth anniversary of the—"

"This isn't story time. Now, I'm not saying that whatever you're about to yammer on about isn't interesting—wait. That's exactly what I'm saying. Get to the point!"

Passengers turned to stare when Zady raised her voice. The flight attendant came over and asked if everything was alright. Larson waved her off. "The point is," he resumed, smiling idiotically until she was gone, "somebody there claimed Ezekiel was the first Essene though he'd lived long before, that he had a huge impact on the community at Qumran. This scholar said Ezekiel's visions informed the rules the Essene priests followed at Qumran, the way they dressed, the way they wore their hair, the ban on worldly goods, their whole theology, really. And..." He trailed off, deep in thought.

"You're doing this on purpose, right? Trying to piss me off?"

"The temple," Larson said. "There was something about the temple."

"What temple?!"

Larson shushed Zady with a finger to his lips, leaned close, and said quietly, "The Qumran-Essenes, at the time of Jesus and John the Baptist, rejected the Temple in Jerusalem. They placed more stock in Ezekiel's visionary temple than the real one that existed in Jerusalem."

"Okay, Scott," Zady said in a hushed harsh voice. "All right. I'm gonna give you one more chance. What, for fuck's sake, does any of this have to do with Moses' treasure?"

"First, my name's Lester. Second, I'm not sure. But I think we need to compare the chapters from Ezekiel with the Temple Scroll."

"So, it's back to the library. Let's wait until we land in Cairo to figure out which one. No digital trails."

"But you just used your phone."

"That didn't have anything to do with where we're going."

"Okay."

Then he had a thought. A terrible thought. One so awful he wished more than anything he could unthink it. But the harder he fought to suppress it, the more it seemed a distinct possibility. And if it were true, it would change everything. The thought was this: When it came to both envelopes—the one on his seat and the one in the hotel—Zady's proximity was the common denominator. Could she be the source of the cryptic messages? Was she involved in all of this in some nefarious way? She'd said he was the only person she could trust, but the real question was, could *he* trust *her*?

40

It wasn't working. Or rather it wasn't having the effect she'd believed it would, but Brynn consoled herself with the thought that things were going according to God's plan, that whatever He had in store was the best possible outcome, the only outcome.

She sat upright in bed, leaning her aching back against the headboard. A gamey smell filled the room. Her ankle was raw; she wanted nothing more than to rub it with aloe. She could almost feel the burning, cooling sensation it would bring. But she kept her physical discomfort at bay by focusing on God and the man standing at the foot of the bed who maintained a silence that was like the loudest noise in history.

The attempt to demonstrate compassion, to show empathy, had been met by a stony silence. She'd tried pressing him for details on his life, his youth, and family. When that had failed, she asked him to elaborate on what he'd said about domestic terrorism in the U.S., thinking he might take the opportunity to at least vent his anger and frustrations with the country he saw as the source of all his trials and tribulations, but he hadn't been forthcoming. Now she imagined herself wrapped in the loving arms of God and listened for the still quiet voice inside her that always spoke if only she opened herself up to it.

"Muslims, Christians, and Jews all claim to believe in the same God," she said. "Still, we fight."

The man drew up the chair next to the bed and took a seat. He leaned so close, she could feel his breath, smell it, a fetid combination of spoiled milk and sweaty socks. Then she thought how her breath was probably none too pleasant at this point either—it had been a while since she'd brushed her teeth.

"You don't get it, do you?" he asked.

"What don't I get? Please tell me," she said.

"Allah, praise be His name, is a just God. Until justice prevails, there will always be struggle, conflict, war. Foreign occupation is never just. Never!"

She wasn't sure if he was referring to the American military presence in Iraq or the Israeli occupation of the Gaza Strip and West Bank. At the end of the day, both were unjust. "But is terrorism?" she asked. "I mean, in your eyes, is it okay to kill innocent people who have no active role in the occupation?"

"Everyone has a role in the occupation. By letting it continue, by doing nothing to stop it. I could tell you stories of people I know, family, friends, killed in the name of freedom. But it's not worth it."

"But I want to hear. I want to understand," Brynn said.

"It does not matter."

"But it does. It's the only thing that does."

The man waved her off. "It does not matter to you."

"But—"

The man shot from his seat. "I said, no!" His eyes rolled like a wild stallion.

"Why?" Brynn pleaded.

"Because in less than three days, if I don't get the name-plate, you—" He stopped and cocked his head. "Did you hear that?"

"What? What did you hear?"

"It sounded like movement outside. I go and check." He reached under the bed, pulled out an automatic rifle, and fled the room.

Brynn didn't know whether to be more afraid or take comfort at the thought of someone else coming. She stared up at the ceiling and begged God for His will to be done. Then held her breath and waited.

41

In a stuffy surveil van on a woodsy trail, Aleister Mabrey watched the monitor, his heart racing, as a few hundred feet away an assembled team of men outfitted with helmet-cams approached a tiny log cabin in Snowshoe, West Virginia. All that was left before the cabin was breached was the final countdown.

Uttering the word "ten" to begin it was a simple act, but saying it felt as hard as all of Hercules' labors. What if this effort ended in Brynn's death? If it did, Mabrey couldn't go on. It was as simple as that. And the more he thought about that outcome, a very real possibility, the more it felt as if someone had plunged a rusty dagger into his heart and given it a good, hard twist. He fumbled inside his shirt and grasped the silver key hanging from his neck, the one that opened the desk drawer in which he'd placed the letter to his nieces he'd finally finished just a few hours ago. He hoped it said everything; hoped it was enough.

With a bone-crunching squeeze of his hand around the key, he croaked out the word, "Ten," and stared at the monitor. His stomach lurched as if he were falling down an elevator shaft.

Worries ripped into his mind in the silence between each number that was like a pause between lightning and thunder.

"Nine."

How could I have let my sister die like that?

"Eight."

I should've chosen differently.

"Seven."

I must save what's left of my family—that's something I still can do.

"Six."

Brynn and Zady, see them play.

"Five."

Zady and Brynn, all grown up.

"Four."

What will the truth do to them?

"Three."

How will they react?

"Two."

At least I'll be dead when they read it.

"One."

Beautiful Masika, the key to it all. He pictured her dark, elegant features, like an Egyptian goddess.

Then everything happened separately and all at once:

The downpour.

The lightning flash.

The burst of thunder.

The cabin door smashing.

The men entering.

The main room: empty.

A bedroom: empty.

Another bedroom: empty.

The bathroom: empty.

Brynn wasn't there.

Heartache.

42

U sing their fake passports, Larson and Zady made it through customs at Cairo International unscathed. But Larson struggled with his suspicions; if Zady was the source of the two wax-sealed envelopes, if she knew more than she let on. He'd found it especially odd that after finding the one on the plane, she'd said nothing about the people on board, didn't even talk about trying to find out who might have left it.

Yet if she had left the envelopes, did that make her bad? Or complicit in her sister's abduction? Her concern for Brynn's welfare seemed genuine—that was a good sign. And she was conflicted about contacting Aleister again because she thought he might be holding something back. But if Aleister couldn't be trusted, who could? And if he hadn't called off the guards at Ben Gurion, who had?

Zady exchanged dollars for Egyptian Pounds at the Banque Du Caire inside the terminal. Then they hopped into a taxi parked outside and headed to the American University which, after very little discussion, they'd agreed was the best choice.

It was just past seven o'clock and the evening streets were crammed with a hodgepodge of vehicles: cars, buses, commercial trucks, a donkey cart lit by a flashlight strapped on with duct tape. A cacophony of horns, syncopated pistons, and sirens violated the night, and blared through the half-open windows of the taxi. Coffee shops, squalid apartment risers, ramshackle two-story houses with once-grand ancient facades, rainbow-colored street markets selling handkerchiefs and jeans, minareted mosques, all passed by, a writhing, squirming mismatched combination of the ancient and dated. A musky, pleasant aroma, like church incense, permeated the air. But just underneath lay hints of the smells it masked: body odor, rancid meat, cloying poverty.

Along the way, Larson asked the driver about the layout of the campus and an hour later the taxi reached AUC Avenue, in front of the university. Zady paid the fare and she and Larson got out. They walked past a squat building with a geodesic roof and onto a brightly lit, immaculate promenade. The walkway was lined with short, well-trimmed trees laden with bouquets of yellow-orange flowers. They passed a large Neo-Islamic building on the right, then emerged into a plaza, larger than a football field, with palm trees, white-lighted fountains, water gardens, and intricate stone cladding. Across the plaza stood the main five-story library, its square front compartmentalized like cubbyholes.

They didn't meet security, but Larson didn't know how long their luck would hold. As they neared the library's steps, he told Zady to walk in like they owned the place. Inside, a lofty common area was kitted with wooden tables and latticed chairs. White columns were interspersed throughout. Black ovals dangled from the ceiling in orbital satellite paths.

Zady pointed Larson to an empty table and said she'd be right back.

"But—"

"I'll get what we need," she called over her shoulder.

Larson spent the time she was gone brooding over the fact that she'd taken her tote bag with her: it kept him from rummaging through it for more red wax-sealed envelopes, or other incriminating evidence. His body was tense. He didn't know if anyone was watching him, waiting for the right moment to pounce. He still wore his disguise. At first, it'd been annoying, but he'd come to accept it, and now he stroked his beard like a nineteenth-century Russian novelist.

Zady returned to the table with three books, handed him two—a Bible and a copy of the Dead Sea Scrolls—and kept the third, another Bible.

"The Vermes translation, right?" she said, seating herself across from him.

He nodded.

"You look up what you need to. I'm gonna read the chapters in Ezekiel. Not everyone has them memorized."

Larson picked up the book and turned his attention to the Temple Scroll to refresh his memory.

"When did Ezekiel have his vision of the temple?" Zady asked.

"When he and the rest of the Hebrews were exiled to Babylonia after the destruction of the first temple and the sack of Jerusalem in 586 B.C. by King Nebuchadnezzar."

"So, these chapters deal with what a rebuilt temple would look like?"

"That's right," Larson said. "What God showed him."

"Well, call me a skeptic, but who the hell has visions this specific? I mean unless God gave Ezekiel blueprints and a giant tape measure, how could he have known the exact measurements of the building and everything in it?"

"There's something else," Larson said. "The temple Ezekiel describes—and the one in the Temple Scroll—is much too big to fit on the Temple Mount. We seem to be dealing with a temple other than the one in Jerusalem."

"But what other temple would be so important to Ezekiel and the Essenes?" Zady asked. "You said the Essenes rejected the temple in Jerusalem. If that's the case, then what temple are they referring to in their scroll?"

Larson was stumped.

"Maybe it has to do with what you said about that date," Zady suggested. "The one that was so important to the Essenes."

Yes. It had temporarily slipped his mind: 1350 B.C. The year Akhenaten became pharaoh of Egypt. "But why would the Essenes be so concerned with an Egyptian pharaoh who'd been dead for hundreds of years by the time the Dead Sea Scrolls were written? We're going to need more sources."

43

To Pope Innocent, it was bad enough that the *sedia gestatoria*—the ornate sedan chair in which popes used to be carried—had been done away with years before he became the Supreme Pontiff; being carried on the shoulders of twelve footmen via long poles denoted all the glory befitting God's sole representative on Earth. What was even worse, however, was the mediocre papal apartment in the Apostolic Palace consisting of a kitchen, dining room, study, private chapel, guest bedroom, and a couple of other rooms that were completely inadequate for the world leader with the most followers. The sparsely furnished "master bedroom" was most insulting. He'd swapped the twin bed and—horror of horrors—particle board desk for a queen-size canopy and a 17th-century French Mazarin writing desk, but the accommodations were still unsuitable for a person of his holy stature.

In his time as pope, he'd done his best to transcend the stifling quarters by spending as much time as possible in the more spacious areas of the palace and at the idyllic summer residence in Castel Gandolfo. For the past few days, however, ever since his last communication with the Council in the secret bunker of the Vatican archives—a bunker that had mysteriously vanished—he'd confined himself as much as possible to his apartment, particularly this bedroom, where he'd holed up with Bisschen. He insisted on having all his meals here, brought by his butler, and eaten at the priceless writing table he'd covered with a white cassock that left some of the apes, lions, angels, and dancers on the Boulle surface visible.

It was where he sat this evening, pondering his fate, when a knock at the door sounded.

Bisschen let out a sharp, quick bark from his regal recline on the canopied bed. The knock-bark caused Innocent to jump in his chair. He glanced at the clock on his desk: eight o'clock. His appetite had abandoned him as of late and he realized, much to his relief, that it was long past suppertime, and that the knock on the door was most likely his butler, asking if he was ready to eat.

"Come in," he said, in a voice higher than usual.

He relaxed a little when the young butler, tray in hand, opened the door, but froze when Cardinal O'Rourke followed closely on his heels. The butler set the tray on the desk, bowed, then left, leaving the pope alone with the creepy head of household. Innocent hated the moments alone with Amos, as he thought of him, since he was so much like an oversized prophet in a Renaissance painting.

As O'Rourke approached the desk Innocent stood, disliking the fact that his knees wobbled. Despite his stoop, Amos towered above him.

"I had Alan prepare your favorite dish, Your Holiness," he said. He talked without moving his lips, which kept his long beard stationary, and lent him the air of an old ventriloquist. "The Lord 'upholds the cause of the oppressed and gives food to the hungry,' as the psalmist says."

The smell of the chicken, bacon, wine, and garlic of the coq au vin was strong, despite the covered dinner tray. Normally it would've made Innocent salivate, but in the cardinal's presence it was sickening. Innocent's insides clenched like a fist and for a moment he was sure he'd vomit. The nausea only subsided when the pope focused on Bisschen's tiny face, tilted to the side, eagerly anticipating a share of the spoils.

Innocent's nausea passed, but his suspicions remained. Was there something in the food or the cup? Had Amos slipped poison into the chicken or wine when the chef's back was turned? Or had he done it with the cook's assistance? The butler's complicity? Certainly, the man who stood—or stooped—before him wanted him gone.

"Thank you," Innocent said perfunctorily. But Amos just stood there, staring. "You may go now," the pope said, nodding at the door.

What felt like eons later, Amos bowed slightly and went to leave. But after opening the door, he stopped, turned, and faced Innocent.

"'For the wages of sin is death,'" he said then left.

An ice-cold frisson shot through the pope. He collapsed in the chair, hugged the desk, then dropped his head on his folded arms as if it were nap time in kindergarten. Bisschen, sensing his dismay, jumped off the bed, waddled over to his human's feet, and stared up at him expectantly.

With his head still on the desk, Innocent glimpsed the dog out of the corner of his eye. At least he had Bisschen. He reached down and the little dog licked his hand.

"Good boy. It'll be alright," he tried to reassure the dog and himself. Even if people were out to get him, the dog loved him and would continue to do so, even if Innocent was going insane.

Then he had a thought. There had to be a way to test if he were imagining things, or if the circumstances were really as awful as they seemed. Maybe someone wasn't out to get him. Maybe he was just being paranoid.

He raised himself to a full sitting posture and lifted the lid on the tray. The food smelled better, almost appetizing.

But no matter how badly he needed the nourishment, he knew he couldn't take the chance.

He considered for a moment then set the plate on the floor. He called Bisschen to it and watched as the dog set to with gusto.

44

Madge Roberts had every intention of using the lunch hour to go to her office in the Russell Building and open the envelope her chief of staff had texted her about. But when she left the Senate chamber, the media pounced, pumping her for insights into the morning's proceedings and what the afternoon might hold in store. She did her best to answer the questions, but once she had, she realized she'd never make it to her office and back again before the trial resumed.

She had just enough time to placate her growling stomach with vending machine fare before returning to the chamber, seating herself just as Ananya Chandler continued the case against the imperiled president.

"Now, some people claim," Chandler said, "that John Paul Jenkins has done nothing wrong in his latest executive order, that it is simply a recognition of the obvious. And to some extent, that is correct. Most people in this country *do* adhere to elements of the Judeo-Christian tradition. And since we live in a democracy, where the majority rules, some would argue that there is nothing wrong with declaring the United States a Judeo-Christian nation.

"But when it comes to the Constitution, it is vital that the majority does not—indeed, should not—rule. For the very essence, the foundation of our democracy is the preservation of minority rights. That is what it's all about, what it all comes down to. Because in the absence of minority rights, whatever group happened to be the majority at any given time and on any given issue could impose its will on the rest of the people.

"This is true when it comes to what some perceive as the foundation of Judeo-Christianity—namely, the Ten Commandments. Now at first glance, it might seem that no one would argue with these time-tested tenets: injunctions against killing, lying, stealing, adultery, and so forth. Surely anyone can see such laws are necessary for society to function. But even in the case of something so clear-cut, there is a problem. For not everyone subscribes to all of the commandments. Buddhists and Hindus object to worshipping one deity. Muslims see the Bible as true up to a point but believe the Quran necessary for the ultimate revelation of God's word. Then there are those who see the Bible as myth and point to the lack of proof for many of its claims.

"If one considers such people to be in any sense 'less American,' less deserving of government funds and social acceptance than Christians and Jews, then let me pose this question: What does it mean to be American? Certainly, the Founding Fathers were American, despite their belief in a non-denominational God, a watchmaker of the universe, who set the world in motion and then stepped back. And who could be more American than the Native Americans? Yet their idea of God is different from ours, as the European Christians who landed here were quick to point out before reducing the indigenous population from eighty million to ten million people in fifty years."

Roberts' phone buzzed. She slipped it out of her jacket pocket as discreetly as she could and peeked at the text under her desk. It was another message from Carl:

Hello? Where are you?

Her chief of staff was obviously upset that she hadn't stopped by her office at the noon recess. Roberts shook her head and refocused her attention.

"Let me add something here," Chandler said. "In the past, the Supreme Court has recognized that keeping the government out of religion is best for everyone. In *Everson v. the Board of Education*, *Engel v. Vitale*, *Abington Township v. Schempp*, and *Lee v. Weisman*, the Court called for a strict separation of church and state in public schools. Recently, however, the trend to improve morality has led to a blurring of the line between the sacred and the secular, the private and the public. Legislatures across the country are passing laws and resolutions to display the Ten Commandments in public places. There are bills in Congress to amend the Constitution to include Jesus and to promote prayer and devotionals in public schools. And now there's the executive order to provide money to religious schools and institutions that espouse Judeo-Christian values, and to favor immigrants who share those values. As of today, the Supreme Court has abdicated its constitutional mandate of judicial review by refusing to take up President Jenkins' order, and so it has fallen to us, the members of Congress, to act, to condemn these efforts as blatant violations of the Constitution and the Bill of Rights."

Roberts' phone vibrated again. She yanked it out and, without bothering to hide it under her desk, read yet another text from Carl:

Are you getting these messages?

What the hell was this damn fool's problem?

Now, though she tried her hardest, Roberts couldn't follow Chandler's words. She knew she'd be unable to think of anything else until the trial was adjourned and she could go back to her office to open the envelope that was causing Carl so much consternation.

45

"You know the library's closing soon," Zady said.

"I'm aware of that," Larson replied absently, his mind trying to pull together all the info he'd culled from the piles of books Zady had retrieved and that now surrounded him in a literary cordon.

"So, whaddya got?" she asked.

"A lot of ideas, but I'm not sure how many of them make sense, or how everything hangs together."

"Stop qualifying and just spit it out."

Larson took a deep breath. "Okay. Amenhotep IV a.k.a. Akhenaten becomes ruler of Egypt, around 1350 B.C., the date that's so important to the Essenes. Well, in the fifth year of his reign, he does two things. First, he changes his name to Akhenaten. Then he moves the Egyptian capital from Thebes, north, to Amarna."

"What's up with the name change?" Zady asked.

"The new name signified his devotion to Aten, a form of the sun god Re. When he moved the Egyptian capital to Amarna, he began work on a huge temple, half a mile long. Then in the tenth year of his reign he does something really extraordinary, unprecedented. He bans the worship of all gods except Aten,

160

closes the temples of all the other gods, even removes the name of one of the most popular gods, Amun, from all monuments. As you can imagine, this didn't sit well with people who worshipped these gods, especially with the rich, powerful priests who'd attended to them. Akhenaten undercut their power, declaring him and his wife, Nefertiti, the sole intermediaries between the people and Aten."

"So, you're saying Akhenaten was a monotheist?"

Larson nodded. "The first monotheistic ruler for whom there's historical proof."

"I thought Abraham was the first monotheist," Zady said. "Well, him and Moses; you know, the whole first commandment thing, about having no god but the one true God. And didn't Abraham come before Akhenaten?"

"Yes, but as I've said, there's no historical proof for Abraham or Moses. But we have evidence of the pharaohs—the Egyptians were meticulous record-keepers."

"Okay. But how does any of this relate to Moses' treasure or the other messages we've gotten? And, more importantly, how does it help us find Brynn?!"

The few patrons in the common area turned to look at Zady when she raised her voice. She forced a smile to let them know everything was all right.

"I can't pretend to know, because I don't," Larson said. "Not yet. But some things are starting to connect. A lot of what we've been talking about is the temple—Ezekiel's vision and the Temple Scroll. There's also mention in the Apocrypha, in Baruch, and in the Midrash of Moses, of him having a scroll describing a temple."

"So?"

"We said the chapters in Ezekiel and the Temple Scroll mention a huge temple, too big to fit on the Temple Mount. But according to some of these sources," Laron said, pointing to the books in front of him, "the temple Akhenaten built at Amarna matches the descriptions given by Ezekiel in his vision and by the author of the Temple Scroll. So maybe the scroll Moses is said to have had was of the temple at Amarna. The Bible says Moses grew up in Egypt, so it's at least possible."

"*Possible*? Listen to yourself, Scott. Why would Ezekiel and the Essenes be so concerned with an Egyptian temple, built for an Egyptian god, by an Egyptian pharaoh hundreds of years before their time?"

"That's a—"

"Yeah, yeah, I know," Zady said, waving a hand. "It's a good question. Whatever happened to Akhenaten, anyway?"

"Well, the reforms he introduced weren't popular, so he was overthrown, eventually replaced by his son, King Tut, who also changed his name during his lifetime. He started out as King Tutankh*aten*, demonstrating his fealty to the god of his father. He changed his name to Tutankh*amun* after he brought peace to Egypt by bringing back Amun and the other gods his father had outlawed. But no one knows exactly what happened to Akhenaten after he was overthrown."

"But the text said the treasure we're after is silver and gold. Nothing you've mentioned has to do with silver or gold."

"Granted," Larson said. "But how about this? Remember how Moses took a lot of treasure with him when he fled Egypt, you know, to make all the stuff God told him to? What if he got it from Akhenaten? What if it was all the wealth Akhenaten got after he shut down the temples to the other gods, putting the priests out of business? The temple he built at Amarna proves he had access to a lot of wealth. Maybe the silver and gold Moses took with him when he fled Egypt was Akhenaten's."

"You know what I'm going to say, right Scott?"

"I know: 'How does any of this help find Brynn?' Look, from what I've read, there's an archaeological dig going on at Amarna. Maybe we should head there, see if we can learn anything else about Akhenaten and his wealth." He paused. "And I know you're not going to like this, but you need to put aside your suspicions about Aleister and keep in touch with him. It's the only way we're going to know how close he is to finding Brynn."

It wasn't until he said it that he realized he should heed his own advice. Even if Zady was the source of the envelopes, Brynn was still in danger, and they needed to work together to save her. Maybe Zady wasn't telling him everything, but if she'd wanted to harm him, she'd had plenty of chances to do so. Right now, he needed to trust her, just like she needed to trust Aleister.

He didn't know what was behind the scrutinizing look she gave him now, but she was pondering something deep. He was beginning to wonder when—or if—she'd reply, when she said the last thing he expected:

"Okay."

46

Something was wrong with Bisschen.

After devouring the pope's dinner, the little dog ran around the bedroom in circles and, as Innocent watched in horror, started slamming into the walls. Finally, he collapsed at the side of the bed in a small black and tan puddle.

Innocent's loud summons and handclaps failed to rouse him. The pope couldn't bring himself to get up from his desk and physically touch the dog—fear and guilt kept his knees bent. Instead, he slid off one of his ruby slippers, bent over, grabbed it, and tossed it at the dog.

The slipper bounced off Bisschen's tiny head and landed beside him.

He still didn't move.

Innocent's mind raced. Obviously, O'Rourke had poisoned the food—whether in cahoots with the chef or on his own. And that could mean only one thing: Innocent hadn't been imagining things. His suspicions were warranted, someone *was* trying to kill him. There was nothing wrong with his mind. That also meant that his bizarre experiences, the mother-demon he'd seen in the crowd of visitors, the disappearing bunker, were not hallucinations coming from a diseased brain inherited from his crazy mother. Someone must be doing all this, and he'd been right to suspect the creepy cardinal who was always rasping Bible passages, condemning him for his sins.

Yes, the more that he thought about it, O'Rourke *had* to be behind all this. And *that*, in turn, meant the Council was *real*, and that somehow, O'Rourke must be connected to it, acting on its orders at the very least, if not making decisions on its behalf. This attempt to poison him was comeuppance for his refusal to turn over Peter's Pence to the Council.

But what would he do now that his worst suspicions were confirmed? What *could* he do? There was no one he could turn to with any of this. Bisschen, his one true companion, was gone. The mini dachshund had taken a bullet for him. The last act of his little life had been to eat the poisoned food meant for his human. It was such a brave act. Perhaps, at some point, Innocent could martyr him. But right now, other matters needed attending to, like—

A knock at the door sounded.

Innocent did the only thing that came to him. If O'Rourke and the Council wanted him dead, then dead he'd be...at least for now. It was just a delaying tactic to be sure, but more than anything else right now, he needed time.

He reached down and grabbed the plate off the floor, set it before him on the desk, and scrambled to the bed. In a second, moving faster than he ever thought possible, he lay down, closed his eyes, and made his body rigid. He figured the plan to kill him must involve finding him dead in the morning, after suffering a heart attack from a slow-acting poison—the poison had acted quickly on Bisschen because he was so small—for finding Innocent dead too soon after eating would raise suspicions. And if that were the case, then he'd lay here, pretending to suffer the effects of the poison, until he could make good his escape.

He lay still, trying hard to keep from trembling, listening intently as the bedroom door slowly creaked open....

47

Madge Roberts was again accosted by the media as she left the Senate Chamber that afternoon. She said only a few words, eager to examine the contents of the envelope Carl had persistently (the term "pain-in-the-ass" came to mind) texted her about over the course of the day. When she finally made it back to her office, Carl stood at the side of her desk, tapping his foot. If he was impersonating a cat that had just swallowed a canary, it was bang-on. He picked the envelope off her desk, bowed, and handed it to her with the ceremonial flourish of Oscar night.

"Carl?"

"Ma'am?"

"What are you doing?"

"I'm waiting for you to open it."

"I can see that. What I mean is, what are you *doing*?"

Carl considered the question. Roberts watched him struggle as if he were trying to answer a problem of quantum mechanics.

"Aren't you finished for the day?" she said.

Crickets.

"Let me rephrase that. 'Thank you, Carl. You're finished for the day.'"

"But—"

Roberts shook her head. "It's not that I don't want you around, Carl, but—Yeah, I guess that's what it is. Now go run along and have yourself a good night." She steered him by the elbow toward the open door. "If it's something you need to know, I'll call you and we'll talk about it."

It wasn't so much that she didn't want him to know what was in the envelope. It was more like...well, he was a man, bless his heart, and the less he knew the less chance he had of doing something stupid or of hurting himself. God knew that a man, even alone in an empty room, could get himself in grief.

"Promise?" he asked.

She traced a cross over her heart with a finger. "Promise."

Carl walked out then turned around for a parting shot.

Roberts didn't give him a chance. She closed the door, returned to her desk, and sank into the chair. Carefully, she picked up the manila envelope marked **CONFIDENTIAL**. Standard size. No postal marks. Strange. Must've been hand-delivered. She stared at it, suddenly remembering the anthrax-laced letters of 2001.

"Must not use finger," she said, opting for the dull letter-opener she picked up from the edge of her desk. "Any sign of powder, and I am *outta* here." She slowly tore the sealed flap with the opener and, finding no powder, gently removed the contents. It was an old sepia photograph, four-by-six inches, and showed a bunch of white guys, twenty or so, gathered around an ornate table in a conference room. All wore top hats. Half the group wore cutaway morning coats, high-buttoned waistcoats, and high-collared winged shirts. The other half were clad in frock coats. Roberts turned the photo over. In neat script were the words, "St. Ermin's Hotel, London." Below that was the date, "1903."

Before she could think about who the men were or who might have sent the photo, the door cracked open, and Carl thrust his head in.

Roberts jumped a foot off her chair.

"I didn't mean to startle you," he said, trying his hardest to sound apologetic. "But I forgot to tell you something."

Roberts gaped, open-mouthed, hands over her heart, and tried to suck air into her lungs. Unable to speak, she moved her head up and down, which Carl took as a sign to continue.

"Whoever left that envelope must've been a ghost," he said. "I've been here all afternoon, and I never saw anyone come in."

48

More than an hour had passed since Innocent's bedroom door had opened. He could see the time on the gold ormolu clock on the bedside table: quarter to twelve. Whoever it was apparently wanted nothing more than a glimpse of him, to check that the poison had taken effect. Though he hadn't risked peeking, he knew it was O'Rourke who'd come to look; fortunately, he'd left as quickly and as silently as he came.

Innocent stayed still—he was still afraid to move—but allowed his eyes to roam in the yellow pall of the desk lamp. He observed the white cassock that draped his body felt like a winding sheet, the gallows-high canopy bed, the ornate escritoire with its mocking angels and ferocious animals—this was what life came down to: inanimate, lifeless objects that had once seemed pleasant, but now were threatening. Finally, and though he tried his hardest not to do so, he eyed Bisschen, lying in a lifeless heap on the floor. The poor little dog had been faithful to the end.

A warm shame coursed through him. The only solace he could grasp was that he wasn't losing his mind. His worries about inheriting a mental illness from his mother had vanished with Bisschen's death. People were out to get him; he wasn't being paranoid. The Council, the secret bunker, everything—except maybe the horrible vision he'd had of his mother—was real. He still wasn't sure how O'Rourke had made the bunker disappear, but he himself was no bricklayer, no expert in determining if a wall was old or new.

When the door creaked open again, Innocent slammed his lids shut.

This time, the person coming to check on him didn't shut the door and walk away.

This time, he wanted proof the poison had taken effect. The door quietly closed. Innocent recognized the heavy breathing in the preternatural stillness of the chamber.

It was O'Rourke.

The pope felt the cardinal come to the side of the bed, knew —even though his eyes were closed—O'Rourke was staring down at him. Innocent kept still even when the cardinal poked his side, then pressed his head against his chest. Then came the low voice, almost a whisper, into what must have been his cell phone.

"The dove is caged," O'Rourke said quietly.

Innocent heard the door open and close, knew he was alone once again, except for poor Bisschen. It was then he realized a part of him had held out hope that his suspicions were wrong, had wished for insanity rather than the terrifying reality that surrounded him, cornered him, narrowed his options like a nightmarish funnel cloud.

Sometime during his despair, there came a sound at the door. He closed his eyes as it opened and shut.

Then the sound of a muffled shot.

Terrible pressure.

Pain in the chest.

The last thing he heard: a small, weak bark.

49

Roberts didn't share the contents of the envelope with anyone. But as she took the Metro to the Park and Ride near her house in the D.C. burbs, the photo was the sole focus of her thoughts. She was pulling her Prius into her driveway when she thought she saw movement on the meet-and-greet porch of the bungalow. A quick subduing of light followed by a return to its normal glow made it look like someone had moved near the porchlight. She threw the car into park, left it running, and hopped out.

"Who's there?" she called when she reached the stoop, her keys and cell phone in one hand, pepper spray in the other.

The porch was well lit; she saw the entire span. No one was there.

"Way to go, Madge," she said. "Acting the fool." She returned to her car, turned it off, and grabbed her briefcase from the passenger seat.

"That picture's gone and given me the willies," she said going up the steps.

She unlocked and opened the door, tossed her briefcase on the table in the foyer, and turned around to close the door. Then she remembered the mail. She stepped onto the porch with one foot and reached her hand into the brass mailbox. Her fingertips felt envelopes, a magazine, ads, and...something small, plastic. She pulled out the contents. The small plastic object was a black thumb drive.

She went inside and put the rest of the mail on top of her briefcase. She looked closely at the thumb drive. Nothing special. You could buy one at any Walmart. But how did it get there? There was no package. It was just sitting in the mailbox. Must've been hand-delivered....

Like the photo.

"What in the world have we got here?" she said.

The drive's appearance in the mailbox sans postage caused her fear to return.

Maybe somebody *was* on the porch.

Still in her pumps, she clicked on the heart-pine floors from one room to the next, turning on every light as she went. The kitchen cabinets were shut tight, just the way she'd left them. The living room furniture looked undisturbed. The Reconstruction Era dining room table and chairs made by her great-grandfather still stood sentry in their place in the middle of the dining room. The Limoges dishes, propped up on tiny stands on the built-in shelves, were in their normal neat alignment. The French doors to the office at the back of the house were closed. She opened them and flipped the switch that turned on the chandelier over the partner's desk. None of the drawers looked tampered with. She rifled through the metal file cabinets against the wall, unable to detect any troubling signs.

"Okay, nothing out of place," she said hoping that hearing the words would reassure her, convince her that she had nothing to worry about. She sat on the Thomas Jefferson swivel chair on the left side of the desk—the only side that ever got any use—and went to jiggle the mouse to wake the computer, but she couldn't control her hand and almost knocked over the picture of her niece beside the monitor.

"This will not do, lady," she said in Corinne's sweet voice, as though it came from the picture.

"You're right, sweetie," Roberts answered. "Your Auntie Madge is losing it."

She stuck the thumb drive in the USB port of her computer. Just as she did, she thought she heard a noise coming from the front of the house.

She froze and cocked her head. It was a muffled sound. Almost like...

A ringtone.

Yes, that's what it was. She'd left her phone on the table near the door, and someone was trying to call her.

"You're just gonna have to take a ticket and wait your turn," she yelled to the caller. "I already got enough crazy going on here."

She clicked on the USB drive. Files of different types: a PDF and several PNGs. She opened the PDF. A member of the Senate Foreign Relations Committee for several years, she quickly recognized a series of foreign aid budgets, going back decades. Two recipients were yellow-highlighted year after year: Israel and Egypt. It was no surprise. They received the most money.

She knew it was something she'd have to devote more time to, but right now she wanted to see the rest of the files, so she turned her attention to the series of PNGs. The first was a photo of a large-beaded necklace of gold and lapis lazuli. Overprinted in the bottom center of the photo were the words, "Yuya's Tomb – Valley of the Kings, 1905" with "14141" below that. The second PNG was a photo of a slender wooden contraption that looked something like a rickshaw. It had the same words and numbers at the bottom as the first. The third photo, identically labelled, was of some tattered old garments.

The last PNG was a photo of a white mummy-like figurine held in a person's hand, presumably for scale. Three columns of hieroglyphs, circled in white, ran down the legs of the mummy and were numbered 1-3. The numbers were listed in the upper right, followed by a translation of the glyphs: "1 – Bearer of the Ring of the King of Lower Egypt," "2 – Seal-bearer of the King of Lower Egypt," and "3 – Holy Father of the Lord of the Two Lands." This photo had the same identifiers as the others: "Yuya's Tomb – Valley of the Kings, 1905" with "14141" below that.

"Hmm," Roberts said, staring at the screen. "Looks like we're gonna have to find out who the hell Yuya is—or was."

She googled the name. Apparently, Yuya was a powerful Egyptian courtier during Egypt's Eighteenth Dynasty, some-time in the mid-fourteenth century B.C. He was married to an Egyptian noblewoman named Tjuyu. Their daughter, Tiye, became the wife of Amenhotep III.

"All righty then. That tells me...absolutely nothing. C'mon whoever left this. I ain't got time to play Precious Ramotswe here."

Roberts shook her head and picked up the picture of her niece. "Well, Corinne. It looks like your Auntie Madge is gonna be up late tonight."

50

Waverley Banner, President Jenkins, along with the president's communications director, press secretary, and spiritual adviser entered the chief of staff's office, right next door to the Oval Office, that evening. The chief of staff knew the president needed a morale boost after the presentation of the case against him earlier that day. Banner led the group to the long, waist-high table directly across from his standing desk and took his place at its head.

"Mr. President," Banner began calmly, "I know I speak for all of us when I say how sad I am that the trial's been allowed to proceed. But there's one thing I want to make clear: The battle will be won. You will keep your presidency. The country is too divided to withstand the upheaval your removal from office would bring about, especially in this dangerous climate, where more terrorist attacks are bound to come. The people know it. Our friends in the Senate know it. There's simply no way our enemies can muster a two-thirds majority—of that you can be sure."

The communications director picked up the refrain. "And there won't be a problem framing this as another disaster for the Democrats," she said nasally, as if fighting a cold. She paused to yank a tissue from her sleeve and blew her pink rabbit nose. "Their intransigence practically ensures your stay in office. We're still waiting for the results from the latest polls but based on what we've got, two out of three want you to stay. The rally 'round the flag effect is strong."

"Mr. President, if I may," the press secretary piped in, raising two fingers of his right hand. "I know you're disappointed by the trial. We all are. But let's remember one thing. Your executive order was simply an acknowledgment of reality. We *are* a Judeo-Christian nation. That's not to say there aren't other faiths in this country, but they're the minority, the extreme minority. We've always been a God-fearing, Christ-loving nation. And, if the Lord wills it, we always will be. It was past time to make official what's been clear since our inception."

The president's spiritual adviser nodded his gray head. "To piggyback on that, Mr. President, God has a plan for you. He put you in office. There's no way He's going to let you fail. Remember the Lord's words to Jeremiah: 'For I know the plans I have for you, plans to prosper you and not to harm you, plans to give you hope and a future.' And as Paul said in his letter to the Romans, 'There is no authority except that which God has established.' You, sir, have been established by God. There's no doubt about it. These are trying times. Satan is everywhere, prowling like a lion, just waiting for this great nation to slide into the secular abyss."

Jenkins looked fondly at the group. "You know, what you've all just said reminds me of a time long ago, when I was thinking about getting active in politics. I had my doubts. I think Anne did too, but she kept them to herself. Then one Sunday in Cheyenne we heard a preacher say how Moses was at first reluctant to deliver the Hebrews from bondage. I thought if even Moses had hesitated, then my doubts were pretty normal. But I couldn't let them stand in the way of doing the right thing, the thing I knew God wanted me to do, to lead America to greater spiritual heights than she'd ever reached."

Banner nodded. "Absolutely. And in this case, the right thing to do is to stand firmly at the helm. America's number one strength, the ark of our might, is her spirituality, a spirituality that's both the solution to our domestic troubles and the key to our international security. You're doing the right thing, Mr. President, and I, for one, couldn't be prouder to serve you."

The others voiced their assent.

"Thank you, everyone," Jenkins said. "Now, before we go our separate ways, I'd like Reverend Benson to lead us in prayer. Reverend, if you will."

"Heavenly Father," Benson said, after they'd joined hands and bowed their heads, "the battle we're waging is for you. And we know that you, in all your loving grace, are on our side. Please grant us the strength to withstand Satan's forces that come in many guises and would deny you your rightful place at the forefront of our politics, our culture, our lives. We look to you, Lord, for guidance as we do battle with evildoers, at home and abroad. And we ask this in the name of Jesus Christ, your only Son. Amen."

After a heartfelt chorus of amen, everyone shook hands.

Banner followed them to the door then closed and locked it. He crossed the room to the damask curtains that hung over the doors to the spacious patio, larger even than the one off the Oval Office, and drew them closed. He strode back to his long, standing desk that was almost like a delicatessen counter and removed a framed poster of Winston Churchill with the words "Never, Never Give Up" at the bottom. The wall safe now exposed, he entered the combination, opened the small door, and smiled, eyeing the stone nameplate nabbed from the Jefferson Memorial two days before with complete satisfaction.

51

A long time had passed since the man holding Brynn captive had investigated the noise that turned out to have been nothing. It felt like days but was probably just an hour. Now he lazed in the chair at the foot of the bed, arms folded across his chest, legs stretched out in front, fighting what Zady called the Battle of the Nod. Brynn watched as his chin sank slowly to his chest.

It was the first time she'd seen him sleep and despite the scraggly beard, his relaxed face held the innocence of a child. She watched his chest rise and fall beneath the long dirty white shirt; his trouser-clad legs, almost spider-like in their thinness, shuffled slightly to the rhythm of repose. Sleep was a great equalizer. No one could resist its siren call.

Then she thought of the rifle.

After satisfying himself that the noise coming from the front of the cabin posed no threat, the man had returned the gun to its place under the bed.

Could she reach it without waking him?

She chided herself for such a cold-blooded thought. Everything about the life of Christ, the only life worth imitating, told her to turn the other cheek. Meeting violence with violence was never the answer. Besides, she didn't know if she could get the weapon without waking the man, and even if she did, she didn't know how to use it. And she had no doubt he'd take advantage of her ignorance and snatch it from her hands before she could figure it out. Besides, even if she were able to hold him at gunpoint long enough to find the key and free herself from the chain, what then? She had no clue where she was, or if there were other people waiting nearby to recapture her. Worst of all, if she tried to get the weapon and failed, there was no telling what he'd do to her.

She knew what Zady would do: go for the gun and try to fight her way out. But could Brynn bring herself to do something so bold, so rash, so against everything she believed in, everything she tried so hard to be?

Before she fully formed the intent, she rolled onto her side and dangled her arm over the bed. If she went through with this, she'd have to lay on her stomach and see if she could reach the rifle that way—she didn't dare risk climbing under the bed, knew it would wake her captor. As quietly and carefully as she could, she rolled onto her belly and reached under the bed as far as she could. But her grasping fingers found nothing. She was just about to give up when she touched something hard and round.

And froze when she felt a presence.

Craning her neck, she saw that her captor was still sleeping. But she knew with stomach-clenching certainty that someone was just outside the room. Whether for good or ill she didn't know. And now, beyond the sleeping figure at the foot of the bed, through the open doorway, a shadow moved.

Her heart stopped.

But when a camouflaged figure materialized in the haloed light from the bedside lamp, she knew she was safe. The lips pressed against a thick forefinger imploring silence belonged to Lance Sterling, family friend and her uncle's right-hand man. And if Lance was here, Aleister couldn't be far away.

Relief gushed through her. But she kept still, letting her fingertips rest on the barrel of the rifle beneath the bed. If her captor awoke, she'd try as hard as she could to keep him from getting it. Eyes stretched wide, she watched Sterling creep noiselessly into the room and point his rifle at the back of her captor's head. Sterling circled around the man's sleeping body until he stood directly in front of him.

"Wakey, wakey, you son of a bitch!" Sterling shouted, kicking the man.

The man jerked awake and started to get to his feet, but Sterling told him not to move and spoke into the earpiece Brynn saw for the first time.

"She's safe. I got him. Clear for Mabrey."

Through a filmy screen of tears, Brynn tried her best to answer Sterling's questions about her well-being. Then, like a heavenly vision, Uncle Aleister rolled into the room and wheeled around Sterling and his prisoner to her bedside. She threw her arms around his neck, and they wept.

"Are you all right, my dear?" Mabrey asked when he could finally speak.

Brynn bobbed her head against his shoulder until he repeated the question.

She gently pulled away and said, "Yes, I'm okay."

"Good, good," Mabrey said slowly, but looked unconvinced.

"Really, I'm all right," Brynn assured him, kissing his cheek.

"Well, if you're sure." He removed the key from his neck and pressed it into her hands. "Just in case," he said by way of explanation.

She looked at him, puzzled.

"Now maybe we can get some answers as to who's behind all of this," he said, nodding at Sterling.

Brynn followed his nod and watched Sterling take one hand off his rifle, reach into the back of his waistband, and pull out a pistol. The next second there was a pop and Brynn stared with huge eyes as her captor slid off the chair onto the floor, blood pouring from a hole in his forehead.

"What the—?" Mabrey said. "Sterling? Why did you—?"

He never finished. Brynn watched, frozen, as Sterling pointed the pistol at her uncle's chest and fired two rounds.

Mabrey's head dropped forward onto his pierced chest.

Sterling aimed the gun at Brynn. "Make a sound and you're dead." He yanked a walkie-talkie from his pocket. "Secure the perimeter. And pull the surveil footage from the van."

THURSDAY

52

"You sure you can see to drive?" Larson asked Zady, using his hand to wipe the gritty film off the Accord's windshield.

"Scott, for the hundredth time, yes."

"I can't believe you gave that student so much money to borrow this. Even if we don't bring it back, he got the best of that deal."

"What did you expect me to do?" Zady asked. "There's no public transport from Cairo to Amarna. Besides, we need something that blends in. And we can use it to charge our phones."

"Well, there's no doubt it blends in. It's so dirty it's the color of the desert."

"Don't listen to him, Artemis," Zady said, petting the dashboard. "He's just a man and knows not of what he speaks."

"I can't believe you named the car."

"And I can't believe that although we're heading south, we're heading into Upper Egypt. That's just wrong."

"It's the way the Nile runs. The whole civilization was built around the river."

"According to the map, the whole trip is about three-hundred and sixty kilometers. We're about halfway to Amarna now. Footnote: We'd be even closer if you hadn't stopped for food near Beni Suef."

"We have to eat," Larson said, ripping open the bag of chips they'd gotten from one of the many large airy places that served coffee, tea, and snacks along the way. "And gas. Needed that. And the map. Wouldn't have that either if we hadn't stopped."

"All right, all right," an annoyed Zady said, waving a hand, but staring straight ahead, keeping her eyes focused on the endless Cairo Road/Route 75M.

The view was the same as it had been since they'd left the city hub. A limitless expanse of highway straight ahead and, on either side, the never-ending desert, punctuated with clumps of palm trees. The Tariq el-Geish, or Army Road, as it was known, began at Helwan, ran south— parallel to, and east of, the Nile— and consisted of two wide lanes, separated by a strip of sand and concrete barriers to reduce damage from accidents. It was an impressive feat of engineering.

They passed a white minibus—the fifth or sixth they'd seen— packed with people rushing north at reckless speed. It was tailed, too closely, by a flatbed truck piled high with huge, cube-shaped blocks of limestone and granite. Though it was now the middle of the night, they'd passed lots of these vehicles along the way, some broken down on the roadside, piles of enormous stones pushed off the flatbeds and laying haphazardly near to allow for a tire change or other necessary repair. Larson wondered how drivers toppled the blocks off the truck beds and got them back on. Then again, their ancestors had built the pyramids.

"Truthfully," Zady said, breaking his reverie, "I'm not sure what we're going to do when we get to Amarna."

"I think the clues are leading us somewhere."

"Could you be a *tad* more specific, genius?"

Undeterred, he went on. "And I think the temple Akhenaten built there is somehow crucial to all this. You want to try Aleister again?"

"I just tried him ten minutes ago."

"Aren't you worried that he's not answering?"

"Not as worried as you, apparently," Zady said.

"But how else are we going to know if he finds Brynn?"

"*When* not if. And he'll let us know. Besides, the kidnappers have been good at keeping in touch—like letting us know she has until Saturday to live if we don't get them the nameplate, Moses' treasure, or whatever the hell they want. Great, there's a tollbooth ahead. Can you hand me my bag? It's on the floor behind my seat."

Larson reached behind him and grabbed the beat-up tote that was like Zady's extra appendage. The tollbooth was more modest than the one at Helwan, at the start of the Army Road, with its huge pharaonic-style toll gateway. This one looked just like any tollbooth in the States.

"Do you want me to dig out the money?" He relished the opportunity to rummage through the bag. He'd decided to trust her, but that didn't mean he'd stopped being curious whether there was another envelope sealed with red wax hiding in her bag.

"No, just give it to me."

She slowed down, pulled up to the booth, and told the attendant to wait as she dug through her tote. Larson watched as she pulled out a wad of Egyptian pounds then stuffed them into the man's outstretched palm. He gave her a ticket and most of the money back. She shoved the change and ticket into her bag, threw it on the floor behind her, and proceeded along the road.

The moon shone brilliantly as the road dipped from a plateau whose edge was marked by an imposing cliff that ran east-west into the desert below. Suddenly, they found themselves at the top of a ramp, the final descent before the road deposited them in the desert.

"Dropping!" Zady shouted, while Larson held on for his life.

The car fell at such breathtaking speed he wasn't sure the wheels touched the ramp.

When the road leveled, Zady turned right at the signpost for Minia. They soon hit another tollbooth. Larson reached behind him and handed Zady her bag. Once through, they coasted to a T-junction, marked by a small, run-down café, and an equally worn tire repair shop—though calling it a shop was generous; it was more like a corrugated shack—surrounded by old tires.

"Left, or right?" Zady said absent-mindedly. "We're off the map now."

"I think we should go right," Larson said. "The old desert highway looks like it continues there."

"Your confidence underwhelms me," Zady said then turned left. After a steep rollercoaster drop, they hit the valley floor. They continued across fields, past a huge cemetery of domed tombs, to a bridge that crossed the Nile.

"It all started with that river," Larson said, watching moon-light glitter on the water.

They passed a large Neo-Islamic building with a huge entrance portal. A barbed wire fence ran around the perimeter. Several police SUVs were parked at various angles nearby. Zady continued, and soon they were riding alongside huge cliffs.

"Oh, no," Zady said.

"What?"

"I have to pee. Must be the river."

When she slammed on the brakes Larson was sucked into his seat. The Honda slid sideways, tires screeching, before coming to a stop perpendicular to the road.

"Nice job," he said, trying to slow his heart.

"What can I say? I told you I had to go."

She threw the car into park with the engine running then reached behind her to grab her tote. She flipped the dome light on so she could find what she wanted. Larson watched in the wan light as she ransacked the bag and pulled out a pack of tissues before tossing the bag on her seat. She unclicked her belt and grabbed her phone off the console. Before Larson could ask why she needed to take her phone, she threw open the door, got out, and slammed it shut. She strode away diagonally, beyond the high beams' swath.

This was his chance to see if her bag held any surprises. He had to know what he was dealing with. If Zady was the source of the envelopes, then she knew something he didn't, and anyway you looked at it, that wouldn't do. In one quick motion, he grabbed the tote and plopped it on his lap. After counting to three, he unzipped it. Near the top, amid a wad of currency and tollbooth tickets, an envelope lay face-up. He pulled it out, praying desperately, with what little faith he had left, that the red wax on the back was broken, that it was one of the two envelopes they'd already found.

A quick intake of breath, and he turned it over:

The wax was intact.

He jumped at the knock on his window.

Zady, bent at the waist, peered inside. She hunched her shoulders, then held her hands open, palms facing upwards.

"What the fuck, Scott?" The closed window muffled her voice.

She stormed to the driver's side, ripped open the door, launched herself into the seat, and slammed the door shut.

"Again, Scott, I say, 'What the fuck'?"

"You're asking me, 'What the fuck'? You're asking me?!" he yelled, thrusting the envelope in her face. Dropping the f-bomb was satisfying, as was the delicious rage coursing through him.

"One of the envelopes we found. Christ, what's your problem? And why the hell are you going through my bag?"

"It's NOT one of the envelopes we found! The wax on this one isn't broken. It's never been opened."

Zady ripped the envelope out of his hand and examined the wax. "Okay, you're right. Somebody must've slipped it in my bag when I wasn't looking. Stop making a federal case over it. God, what is wrong with you?" She used her fingernail to break the seal, but Larson grabbed the envelope before she could finish.

"Just tell me what the hell is going on," he said. He spoke quietly but felt like a pressure cooker about to explode.

"What do you mean? Wait a minute. You think I...? Shit! I can't believe it!"

"Well, what am I supposed to think, Zady? You found the first envelope in your hotel room. The second one ended up on my seat when I went to the can. And now I find this one in your bag. You've been leaving clues all along, haven't you? How long have you and Aleister been stringing me along? Is Brynn even in danger? You want to tell me just what the hell is *really* going on?"

"I can't believe you, Scott. I can't fucking believe you. You really think I'd string you along all this time and go so far as to stage Brynn's kidnapping? What would be my motive?"

"I haven't exactly figured that part out yet."

"Scott, you have to trust me. I have no idea where the envelopes are coming from. I promise you that you know as much as I do. If you want, we can go back to the toll booths. One of the attendants could've slipped it to me when he gave me my ticket and change. I don't remember the bag being out of my sight, but maybe somebody stuck it in when I had my head turned before we hit the road for Amarna. Maybe even at the university. Do you want to go back to the toll booths and check there?"

"No. We don't have to go back," he said, suddenly feeling a little guilty for doubting her. "That would waste time and Brynn doesn't have much left. Whoever gave it to you was probably just doing what he was told. Or somebody slipped it to you before that." *And,* he thought, *if you are lying, whoever did is on your—or your uncle's— payroll.*

But even if she wasn't being truthful, what could he do about it now in the Egyptian desert in the middle of the night? He figured his best chance of getting through all this alive was to just go along for now as if he trusted her, in the belief that eventually, truth would will out. There didn't seem to be a better option on the horizon.

"I think you should open it," Zady said.

It was only then he realized he was still holding the envelope. He turned it over, broke the rest of the wax, and tore open the flap. Inside was a single sheet of paper. The precise, calligraphy-like words were the same as the others:

So, Joseph died at the age of a hundred and ten. And after they embalmed him, he was placed in a coffin in Egypt.

"What's it say?" Zady asked.

Larson read it to her.

"Thoughts?"

He reread it to himself. "It's the last passage of Genesis, chapter fifty, verse twenty-six. It refers to Jacob's son, Joseph, whose brothers sold him into slavery. But he went on to become pharaoh's right-hand man."

Zady bit her lip. "What does Joseph have to do with anything? It's the same name that's on the nameplate we tried to hand over to ISIS. But I thought that was a reference to Jesus' brother Joseph. Anyway, aren't we supposed to be looking for Moses' treasure? And didn't Joseph live long before him, according to the Bible at least?"

"Yeah," Larson said. "I don't know, maybe the number one-hundred-ten is important, or fifty, or twenty-six."

"But how does Joseph tie in with Moses?"

He shook his head. "Wait a minute. Remember the other day when I mentioned *The Assumption of Moses* and its strange reference to TAXO?"

"The one that scholar said could be translated to 'Asaph,'

who you said might be the Teacher of Righteousness in the Dead Sea Scrolls?"

"Yeah. If I remember correctly, 'Asaph' can also be rendered as 'Joseph.'"

"Interesting...not. C'mon, we need something concrete. The passage refers to Joseph's burial. Where in Egypt was Joseph allegedly buried?"

"The Bible doesn't say. But before he died, Joseph made the Hebrews promise that when they left Egypt, they'd take his bones with them. Moses did just that when he fled Egypt. Eventually, the bones were interred at Shechem, where Joseph and his family lived before going to Egypt. The Israelis and Palestinians have fought over a tomb there for years, though there's no archeological evidence that it's Joseph's. Several other locations have been put forth as his tomb."

"But the passage in Genesis talks about his coffin in Egypt. Is there any place associated with his burial here?"

"Not that I'm aware. Wait. I remember reading at the library that a bunch of clay tablets were found near here in the early twentieth century, including a record of Akhenaten's diplomatic correspondence. The Amarna Letters, they're called."

Zady held up a hand. "While I admit, you're a veritable suppository of information—"

"You mean repository."

"No, no, I said what I mean. But how—?"

"I'll tell you. Shechem, where Joseph's bones might be, is mentioned in the Amarna Letters."

"And this would be helpful how?" Zady asked.

"I'm not sure. But at least it shows a connection between Amarna, where we're heading, and the location, or at least *a* location, associated with Joseph's tomb. It might not be much, but it's something. The good news is we're heading to Amarna, so maybe we're on the right track."

"And now for the bad news," Zady said, as an SUV pulled

alongside them on the shoulder of the road. "Looks like the police are here."

53

I t was well past midnight, and Madge Roberts was still ensconced at her desk. She knew she needed sleep. As her mother always said, "One hour of sleep before midnight is better than two after." But she felt compelled to keep digging into the contents of the thumb drive she'd found in her mailbox. She couldn't say how, but she felt that it, along with the photo of the men at the London hotel in the early twentieth century, were crucial to the president's trial, which resumed in just a few hours.

She reviewed the summary of what she'd discovered so far, handwritten notes on a yellow legal pad, scribbled while guzzling cup after cup of very strong coffee. Her mind buzzed as she read her notes on the PDF document, the listing of U.S. foreign aid to Israel and Egypt from the late 1940s to the present:

—Israel and Egypt top recipients of U.S. foreign aid, military and economic - why these two countries?

—Aid to Israel makes sense, but aid to Egypt doesn't - these two countries have been at odds since Israel's creation - Why aid both sides? Payoff? Hush money?

—Interesting fact: foreign aid to Israel nearly doubled from 1965-1966, from $65 million to almost $128 million - 1966 was the year prior to Israel's epic Six-Day War, in which it captured the West Bank from Jordan, the Gaza Strip and Sinai from Egypt, and the Golan Heights from Syria

—Interesting fact: The Dead Sea Scrolls have been under the control of the Israeli Antiquity Department since the fall of East Jerusalem in the Six-Day War, Prior to that they were under Jordan's control - Did the Scrolls play any part in the war?

She still felt like she had more questions than answers, especially when she reviewed her notes on the photos:

—Yuya's Tomb - Discovered in the Valley of the Kings in 1905

—Yuya: Egyptian courtier, Eighteenth Dynasty, c.1390 BC; married to Tjuyu, an Egyptian noblewoman; daughter Tiye = wife of Amenhotep the 3rd (c. 1425-1350 BC)

—Tomb contents, photos: 1) gold necklace; 2) chariot;

3) garments; 4) small, mummy figurine/ushabti-hieroglyphs: a) Bearer of the Ring of the King of Lower Egypt, b) Seal-bearer of the King of Lower Egypt, c) Holy Father of the Lord of the Two Lands

—Significance of 14141?

She was particularly stymied over that last number, which appeared in the bottom center of all the photos. What could it refer to? A date didn't make sense. Was it the combination to a lock? A password? Coordinates? Numbers that needed to be rearranged before their meaning could be discerned?

The year 1905 was two years after the photo of the men at the London hotel. Were they responsible for finding Yuya's Tomb? But why was Yuya so important? Obviously, he was a top official during the reign of Amenhotep III, but what did that have to do with foreign aid to Egypt and Israel centuries later? And what did any of this have to do with Jenkins' trial?

Completely at a loss, she spent the next two hours doing more research, talking to the picture of her niece as she tried to put the pieces together. When the computer clock showed 2:12 she got up from her chair and headed to the bedroom. She doubted she could sleep, but she owed it to the American people to be as fresh as she could when the trial resumed in seven hours.

54

"What fresh hell is this?" Zady asked.

"I wish I knew," Larson said.

The cement room in the Egyptian police station reeked of mustiness and sweat. A small metal table and the two wooden chairs on which they sat were the sole furnishings. They'd been deposited here by two policemen in khaki cotton uniforms, who'd left as soon as they were seated. But that had been a while ago—impossible to tell exactly how long because there was no clock on the wall, and the cops had taken their phones. And Zady's bag. And their fake passports. At least they'd thrown out their real ones when they'd gotten off the plane. But after using the library at the American University in Cairo they'd ditched their disguises and now there was little chance they'd be taken for the people in their phony passport photos.

"Do you even know where we are?" Zady asked.

"A police station," Larson said.

"No, genius, I mean where, like in what town or city."

"I don't know. They drove us south, though, so I don't think we're too far off course. I'd say we're closer to Amarna than when they picked us up." He tried to keep his voice steady, but it trembled toward the end.

Just then the heavy metal door opened and one of the policemen entered carrying a black metal-framed upholstered chair. He set it down at the table across from them and turned to leave. But the door hadn't fully closed when it swung open again, and a short slender man came in. It was hard to tell his age, but his dark skin wrinkled at the corners of his eyes, his broad forehead, and the top of his throat—the rest of his neck was covered by a stiff, white collar and dark tie. Though balding, some hair had migrated south to form a thin, Hitler-like mustache above long, full lips. His many decorations stood out in a rainbowed rectangle on the chest of his black jacket. The black cap he carried in one hand and the attaché case in the other lent him an officious air.

After scrutinizing Larson and Zady, he set his cap and case on the table then seated himself in the upholstered chair with such military aplomb Larson almost saluted. With small, perfectly manicured hands he took their passports out of the attaché and set them on the table.

"Good morning," he said in a reedy voice. "I've been told you speak English..."—his eyes scanned the passports—"Mr. Baumgarten and Miss Ansel."

Nodding and smiling idiotically, Larson shifted uncomfortably in his chair.

"And you are...?" Zady said.

"I will ask the questions," came the terse reply.

"And we'll only answer them if you tell us who you are," Zady shot back.

Larson bumped her knee under the table and shook his head when she looked at him.

"What...Lester?" she asked wide-eyed. "We get taken from our vehicle at gunpoint, dragged here, wherever the hell here is, have our shit confiscated, and we've been sitting here in this empty godforsaken room for eons, and you expect me to—"

Larson cleared his throat. "What Dominique means is we're curious to know why we're being held."

"All in good time, Mr. Baumgarten, all in good time," the man said, stressing the surname. He stared back and forth at Larson and Zady. It was hard to say which was worse: the look in his eyes, or the silence that lengthened into darkness like shadows on a wintry afternoon.

"So..." he said, the syllable gradually fading into the preternatural stillness of the room.

"What do you want with us?" Zady finally snapped.

"You are carrying a great deal of money with you," he said, pulling out wads of currency from the attaché case and piling them on the table. "Egyptian pounds, Israeli shekels, American dollars, Euros, you appear to be on an international... expedition."

"We're travelers," Larson said. "We're, um, traveling." He could almost hear Zady's eyes roll.

"I see," the man said slowly. "And this traveling, I assume, is for pleasure?"

"Yes," Larson said, at the same time Zady said, "No."

They looked at each other. Larson continued. "It's both, actually. It's pleasure in the sense that all travel is rewarding, but business because we're writing a book on ancient Egypt and we're doing research. You see, research is a form of pleasure. That is, there are many forms of pleasure, but we're not here for all of them. I mean, well, we're not pleasuring each other..."

"Oy vey, Lester," Zady said, smacking her forehead with her palm. "What this tongue-tied jack—er, Lester, is trying to say is that we're collaborating on a book. On Amarna. Where we're heading. Um, south."

We're heading south all right, Larson thought. But he had to admit Zady was doing better than him.

"There's no law against research," Zady said. "Isn't that right, Anwar?"

Or maybe she wasn't. Larson kicked her under the table,

though he had to admit the guy could've been Anwar Sadat's twin brother. Zady promptly kicked him back—much harder.

"That depends," the man replied.

"On what?" Zady asked.

"On what you are researching. What it is you're trying to find. In Egypt there are many laws, some of which you won't find in Israel, France...or America."

Did the reference to the U.S. mean he knew their true identities?

"Tell me something," the man said, leaning forward. "Why come to Egypt now? There has been *trouble* here; there might be more *trouble* ahead."

The emphasis on the word caused Larson to wince.

"Could it have something to do with these?" the man asked, reaching into the case, and pulling out the envelopes. He placed them on the table one at a time, next to the currency. "Tell me what these are," he said, pointing a thin finger at the envelopes.

It was a good question. Larson took a little comfort in the fact that he'd counted three envelopes as the inquisitor put them on the table—that meant Zady didn't have any in reserve, waiting to dole out at some point or points in the future. Maybe she was on the level after all. Then again, she and/or Aleister could have arranged for more envelopes to be "found" during their journey, like the guy in the toll booth who'd passed along the last one—if he had.

Unsurprisingly, Zady spoke before Larson could think of a semi-plausible response. "Those are part of a scavenger hunt," she said. "Just trying to keep entertained as we go along. You know, fight the boredom of the road, what with all the sand. Keeps our minds sharp. Our colleagues are always finding new and creative ways to challenge us, eh, Lester?" She jabbed an elbow into his ribs.

Larson tried to smile but felt sick to his stomach.

"So, there are others with you on this...research expedition?" the man said suspiciously. "What are their names?"

Larson listened as Zady reeled off a litany of the names and titles of people accompanying them. Her glibness did nothing to quiet the voice of doubt inside him; she was a good liar. The sour taste of bile rose to his throat, as he struggled to think of a way out of this mess. There was a good chance they were heading to jail, maybe prison, *Egyptian* prison. There was nothing good about that—not for him, and especially not for her.

Then something unexpected happened. Sadat—great, now she had him doing it—nodded slowly, as though believing Zady's every word. "I see," he said. His face relaxed; his ramrod posture slackened. "Well, I guess there is no harm done." He smiled and his lips peeled back to reveal crooked yellow teeth. He returned the money and envelopes to the attaché case, closed the lid, and placed his elbows on the table so his knuckles met.

"Before we finish, I would like to ask one question," he said, leaning forward, his face transformed into an imperturbable stone mask. "Do you think I'm stupid, Mr. Baumgarten and Miss Ansel...or should I say Mr. Larson and Miss Jones?"

"Actually, it's *Doctor* Larson."

"Oh, shut the fuck up, Scott!" Zady snarled.

They were led to adjoining cells—separated only by bars—by the two policemen who'd brought them to the interrogation room. They weren't told why they were being held. The major general (Larson learned his rank when one of the policemen addressed him as such) simply said they were on their way to prison.

Larson looked around his cell. Concrete blocks made up two walls. A bucket in the corner served as the toilet; half-full of nastiness, the stench curled his nose hairs. A few blocks protruded from the wall at the end to form a small platform where a moth-eaten blanket smelling like wet dog was rolled into a loose ball in the middle. There were no windows or ventilation of any kind. The only saving grace was he could see Zady through the bars.

"Cheer up, Scott. At least we don't have cellmates," she said.

He was facing the back wall of his cell, staring numbly at the platform-bed. Her words didn't even make him turn his head, which felt incredibly heavy, to look at her. His eyes were dry; he wasn't blinking much—a sign, he'd once read, of depression—and though it'd been hours since he'd eaten, he wasn't hungry. He assumed his bodily processes were starting to slow. Time felt heavy, tangible, each moment interminable. The confinement made him think of the hell Brynn must be going through and the thought of her made him feel even worse because now he and Zady couldn't help her. Everything his eyes and mind registered was tinged in black.

55

I t was early, just a few minutes past six, and White House Chief of Staff Waverley Banner was already in his spacious office. From behind his standing desk, he spoke into a burner phone. "Everything's in place. The final vote's Saturday. Jenkins will be acquitted."

"Good, sir," Sterling said. "I've held up my end, too."

"Has anyone tried to contact him?"

"His niece, several times, but not for the past few hours."

"Because the Egyptians have her," Banner said. "She and her friend are on their way to prison. We're not going to have a repeat of the Israeli airport. You can dispose of the other one any way you see fit."

56

"One of the worst parts about this is not knowing what time it is," Zady said as she leaned against the bars, her legs balanced on her shelf-bed. "We have no way of knowing how long Brynn—not that we can do anything about it, but—oh, shit, I don't know."

"I understand," Larson said, watching her closely from his side of the bars. Now that he'd regained some sense of composure, he wanted to comfort her, but his mind kept churning over the clues in the wax-sealed envelopes, what it was they were trying to find, who wanted to stop them, the nature of Zady's involvement in all of it. It bugged him that he still fretted about the last one, but he couldn't help it—though he was certain getting captured by the Egyptian police wasn't a part of her plan, if she had one.

He was still looking at her when she raised a finger and pointed ahead. He turned to see. The heavy metal door down the hall opened and the two policemen entered. One of them locked the door behind them, while the taller one strode to Larson's cell. He was soon joined by his cohort, who stood before Zady's. The taller cop pulled a key from his pocket and inserted it into the lock of Larson's cell, while the other drew his pistol and kept it trained on him. Once the lock was opened, they entered. The tall one shoved Larson against the wall and yanked his hands behind his back.

Larson winced as the handcuffs bit into his wrists. He turned to look at Zady, who wore the most terrified expression he'd ever seen.

"It's all right," he said gently, managing a weak grin. "Just keep your eyes on mine. Look at me, Zady."

He kept his eyes on hers as the cops strong-armed him out of the cell and into the corridor then watched helplessly as they dragged Zady out of her cell and shoved her next to him.

"Where are you taking us?" he asked.

"Prison," the shorter one said.

"Scott?" Zady pleaded.

The way she called his name, like a final SOS on a sinking ship, would always stay with him. "You're doing great," he said.

He kept his eyes locked on hers until they left the building. When they were pushed into the bright sunshine, he blinked rapidly, his eyes trying to adjust to the photons stabbing his pupils. It had to be mid-afternoon. Once his eyes adjusted, he saw they were in the sandy parking lot in front of the station. Except for the barbed wire fence surrounding it, the building looked very much like the ones on campus in Cairo.

A few SUVs dotted the lot, but what caught his eye were two vehicles straight ahead. One, a white van—obviously, a transport vehicle, what with the windows on the back doors covered in steel mesh—was no doubt their intended destination. But what really surprised him was the vehicle parked next to it: the dirty Accord they'd gotten from the student. The police must have sent someone to retrieve it. It was like seeing the ghost of a loved one. For all its ugliness, the car took on an almost sacred preciousness he could barely comprehend.

The tall cop pushed him toward the gaping maw of the van and shoved him inside. He leaned against the wall on the bench and watched as Zady was thrust into the vehicle. She sat next to him and nestled her head against his shoulder. Her body trembled. As if their heads were connected by an invisible wire, they stared out the back windows, through the steel mesh, at the Honda, as the van pulled away.

Larson was so focused on watching the Accord become smaller and smaller that he heard the gunshot before his eyes were yanked to its source. The Lieutenant General stood just outside the station's entrance, pointing his pistol at the sky. A cloud of smoke drifted lazily from its barrel like an orison.

The van screeched to a halt. Larson and Zady tumbled off the bench and onto the floor. They struggled to their feet then watched through the mesh as the driver came into view and approached the lieutenant. Larson couldn't hear what they were saying, but the lieutenant yelled something at the driver, who cocked his head in confusion.

"He's got my bag," Zady said.

Larson nodded. "What the—?"

"Fuck!" Zady finished.

"Yeah, that," Larson said.

For a moment they stared at each other, then turned their attention back to the men. The lieutenant handed Zady's tote bag and a key he took from his jacket to the driver and nodded at the van.

"Um, what's happening?" Zady asked.

"Be damned if I know," Larson replied. They watched in utter disbelief, as the driver approached the van, set Zady's bag on the ground, opened the back doors, and climbed inside. He took a key from his front pocket and unlocked Zady's handcuffs then Larson's and motioned them out. Once they did, he jumped out of the back and stood before them.

"You're free to go," he said. He reached into his pocket and pulled out the keys to the Honda.

Zady was the first to act. She grabbed the keys with one hand and snatched her bag off the ground with the other. She elbowed Larson then raced to the car.

Stunned by what had just happened, he was unable to move, until Zady shouted at him from over her shoulder.

"Now, Scott! Move!"

Instinctively his feet carried him to the passenger door. He opened it and collapsed inside. Zady tossed her bag in the backseat, plunked herself behind the wheel, slammed the key into the ignition, and revved the engine.

"What the...?" was all he could manage.

"Fuck!" Zady said giddily. "The word you're looking for is 'fuck!'" She let out a short maniacal laugh.

"Are you okay?" he asked gently, touching her arm.

"Never better." She yanked the car in reverse, spun it around, and tore off, leaving a thick swirling dust cloud that completely obscured the jail.

"Where are we heading?" Larson asked.

"Away from here. Grab my bag from the back and see if our phones are inside."

He reached behind her seat and pulled the bag onto his lap.

"You sure you want me to go in this?" he asked.

"Of course, Scott. I told you. I have nothing to hide."

He opened the bag and rummaged through it. At the bottom, amid all the currency, were their phones. He also saw three envelopes with broken red wax—no more, and no less. He grabbed the phones and closed the bag.

"Everything's in there. Our phones, the money, the envelopes."

She took her phone from Larson. "Well, no calls or texts," she said, setting her cell in the center console, next to the mini trash can the car's previous owner had put there.

When Larson checked his, he discovered he hadn't received any calls or texts either, but a headline he glimpsed on his newsfeed made him catch his breath. "Oh my God," he said, "the pope's dead."

"Holy shit!" Zady said. "What happened?"

"It says he died overnight of natural causes."

"We're going to have to put a pin in that and come back to it. Right now, we need to figure out how far we are from Amarna." She pulled over to the side of the road. "Give me the map. Also, what happened back there?"

"I have no idea," he said, handing her the map, which had been folded up neatly in the back seat. "All I know is someone or something is looking out for us. Remember what happened at the Israeli airport? And now this. You think it's Aleister?"

"I'd like to think so except he didn't know about our change of plans. He thought we were going to Alexandria, remember? I haven't been able to get ahold of him, so I doubt he knows where we are, or that we were headed to prison. I should try him again." She picked up her cell, speed dialed, then turned on the speaker. It rang...and rang...and rang.

"This is ridiculous," she said, ending the call with her thumb. "I don't know why I didn't think of this before." She pushed another button on her phone and waited as it rang.

57

P resent at the creation...

That was how Lance Sterling framed it in his mind whenever he thought of how he'd met Aleister Mabrey. Though "met" wasn't exactly the right word; for his involvement with the Brit was preordained. Mabrey had just started DoveCo. when Sterling was tasked to keep a close eye on him, make sure he behaved, above all that he never divulged the existence of the organization Mabrey had left—the one whose American counterpart had hired Sterling to keep an eye on the old Brit.

And now he'd gone rogue.

It hadn't been easy, faking devotion to Mabrey and his nieces, a couple of brats if ever there were ones. Even though the one he now observed lying on the bed, her ankle chained to the floor, ended up becoming a nun. Or a junior—whatever the fuck you called the pre-nun phase, other than stupid, which is the only thing a person could be to want to become that involved with any religion. Both bitches were spoiled by their dead uncle. The older one was more worldly than this inert lump, but neither had been told the truth about their parents. And their deaths. No, they were far too precious, too fucking delicate for that, so Mabrey had treated them like mushrooms, kept them in the dark, and fed them shit.

But with the snarky bitch and the pain-in-the-ass priest locked in prison—and an Egyptian one at that—the only thing left to do to end the threat Mabrey and company posed and clear the final hurdle to his own personal ambition was to do away with the godforsaken mess on the bed. Sterling rose from the chair and strode to the bedside. This one was too hot to be a nun anyway. Even now, in her piss-poor state, she was a looker: long, raven black hair, classic, angled features, eyes like a clear summer sky, body to kill for. Maybe before he offed her, he would show her just what she'd missed by marrying Jesus. There'd be something so profane and sacrilegious about it, something delicious.

At the sound of a knock, he whipped his eyes to the door so fast he felt a tug on his nerve stalks. Quinn stood at the door eyes wide, eager to please, stupid, and gullible—the winningest combination. One of several dupes he'd easily turned against Mabrey.

"What?" Sterling said sharply.

Quinn spoke in the high-pitched, excited manner that made Sterling want to shoot him in the face. "Sir, is there anything I can do, sir?"

Sterling eyed the young man from head to toe. He would just as easily have sat on him if there was no furniture in the room. "No, Quinn. There's not."

"Sir!" He executed a perfect salute, turned on his heel with SS-adroitness, and vanished as quickly as he'd come.

Back to his thoughts. The bitch *was* hot. But the important thing was to waste her... Of course, afterwards, he could always —No, he couldn't. *That* was a bridge too far.

He raised his pistol at the bed-lump wrapped in the sheet, head visible at one end, bare feet, left ankle chained, at the other. Besides a gag he'd stuffed in her mouth and the rope around her wrists, he'd made no changes to the condition he'd found her in. He'd briefly considered moving her to another safehouse, but then Banner had called and given him the go-ahead, so he could just as easily snuff her here.

She'd spent the time since he'd killed Mabrey curled in the fetal position, facing away from him. Now, maybe sensing her fate, she turned, stretched to her full length, and fastened her eyes on him. She showed no sign of panic, her blinking remained slow, lethargic. She was practically dead anyway.

Standing at her bedside, he pointed his pistol at her head and started to squeeze the trigger.

But she uttered something through the rubber gag. From her body posture he could tell she wasn't straining—she wasn't trying to scream or curse at him. No, this was more like talking; calm, considering how close she was to death.

What the fuck is she saying?

The fact that she wasn't struggling bothered him more than if she'd thrown a fit. This sound—the slow, steady, annoyingly rhythmed cadence—was unnerving. He couldn't tell what she was saying, but it almost sounded as if she were...

He had to know. He dropped the pistol and ripped the gag out of her mouth.

"What are you blabbering about?!"

Her face bore little sign of stress. She looked radiant, glowed with a light from within.

"Praying," she said quietly, "for your soul."

He backhanded her across the face, smearing her lips with blood, then stuck the gag back in her mouth.

"Don't pity me!" He jabbed the barrel of the pistol against her forehead. "Don't you dare pity me!"

He was about to squeeze the trigger and finish her off when one of the phones in his pockets rang. Thinking it was Banner on the burner, he lowered his gun, yanked the phone out of his pocket, put it to his face, and barked, "What?!"

But no one answered. And the ringing continued.

Some idiot was calling his regular phone. He tore that out of his other pocket and screamed, "What!" again.

"Lance? It's Zady. Are you okay?"

His heart froze. How the fuck was Zady calling him? Were Egyptian authorities now allowing prisoners a final phone call? Fucking liberals! They were able to infiltrate themselves everywhere. Instinctively, and in one fell motion, he stepped into the other room, shut the door behind him, and ran his finger across his throat to silence his men.

"Yes, I mean no," he said, trying to tamp the harshness in his voice. "That is, I'm all right. But I'm afraid your uncle isn't."

"What happened?"

"Me and a small group of men went to one of the locations Aleister thought Brynn might be—a warehouse, down by the Potomac. He stayed in the van while we surrounded the building. There were guys inside, lots of them—ISIS—but no Brynn. There was a firefight. I was the only one that made it. When I went out to the van, I found your uncle. I'm sorry."

A long silence followed.

Finally: "Scott and I'll head back to the States."

"No, no, don't do that," Sterling said.

"What do you mean?" Zady asked. "Arrangements need to be made."

"Look, one of the last things your uncle said to me was to make sure you guys stayed on the trail in Egypt. Felt Brynn's life depended on it, that the nameplate, Brynn's life, and Moses' treasure were all connected. Let me make the arrangements here. I've got a good lead on Brynn. I'm almost positive I know where she is. I'm just rounding up some guys now and then we're heading there."

"Where?" Zady said.

"I don't want to say over the phone. But like I said, Aleister believed that whatever you're looking for in Egypt is crucial to Brynn's survival. That even if we find her, we're still going to need it to seal the deal."

"Christ, Lance. We don't even know what we're looking for. We got some clues and Scott thinks we should head to Amarna. That something there might help us figure it out."

"Well, trust his hunch. Go and see what you can find. I'll do everything I can on my end to find Brynn. With you working there and me working here, we should be able to save her by the deadline."

A plan had formed in Sterling's mind. With Zady and Larson on the loose, he had to keep them out of the way until ISIS' deadline passed. After that he could kill Brynn and blame it on ISIS.

Wait...

Maybe he could get rid of all three of them. He could use Brynn to lure Zady and Larson back to the States, to some designated location—here might work—then finish them off. He knew the provisions of Mabrey's will. After Zady and Brynn, he was next in line to get control of DoveCo. and the rest of the old fart's vast resources. Plus, he'd have whatever Zady and Larson were looking for in Egypt—assuming they found it and brought it back to the States.

"You need to trust me, Zady. It's the right thing to do."

"All right," Zady said. "Call me the second you find her. I'll touch base soon."

"Yes," Sterling said. "Make sure that you do."

58

Zady and Larson sat in silence. Outside the car, the sun shone brightly, drenching the surrounding cliffs of the desolate terrain; there was a strangeness about it, like being on another planet.

"Zady," Larson finally said, breaking the silence. "I'm so sorry." He reached out to touch her.

She batted his hand away. "Don't. Just, please, don't." She placed an elbow on the steering wheel and cradled her head in her palm.

He didn't know what to say. He suspected her recent suspicions of Aleister played a large part in the tangle of emotions she must be feeling.

"So, what do you want to do?" The words were out of his mouth before he could stop them.

She raised her head and stared at him, her gaze as penetrating as a star.

When she didn't speak, he said, "How much do you trust this Sterling guy?"

Her brow furrowed and she wet her lips with the tip of her tongue. "About as much as I trusted Uncle Al, or at least as much as I used to trust him. No, I don't mean that. I *do* trust Al

—or, rather, did. I mean it's still weird how he knew the spell number of the clue we got at the hotel, but that doesn't mean... I don't know. Right now, I just feel like shit for doubting him."

"If you think we can trust Sterling, then I think it's clear we stay on the path we're on and get to Amarna. It's what Aleister wanted."

"But what are we going to do? Just mosey on up to the head of the expedition there and say, 'Hey, do you have an envelope with a clue telling us where to go next?' The guy doesn't even know we're coming."

"That was intentional," Larson said. "Remember, we didn't want anyone to know our location."

"Yeah, well, now they do. At least Sterling does. And I just thought of something else. If Aleister's dead, then who the hell's responsible for the get-out-of-jail-free card we just got from the Egyptian police? I already thought it was a long shot because he didn't know exactly where we were, but he's the only person I can think of that might've been able to spring us. I mean, it's possible he pulled strings to turn off the heat at the Israeli airport, but he couldn't have helped us here, not if he's dead."

"True. But at this point, I think we just have to be grateful for however it happened and just keep on going. And maybe the expedition head at Amarna will be able to tell us something about Akhenaten, his temple, or his treasure. I know it's a little awkward, his not knowing we're coming, but it's not like I'm a complete unknown in the academic community. Lots of people have read my work, even those outside my field."

"You're a legend in your own mind," Zady said dryly.

"Ouch. Lucky for you I'm callous and insensitive. But one of these days you're going to say something I might take offense at."

"Bullshit. You're very sensitive. Almost everything I say offends you."

"Touché."

She reached over and squeezed his hand. "I'm just sick over this whole thing. Uncle Al, Brynn."

"Me, too," he said, squeezing back. "But I think the best thing to do is to keep moving. We're going to figure out how everything fits together. And we're going to do it in time to save her. Sterling says he's got a good lead."

"I like the new, confident you, Scott," she said, then started the car and pulled onto the road.

59

As they drove to Amarna (the map showed they were close), Larson grew concerned with Zady's reaction to Aleister's death. She hadn't cried, didn't try to deny it, or even question it. Just accepted it and moved on. A little voice gnawed at the back of his brain: Was Aleister really dead? Or was this all part of the plan, one more piece of the giant trap being set for him?

But he trusted Zady. And people handled grief differently. Her relief at being released from jail may have quelled some of her sadness over Aleister. And losing her parents at such a young age must have hardened her from the get-go. Given recent events, she could also be on an adrenaline high. Maybe he was too.

"This is it," Zady said, pulling off the asphalt road and onto the dirt shoulder. "The place where Akhenaten built his temple."

To the right stood a little group of self-built houses of brick, mud brick, and wood. A ramshackle chicken shed leaned amongst them. But otherwise, the landscape was disappointingly empty, just a huge expanse of flat, featureless terrain. The only trace of the temple was a partially reconstructed foundation, made from limestone blocks, of an enormous rectangular building that faced the road. A low platform ran down its central length; large circles of limestone rose slightly above the desert floor on either side. A few people milled about, mostly young, presumably future archaeologists, and a couple of locals. They stared at Zady and Larson as they pulled up.

"That's it?" Zady said.

"Not exactly." Larson jerked a thumb in the direction of an approaching guard. He was draped in a long-sleeved, wide-cut, light-bluish garment. A white turban covered his head, and an antiquated rifle was strapped to his side.

"Where'd he come from?" Zady asked.

"I don't know. Seems like he just appeared."

"Maybe it's a mirage."

A knock at Larson's window dispelled that notion. As he lowered the window, the guard unleashed a barrage of questions, of which he only caught the tail end.

"Good afternoon," Larson said. "Allow me to introduce myself. I'm Doctor Scott Larson. You may have heard of my work on—"

"What's your business?" the guard growled, starting to unshoulder his rifle.

"Another adoring fan," Zady quipped.

Larson cleared his throat. "Never mind. We're looking for Michael Green. Do you know where we can find him?"

At the mention of the expedition leader, the guard relaxed and re-shouldered his rifle. "Nekhu-em-pa-Aten's house."

"No, Michael Green's house," Larson said.

"Nekhu-em-pa-Aten's house."

"No, we're—"

"Look out, Scott," Zady said, leaning over him so she could address the guard. Does Michael Green live at Necca—er, Necco Wafer—um, whoever's house you said?"

The guard nodded.

"Great," Zady said. "How do we get there?"

"I was doing fine without your help," Larson said, as they followed the directions the guard gave them.

"Yeah, you were doing just great. Another minute and he would've blown your head off. On second thought, given the relic he was toting, it would've been more like a close shave, which by the way you could really use. Anyway, it shouldn't be far from here. He said it was about a kilometer from the village, right?"

"That's it," Larson said, pointing to a large white complex just up ahead. The façade of the main building had a high, crenellated wall. Two great arches marked the entrance. The compound stretched back several yards. Past the arches, a long thin extension ran parallel to the façade. Domes punctuated the building, their long thin cones rising to crowned points where flowerpots perched, lending it a somewhat lewd look.

"Hey," Zady said. "Those domes look like erect—"

"I know what they look like."

"The whole thing reminds me of a hacienda after too much peyote. Oh, look, more guards. This should be fun."

As Zady pulled into the driveway, two armed guards, exact replicas of the one they'd already encountered, came from behind the high wall. They pointed their outdated rifles at the car.

"These two seem even less friendly than the first. But don't worry, Scott. Once you tell them how famous you are, it'll be fine."

Larson swallowed hard. "Maybe we *should've* called ahead."

60

Larry Miller's bristly hair was dyed jet black and held so much product he looked like an upside-down scrubbing bubble, Madge Roberts mused—an image only reinforced by a weak handlebar mustache. His jowly face drooped in hound-dog folds and large deposits of fat threatened to squeeze out of his tight, tight suit at the first sign of a worn thread. Tall, wide, and icky (his overall bearing made Roberts think of a portcullis to a sex dungeon) the president's defense counsel loomed large at the table before the Republican senators. But caught up in her musings over the contents of the thumb drive she'd found the night before, Roberts could only pay scant attention to his opening words.

"Now, I know I'm not alone in my astonishment," he said. "The articles of impeachment claim that the president's latest executive order violates the First Amendment's Establishment Clause and Free Exercise Clause. But that's not the case. That is not what's really happening here. What we do have is a partisan, secular attack on a man whose firm belief is that the Judeo-Christian tradition is the core of our nation's moral fiber and that it represents the greatest hope we have for ensuring our safety, our very survival in the world today. What I intend to do is paint a portrait of the values embodied in the person of President John Paul Jenkins, values that are our greatest hope at preventing a precipitous slide into the amoral abyss of secularism, values that represent a return to the principles for which America has always stood."

This oughta be good, Roberts thought. Time to lace up the hip boots for the bullshit headin' this way.

"Now it's true the Constitution doesn't mention God explicitly," Miller continued in a reverberating baritone. "But what we do have, over the course of the last half-century in our great country, is an increasing recognition of the desperate need for God in our government. It all started right after World War II when President Eisenhower famously declared that 'our government makes no sense unless it is founded in a deeply felt religious faith.' Around the same time, the Supreme Court declared that 'we are a religious people, whose institutions presuppose a Supreme Being.' And since Jimmy Carter, our leaders have spoken in detail of their religious faith, of being born again in Jesus Christ. John Paul Jenkins is simply the last in a long line of presidents unafraid to declare their faith and the need for God's guidance at home and abroad.

"And let me ask you this, which goes to the very heart of the matter. If we are not a Judeo-Christian nation, then what are we? A huge percentage of Americans believe in the Ten Commandments and most believe in Christ's sacrifice as the only way to salvation. I submit to you that *not* recognizing this tradition as the bedrock of our society, of all democratic societies, is undemocratic. Can we really afford to do so when the stakes are our very own survival?"

The last thought Roberts had before she tuned him out was how the term Judeo-Christian tradition was an oxymoron. The first half of the tradition denied what the second half deified. It was akin to democratic-authoritarianism or capitalist-communism.

But then her mind turned back to the photo and the thumb

drive. How did everything fit together? And how was it relevant to the trial? It had to be or else she wouldn't have received them when she did.

Keep thinking, Madge, keep thinking. Your momma didn't raise any fools. She chuckled when she started asking the Lord for help and tried to refocus on Miller's words, as much of a losing battle as it was.

61

The guards approached with their rifles pointed directly at the Honda. One came to Zady's side, the other to Larson's. He lowered his window but told Zady to keep hers up. He greeted the guard in Arabic, hoping that would improve his odds, and told him they wished to see Michael Green.

At the mention of the name, the guard lowered his rifle and nodded for his companion to do the same. "Do you have appointment?" he asked.

Larson smiled weakly. "No. That's just it. He doesn't know we're coming—we didn't know we were coming until recently. But I'm sure if you mention my name, he'll be more than happy to—"

"Go check to see if foreigners are welcome," the guard told his colleague, who nodded and made his way through the arched wall to the building.

"But you didn't even give him my name," Larson said.

"If he agrees to see you, you can tell him yourself."

"I think these guys need to hone their welcoming skills," Zady said.

"You think?" Larson replied. He watched as a slight, gray-bearded figure emerged beneath the façade and, with one hand shielding the sun, peered at the car. He ambled forward in short confident strides. Seeing Larson's window open, he stopped a foot or so away and addressed them with a smile.

"How may I be of assistance?" he asked.

"Hello, Doctor Green. Allow me to introduce myself and my colleague." Larson's outstretched hand was lightly taken by the elderly archaeologist. "I'm Scott Larson and this is my research associate Zady Jones." Zady gave a short wave. "You might be familiar with my work on the Dead Sea Scrolls," Larson said.

"No. I'm not familiar with your work."

"You sure?" Larson said.

Zady's elbow jabbed into his side. "Just another starstruck admirer of your work."

"Yeah, well, anyway," Larson continued, "we're writing a book on Amarna and Akhenaten's temple and we're wondering if you'd be willing to answer a few questions."

"Possibly, possibly," Green said, tugging his beard. "Why don't you come inside."

The area into which he led them was a large workroom with long rectangular tables, one of which was a modified picnic table. A cross with a loop at the top hung on the wall. Artifacts, computers, and endless piles of papers and folders were balanced precariously on top of every horizontal surface.

"Most of my assistants are at the temple site," Green said, directing them to chairs on either side of a table. The three sat, Green at the head. "This site belonged to Akhenaten's chief bowman Nekhu-em-pa-Aten."

"Ah, so that's what he was saying," Zady muttered.

"Yes," Larson said, looking at Green. "We stopped at the site of the temple first, and the guard said this was the house of Neka, um, the person you just mentioned."

Green nodded. "It's also the site of the original dig house built by the German expedition in 1906. They were the first to excavate here. Man by the name of Ludwig Borchardt led it.

Over the years, we've added to the compound. Built several bedrooms, installed plumbing, the two long storehouses along the sides. We've even added a court and a beautiful garden—not quite a British garden, but lovely, nonetheless. We're quite proud of what we've done, though I prefer my shallow tin bath in the privacy of my own room. But the younger generation, well..."

Larson caught the wisp of a thoughtful smile on Zady's lips brought on no doubt, by Green's avuncular demeanor and British accent.

"I read that you've been excavating the site since the late 1970s," Larson said, hoping to direct the conversation onto a more fruitful path. "We saw the work you've been doing at the temple. It looks amazing."

"Yes, we're building up the foundation to about knee-high, atop a layer of lime and gypsum, to show the area where it once stood. And to demarcate it from the modern cemetery that threatens to encroach. Eventually, we hope to show what the entire façade looked like."

"What are you using to restore the original foundation?" Zady asked.

"Rectangular limestone blocks, called talatats. Akhenaten used them to build the temple, to build the entire city, really. He had them made the same size, roughly 27" by 27" by 54", each weighing about a hundred pounds. Their uniformity and relatively low weight accounts for how the buildings were put up so quickly."

"How big was the original temple?" Larson asked.

Green narrowed his eyes. "The outer enclosure was about 800 by 300 meters, but much of it was empty. Of course, the ancient Egyptians used different measurements—cubits and what they called a *ris*, equivalent to 350 cubits. The temple consisted of two main buildings: the Long Temple and the Sanctuary. The Long Temple was divided into six courts with as many as a thousand offering tables. The sanctuary behind it was the largest element, meant for gardens or tree plantations."

"Did the city's inhabitants worship in the temple?" Zady asked.

"That's hard to say," Green replied. "According to most accounts, the people were not allowed to worship Aten directly. They had to approach him through the intercession of Akhenaten and his wife, Nefertiti. Akhenaten's chief priest, Meryre, also played a large part in the daily functioning of the temple."

"That's interesting that Nefertiti was given such prominence," Zady said.

"Oh, yes," Green said. "In many ways she was on a par with the pharaoh himself. There were at least six female pharaohs in Egyptian history."

"Ancient equality of the sexes," Zady said. "How about that?"

"Yes. And goddesses played a crucial role in all aspects of life, including creation," Green said.

"Would you show us the site?" Larson asked.

"There's not much to see," Green said. "In fact, what you saw from your auto is about all there is."

"Just the same," Zady said, "would you be willing to show it to us?"

"I'm afraid I really can't spare the time. However, there's nothing keeping you from going back and looking around."

Zady shot Larson a look. She, too, must have picked up on the change in Green's demeanor. He suddenly seemed more reserved, less willing to help. Even some of the color had fled his cheeks above his beard. Green kept looking over Zady's shoulder, out the window, to the front of the compound where the Honda was parked. Larson turned to follow his gaze, but there was nothing to see. No one in sight.

Green stood up. "I'm afraid that's all the time I can spare. I didn't realize how late it was." He glanced at his watch for the first time. "Thank you for stopping by. I wish you luck with your research."

"Talk about a bum's rush," Zady said, after Green had ushered them out the door and slammed it shut.

Larson nodded. "He went from hot to cold in a flash. We didn't even get a chance to ask him about Akhenaten's wealth, let alone anything about Moses."

"I think we should go back to the site," Zady said. "There may not be much to look at, but my intuition tells me we should."

Zady unlocked the doors and Larson walked to the passenger's side. As he opened the door and plopped on the seat, he tried to piece together his thoughts, exactly what he was going to say to Zady when she said, "Holy shit!"

He turned to look. She sat behind the wheel, tote bag in her lap. In her right hand was a wax-sealed envelope.

62

"It was on the seat," Larson said, halfway between a question and a statement.

"Yes!" Zady said. "Someone must've put it there when we were talking to Green."

Or you just took it out of your pocket. Or someone you're in cahoots with put it there. Would this nightmare ever end? He considered confronting her with his suspicions but decided against it. He was in for the duration, no matter who or what was involved. Maybe a stranger had put the envelope in the car. Maybe Green had witnessed it and that's what accounted for his sudden change in behavior. He *had* kept looking out the window.

"So, what does it say?" he asked Zady, once she'd broken the red wax and taken out a sheet of paper. Her eyes scanned the page. Without saying a word, she handed it to him. The neat print was exactly like the others:

Exodus 24:13
Mark 9:2-4
1 Corinthians 10:1-4

The Luxor Nativity

"Well?" she said.

"I don't know yet. But let's not sit here. Let's go back to the site."

As Zady started the engine and turned the Honda around, Larson used his phone to pull up a Bible. He was sure he knew the passages by heart but didn't want to chance it, not if the slightest nuance helped lead them wherever they needed to go next. Brynn's life was still at stake. The passage from Exodus wasn't a surprise, but references to the New Testament? How was Jesus relevant to finding Moses' treasure? Yet there were stranger things in heaven and earth, Horatio. And just what was the Luxor Nativity?

"The first passage," he said, "from Exodus, reads, 'So Moses rose with his servant Joshua, and Moses went up into the mountain of God.'"

"What about the ones from the New Testament?" Zady asked.

"Give me a second. Okay. Here are the verses from Mark. They're about the transfiguration: 'And after six days Jesus took with him Peter and James and John and led them up a high mountain apart by themselves; and he was transfigured before them, and garments became glistening, intensely white, as no fuller on earth could bleach them. And there appeared to them Elijah with Moses; and they were talking to Jesus.'

"And here are the ones from Paul's letter: 'I want you to know, brethren, that our fathers were all under the cloud, and all passed through the sea, and all were baptized into Moses in the cloud and in the sea, and all ate the same spiritual food, and all drank the same spiritual drink. For they drank from the spiritual Rock which followed them, and the Rock was Christ.'"

"Okay," Zady said. "So, the passage from Exodus talks about Moses and Joshua, his successor. And the ones from the New

Testament are about Jesus et al. and Moses. Any connections you can think of?"

"The only thing that comes to mind is that Joshua is Hebrew for Jesus. It means 'the Lord is salvation.' Early editions of the Bible even used the name Joshua instead of Jesus."

"I wonder why the message focuses on placing Joshua-slash-Jesus and Moses together," Zady said.

"It's hard to say," Larson admitted.

"And what's up with the Luxor Nativity? How does that fit into anything?"

"Let me see what I can find out," Larson said, doing a search. "Looks like there are scenes on the walls of Amun's Temple in Luxor, about two-hundred-fifty miles south of here. They show the birth of Amenhotep III, Akhenaten's father, in a way similar to the Annunciation, Conception, Birth, and Adoration of Jesus."

"Hmm," Zady said. "*That's* interesting. Who was Amun?"

"One of the gods worshipped by Akhenaten's father. And Luxor was an important city. At some point, I think it was even the capital."

"'Amun' sounds a lot like 'amen'," Zady said.

Larson nodded.

"I think we're wasting our time here," Zady said. "We already got what we need. We should head to Luxor, check out the nativity. I feel like that's where we'll get the next clue. I'll call Sterling and let him know. Hopefully, he's close to finding Brynn."

63

When the trial reconvened that afternoon, Madge Roberts continued puzzling over the photo and the contents of the thumb drive she'd found in her mailbox the night before. Miller loomed large before his conservative compatriots as he launched into the next phase of the president's defense.

"In the case against President Jenkins," he began, "Congresswoman Ananya Chandler claimed that Executive Order 15721 violates the Establishment Clause, the Free Speech Clause, the Free Exercise Clause, and the Equal Protection Clause of the Bill of Rights. But let me ask you this: Does it really?"

Of course, it does, ya fool! Roberts mentally screamed. *Where'd you get your law degree, jdformydumbass.com?* After reviewing Miller's genealogy, in which neither he nor his mother fared well, she wrested her attention back to his defense of Jenkins. A certain surrealism set in as she listened to the semantics that spewed from his mouth.

"Technically the Constitution states that '*Congress* shall make no law respecting an establishment of religion,' Miller boomed. "I repeat: '*Congress* shall make no law respecting an establishment of religion.' The document says nothing about the executive branch doing so. Nor does the president's order establish a particular religion. It simply states the obvious: that the United States is a Judeo-Christian nation. It doesn't establish Judaism or Christianity as the country's official religion. The order simply references a tradition."

Roberts fought hard not to throw her shoe, but the only sign of disagreement she gave was a slight headshake. She glanced at her colleagues' faces on her side of the aisle. All wore looks of disbelief. But across the aisle heads bobbed up and down like oil drills. And for one of many times during Jenkins' presidency Roberts half-expected Alan Funt to jump out of the shadows and yell, "Yes, Madge Roberts, you and the rest of America are on *Candid Camera!*"

She was so incensed she had to shut Miller out just to maintain the shred of sanity she had left. Back to the thumb drive. The huge amount of foreign aid to Israel and Egypt over the years was puzzling—less so in the case of Israel, but much more so when it came to Egypt. It was almost like a payoff to both sides of the conflict, a form of hush-money.

The more she thought about it, the more she believed it somehow had to do with Yuya's tomb. After all, the tomb was in Egypt. But what did the burial spot of an ancient pharaonic official have to do with the never-ending conflict in the Middle East? Was there something significant about the year 1905, when the tomb was found?

From her recollection of history, at the turn of the twentieth century, the U.S. was emerging as a major power while Britain was in decline, after the Boer War had stretched the island nation beyond its capacities.

Wait...

The photo of the men at the London hotel was taken in 1903, two years before Yuya's tomb was found. There *had* to be a connection. But what about the contents of the tomb? A gold necklace, a chariot, remnants of garments, and the figure marked with the hieroglyphs of all those titles: bearer of this, and holy father of that. And the number on each of the photos of the tomb's contents, 14141, *had* to mean something.

But no matter how hard she racked her brains she couldn't figure it out. Then she remembered that if you put whatever you were trying to figure out on your mental back burner, let your subconscious take a whack at it, the answer often came. She turned her attention back to Mr. Scrubbing Bubble who was working hard so the president didn't have to.

Miller babbled something about the "ark of our might," how it was part and parcel of America's spiritual arsenal. Said we'd use it to vanquish our enemies, especially the Islamic extremists who threatened our survival and our spiritual way of life. He directed those not familiar with the phrase to 2 Chronicles, chapter 6. Said it was the fourteenth book of the Bible, sixth chapter, forty-first verse.

Roberts was enraged by the biblical reference in a trial accusing Jenkins of having violated the separation of church and state. True, Chandler had also referenced the Bible, but she'd done so ironically. This clown was serious. Still, she wanted to look up the passage he mentioned, so she jotted down a shorthand way to remember it: 14-6-41. She'd look it up later when she was devising questions for the—

Wait a minute. Wait *just* a minute.

She stared at the numbers she'd written: 14-6-41. The fourteenth book of the Bible, sixth chapter, forty-first verse. Was there a chance that the number on the photos of Yuya's tomb referred to a biblical passage? The number on the photos was 14141. Could it stand for 2 Chronicles—again, the fourteenth book, first chapter, forty-first verse? She furtively pulled her phone from her jacket pocket and brought up an online Bible. She clicked on 2 Chronicles. No, that couldn't be right. The first chapter only had seventeen verses.

But what if the number referred to the first verse of the fourteenth chapter of 2 Chronicles, as in 14-14-1? She scrolled down and read the passage: "And Abijah rested with his fathers and was buried in the City of David. Asa his son succeeded him as king, and in his days the country was at peace for ten years." Who in the world were Abijah and Asa? And what did they have to do with anything? She was angry and discouraged. At this rate, she'd never figure it out.

She might as well just hang it up because there was no way her party had enough votes to convict Jenkins. What the hell was the point? He'd stay in office and the country would continue its descent into—

But there was one other way the numbers could be arranged; she saw that now. The last chance was a reference to the first book of the Bible, the forty-first chapter, and the forty-first verse. She went back to the table of contents, clicked on Genesis, and scrolled down until she found the right place:

"So Pharaoh said to Joseph, 'I hereby put you in charge of the whole land of Egypt.'"

Roberts nearly gasped when she read the next two verses: "Then Pharaoh took his signet ring from his finger and put it on Joseph's finger. He dressed him in robes of fine linen and put a gold chain around his neck. He had him ride in a chariot as his second-in-command, and men shouted before him, 'Make way!' Thus, he put him in charge of the whole land of Egypt."

It was all there, the contents of Yuya's tomb: the linen garments, the gold necklace, the chariot. While there were no photos of a signet ring on the disc, there was the picture of that figurine inscribed with the hieroglyphs for ring-bearer. It couldn't be a coincidence, could it? Was Yuya really Joseph the biblical patriarch, and was it his tomb that was discovered in 1905? If so, why the cover-up? And how did it relate to what was going on now?

64

"Stopping here," Zady said, pulling into the first gas station-cafe they'd seen in a very long time. It was completely devoid of patrons. "Artemis is thirsty, and I have to pee. Grab us something to eat."

"What do you want?" Larson asked.

"Something salty, something sweet," she told him. She got out of the car and started fussing with the pump.

Larson stepped into the mild night air. He reached into his pocket and glanced at his phone. It was 8:05. It wouldn't be long till they reached Luxor. Inside the clean, well-lit café, his bladder told him to stop before he shopped. He looked through the window and saw Zady rushing toward the café, doing what she called "the pee-pee dance;" apparently, she couldn't wait until Artemis was full. When she raced past, he told her that he was also heading to the restroom. She nodded briskly as she wiggled to the back, a look of extreme discomfort on her face.

The man behind the counter was fidgety and eyed him suspiciously, so Larson assured him in Arabic that he and Zady were going to purchase gas and food, as soon as they'd used the toilet. The clerk shot him a toothless grin and vigorously nodded. Larson headed to the men's room.

It was neither cleaner nor dirtier than he expected. But as he unzipped his pants, the relatively fresh urinal cake was no competition for the stench emanating from the unoccupied single stall. He tried not to breathe while he relieved himself. But as he did, he realized, alas, that he'd have to do battle with whatever had been deposited in the toilet—though his recent food intake had been minimal. He took a short breath, kicked open the stall door, and flushed the toilet with his left foot. He realized with some relief that the stall itself, including the toilet, was in pretty good shape, but he still laid toilet paper on the seat before popping a squat.

His mind drifted to the envelope they'd found just before the last one, with a reference to the final passage in Genesis, about Joseph's death. No one knew just where in Egypt he'd been buried, and, as far as Larson could remember, his bones were later moved to Canaan, his birthplace. But what did Joseph have to do with Moses and his treasure anyway? He had to think to figure things out before it was too late to save Brynn. He'd shared Zady's frustration when she still hadn't been able to reach Sterling just before they'd stopped here.

He'd finished up and was washing his hands when he heard a rumble outside that sounded like large vehicles. He quickly dried his hands on a brown paper towel then opened the door. Zady stood, hands on hips, staring out the large window. Larson followed her gaze. Several jeeps and military convoy trucks with canvas-topped backs had pulled up, one on either end of the Honda. They were boxed in.

"This doesn't look good," Larson said, his mouth suddenly dry.

"Captain Obvious strikes again," Zady replied.

The men that emptied out of the vehicles were dressed in combat fatigues. From the fluorescent lights outside the café and the bright illumination from the trucks' headlights, they looked like Westerners.

A man resembling a matinee idol from Hollywood's Golden

Age jumped out of a jeep, rushed in, and pointed his assault rifle at them. Larson stepped in front of Zady, who grabbed his hand from behind.

"I wonder what he wants with us," Zady whispered.

"Move it," the man ordered, poking Larson in the side with the barrel of his gun.

"Move what where?" Zady asked, letting go of Larson's hand.

"I'm only going to say this once, Miss Jones," he said. "You and your boyfriend: out the door and into the truck."

65

Sterling relished watching her on the bed, chain wrapped around her ankle. He'd removed the gag; there was no need for it anymore. Just a few minutes more, he told himself. Prolong it for as long as you can, so you can savor it.

His initial shock at hearing Zady's voice on the phone, and learning of her and Larson's newfound freedom, lasted just a moment. He'd regained his composure and phoned Banner after he hung up. His attempt to calm the chief of staff with the words of the Scottish poet, that the best laid schemes of mice and men "gang aft a-gley", were met with the less poetic, "Fuck off!" followed by stony silence. When he'd told Banner of his plan to lure Zady and Larson then kill them, Banner told him to shut up and call Garner Long. Long was the owner of Kobra, the largest mercenary company in the world.

Of course, Sterling had done just that. When he'd told Long the pair's approximate location, Long insisted on capturing them himself. Sterling had considered arguing with him—he wanted to kill them almost as much as he wanted control of DoveCo.—but knew Long's authority superseded his own. Much to his surprise, however, and to his utmost pleasure, Long had ended the call by saying he didn't give a "runny green goose-shit" what Sterling did with Brynn, just so long as she never caused any trouble again.

So, he'd take comfort in that. And pleasure. For as long as he could stand it. Because the anticipation of the kill was as sweet as the offing.

66

It was only when Larson, along with Zady, was perched precariously on a bench in the back of a truck that he figured out who their abductor was. One of the guys had called the man with movie-star looks "Long." That's when he realized it was Garner Long, head of the mercenary company Kobra, who'd captured them. Larson knew that Long, Aleister's long-time nemesis and chief competitor in bidding for security contracts, was driven by a zealous Christian fundamentalism that often found its expression in strong-armed tactics against anyone who didn't share his faith. Long had jeopardized Aleister's evacuation of the Mandaeans from Iraq, exhibiting an especially intense hatred for the group of people often called the "last Gnostics."

The truck stopped. Long forced Larson and Zady out of the back at gunpoint. Larson stared at two wooden platforms in the middle of the tent where they'd been deposited. The platforms were the only things illuminated in the tent, like center ring in some crazy circus; everything else faded into deep shadows. A shudder raced from the base of his spine to the nape of his neck when he saw two tin watering cans on the floor nearby. He wanted to say something to Zady, try to calm her, but he was afraid if he opened his mouth nothing would come out, or, worse, he'd scream and wouldn't be able to stop.

The smell of gas from a generator hit him as two soldiers emerged from the shadows. Garner Long kept his rifle trained on him and Zady as the soldiers strapped them to the platforms. Larson watched Zady for as long as he could, till the gauze covered his eyes. Any second now, the waterboarding would start....

"Which one of you is going to tell me just exactly what you are looking for in this godforsaken desert?" Long's voice came from somewhere far away and muffled.

"Go fuck yourself!" Zady shouted.

"I'm impressed," Long said. "You're much more of a fighter than your parents. They were on the trail to find what you did in Afghanistan, that little blasphemous book. And so, they had to die."

Zady uttered a scream that was not of this world.

Well, Larson thought, *at least she finally had confirmation of what had happened to her parents. She deserved closure... Even if it was the last thing she ever got.*

The sudden water on Larson's face sucked the air out of him. He couldn't breathe. An intense throbbing filled his ears.

Then came the memory flash-burned on his mind's screen: the backyard of the ramshackle house on Albany Post Road in Hyde Park, New York, a couple miles up the road from the Vanderbilt estate. He was five. It was summer and the smell of lilacs perfumed the air. He was splashing around in the above-ground pool, a rickety tin contraption with a blue vinyl base atop a sand mound. His mother was inside, passed out or drunk. His father was...well, nowhere. A five-year-old Scott ran laps inside the four-foot-deep pool, pumping his scrawny arms and legs to see how fast he could go. He never remembered falling. One second, he was running, splashing through the water, the next, he lay face-up on the bottom of the pool.

Stand up, he told himself; all you have to do is stand up.

But he couldn't. The weight of the water crushed him, it felt as if he were encased in lead. The soundlessness was terrifying, noise—like air—completely absent, as if he were in a vacuum-sealed bag. Never had he been so terrified, so completely unable to move. And then, looking up through the shimmering water, he saw it: an outstretched hand reaching over the metal rim of the pool. He couldn't see whose hand it was, but it represented hope. A force surged through him and, with it, the strength to act. He raised his arm out of the water and his body followed. But just as his breath blessedly returned and he reached out to grasp the hand that had saved him, it vanished, and he stood there alone, clutching the edge of the pool, coughing, sucking in air.

He'd steered clear of water ever since.

The water stopped as quickly as it began. He tried sucking air into his lungs through the wet gauze but couldn't at first. Seconds felt like hours. He gasped desperately, trying to breathe in enough air to relieve the crushing weight in his chest.

Finally, he managed a hoarse "wait."

A gap in the gauze around his lips appeared and he gulped greedily at the delicious air.

"I'll tell you everything you want to know," he said in staccato puffs.

"Talk," Long commanded.

Larson shook his head. "Not until you let her go."

"You think you're in a position to negotiate?" Long asked.

"Look," Larson told him, thinking as quickly as he could, though his mind was sluggish from a lack of oxygen. "She doesn't know anything. I'm the one you want. After I tell you what I know, you can do whatever you want with me. Just let her go."

"Don't, Scott," Zady said. His only comfort was that she could still talk. Hopefully she hadn't been waterboarded yet.

A deafening silence filled the air. It seemed to last forever. Long finally broke it with two words: "Very well."

The first thing Larson saw when the gauze was removed was Long, standing at his side, holding Zady's bag, rifle slung over his shoulder. He watched as Long ordered the armed soldier next to Zady to unfasten her restraints and unwrap the gauze from her face. Her eyes found Larson's. She shook her head, begging him with her eyes not to continue his plan, but he reassured her with a nod, mouthed the words "it's okay."

"So, tell me, Larson," Long said, nodding at the bag. "What are the envelopes about? And the messages on your phones?"

Larson drew two conclusions from this. First, Long wasn't the source, and second, he was under pressure to find out who was. "Your guess is as good as mine," he said.

Long's eyes stabbed Larson's. "Put the gauze back on," he ordered the soldier.

"No, wait," Larson said, as the shrouding began.

Long raised a hand. The soldier stopped.

"I have some idea, but I'm not sure. I do know that you're not going to find Moses' treasure without my help. And if you let her go, I'll help you find it."

"Don't do this, Scott," Zady pleaded from Long's side.

"Shut up," Long said, backhanding her across the mouth.

Zady kept her head up and swiped at her bloody lip.

"Who gave you the envelopes and sent the messages?" Long demanded.

"If I knew, I'd tell you," Larson said, looking at Zady. "Just let her go." He turned his gaze back to Long. "We'll have the best chance of figuring this out if you and I put our heads together."

Long considered. The more time that ticked away the more Larson thought he might agree to his proposal. It was the same way with a jury—the longer it took to reach a verdict, the better things looked for the defendant. Of course, either way, things didn't look good for *him*. Even if Long let him live now, he'd kill him as soon as he found the treasure. But if Long agreed to his proposal, Zady would go free. That's what mattered most. That way, she could help Sterling find Brynn.

Without warning, Zady launched herself at Long. She raked his face with her nails and executed a crotch-kick that doubled him over. But he quickly straightened himself and smashed the butt of his rifle into her forehead. She collapsed at his feet.

Breathing hard, Long glared at Larson. "Put his fucking gauze back on," he ordered one of the soldiers. "And put this pile of shit on the other platform," he told the other. Before the soldier could lift Zady off the floor, Long administered a swift, hard kick to her ribs.

The last thing Larson saw before the gauze covered his eyes was the soldier carrying Zady's limp body to the wooden platform. Then came the water and he couldn't breathe. Then came nothing at all.

67

The sun's dying rays through the sagging glass of the mullioned windows in Roberts' home office were the only source of light. As it grew later, increasingly long shadows seeped from the furniture and darkened the walls. Roberts sat bolt upright in the wooden swivel chair at her desk, staring at the black screen of her monitor. She couldn't shake the feeling she was missing something. There had to be more, a way to tie together the photo of the men—she'd counted twenty-four of them—at the London hotel in the early twentieth century and the clues she'd found on the thumb drive. But how?

"Help me, Corinne," she said to the photo of her niece next to the monitor.

She jiggled the mouse to wake up the computer and reached down to her plum cordovan briefcase to get the thumb drive—she carried it with her wherever she went since she'd found it in her mailbox. She stuck it into the USB drive of her computer, then opened the photo of Yuya's a.k.a. Joseph's tomb and peered at it, her chin cupped in her hand. Before she could click on another picture, her hand jostled the mouse, and the cursor zig-zagged wildly over the photo.

That's when she saw—

Wait. That couldn't have been...

Could it?

She wasn't sure, but she thought a little hand had flickered when the cursor skimmed over the photo. Now she scanned the picture slowly with the cursor, moving it deliberately over every centimeter.

There, right there, over the door to the tomb. The little hand with the pointing finger, the tell-tale sign of an embedded hyperlink.

She clicked on it.

A PDF. It took a moment to realize just what she was reading, the import of the words of the transcript refusing to register at first. But as comprehension dawned, it was with the impact of a nuclear blast. Nothing could have prepared her for what she read. Her mind refused to believe it; it was too horrifying. But when she found an audio file embedded in the text and listened to the recording—the audio of the transcript—her doubts lessened. Of course, she'd have to have it verified for accuracy, but she was all too terrified it would prove genuine.

She slumped in her chair, wanting to put her head down on the table like in elementary school at nap time. Just then, her greatest wish was for the innocence of childhood.

Then she thought of Aleister Mabrey.

Why hadn't she thought of him before? It was he who'd informed her of the explosion in Giza. He was the font of all knowledge for covert things, and certainly more forthcoming with intel than anyone in the Jenkins administration. Maybe Aleister could make sense of the contents of the thumb drive, including the shocking information she'd just uncovered. In fact, now that she thought about it, maybe it was Aleister who'd sent it.

She reached into the pocket of her suit jacket and took out her cell. Last year, when Aleister had helped relocate the Iraqi Mandaeans, she'd programmed his number into her phone.

Now she speed-dialed it. It rang for a full minute before a man answered.

But it wasn't Mabrey.

"Yes, who is this?" a brusque voice demanded.

"Hi, I'm...I'm looking for Mr. Mabrey," Roberts said, unwilling to divulge her name or her reason for calling.

"Who is this?" the gruff voice repeated.

"A-a friend, just a friend. Who am I speaking with, please?"

"Lance Sterling. I regret to inform you, ma'am, that Mr. Mabrey is dead."

Roberts' mouth moved, but no words came out. The only thing she could do was end the call.

Something was wrong—very wrong.

Before she pocketed her phone, it rang in her hand, startling her. Her first thought was Sterling must be calling back. She held the phone out at arm's length as if it were a snake. But a quick glance showed her niece's name, so she answered it.

"Hello?" she said cautiously.

"Hey, Auntie Madge. What's the matter? You sound upset."

"Oh, it's nothing, honey." She tried to dispel the thoughts fouling her mind—what she'd just read on the computer, the news of Aleister's death, but the terror writhing inside grew and grew, stretching every muscle and nerve to the breaking point. Nothing would ever be the same.

"W-what can I do for you, sweet child?" Roberts asked. Corinne's parents, Madge's sister and brother-in-law, had died two years ago in a car accident, making Roberts Corinne's closest living relative. And Roberts loved her twenty-one-year-old niece to the point of distraction, always had, always would. The tragedy had only brought them closer.

"I was wondering if I could borrow the car tomorrow morning, around ten?"

Roberts nodded, then realized her niece couldn't see her. "Sure, baby girl. You got a key. You know where it'll be, in the usual spot in the parking garage."

"Got it. Thanks, Auntie. Are you sure nothing's wrong?"

"No, child. Just the mental meanderings of a crazy ole woman."

"Please," Corinne said, with the emphasis only the young can manage. "You know you're not old and you're definitely not crazy...well, not *that* crazy." She chuckled.

Oh, I may not have been crazy before, but I'm sure as hell crazy now. Now that I think about it, I wish I were crazy—at least I could chalk all of this up to a sick mind.

"Thanks again, Auntie Madge. And don't forget dinner on Monday. Love you."

Afterwards, Roberts couldn't remember if she'd told her niece she loved her, too. The thought would never stop haunting her.

FRIDAY

68

"I think he's coming to." Zady's raspy contralto came from a distant planet.

"He'll get there," a deep creaky voice assured her.

Larson was pretty sure his eyes were open, but he couldn't see a thing. He sensed movement, as if he were on a conveyor belt, and felt thin, cold hands caress his face. Then drops of water fell on his forehead and cheeks.

Oh, God, please. Not more water.

But this wetness wasn't suffocating. And there wasn't a lot of it. Just a few drops at a time. The smell of exhaust fumes and ozone came slowly, as if his olfactory senses were working for the first time in a while. He inhaled deeper, but every atom of oxygen felt like a jagged piece of glass slashing his lungs. Then an enormous blue vein directly in front of him as if on a movie screen lit his vision. A boom soon followed the flash. For a second, he thought his eardrums would burst. The second flash —of lightning—for he now knew what it was, lasted longer, gave him a better sense of his surroundings.

He was lying on his back, on a hard, flat surface, his head on Zady's lap. He *was* moving, not because he was on a conveyor belt, but because he was on a truck bed. What looked like a screen or stage on which lightning flashed, was a half-circle view out of the canvas-covered back of the truck. And there was a man, an old man with a beard, kneeling opposite him. Larson tried to sit up but a powerful, burning force inside his chest, one that made it feel like his lungs were on fire, kept him supine.

"Just lie still, Scott," Zady said.

"W-what happened?" The words sounded like they came from underwater and kicked off a violent coughing fit that forced him to sit up and only ended when Zady slapped him on the back. By this time, his eyes were adjusted to the semi-darkness occasionally backlit by another lightning zag that stabbed the huge sky. Slanted drops of rain hit his face, and he noticed for the first time that his shirt was wet. He didn't know what time it was, or even what day. Sharp, painful memories pricked his mind like thorns.

Garner Long. Waterboarding. The fate of Zady's parents.

He wanted to think through these thoughts, but the presence of the man across from him made it hard. Still unable to speak, he pointed a finger at the guy and shrugged his shoulders at Zady.

"I'll let him tell you," she said. "He has quite the story to tell."

Larson nodded and leaned against the ledge of the truck bed.

"Doctor Larson," the man said, "I'm Cardinal James O'Rourke."

As if on celestial cue, thunder crashed.

Larson tried to speak but couldn't. There was something familiar about the old man. The civilian clothes, what looked like khaki pants and a light shirt, threw Larson at first. But now it came to him. The man sitting in the back of a truck careering through the desert, the man, who for all intents and purposes had saved his and Zady's lives, was the Prefect of the Papal Household.

But what was he doing here? And why had he rescued

them? Hadn't he been the pope's righthand man? And hadn't Pope Innocent XIV been...well, not to put too sharp a point on it, evil? It was his Church, after all, that had tried to kill Larson last year.

"I'm sure you have questions," O'Rourke said as if reading Larson's mind. "Let me just say that while I'm a cardinal, I was a close friend of Aleister Mabrey's. We were roommates— 'flat-mates,' as he called us—at Oxford when I was a Rhodes Scholar."

Larson looked questioningly at Zady.

"Wait. It gets better," she said.

"Oh, Mabrey and I ended up going our separate ways, all right, but we kept in touch." The cardinal's light-colored eyes glowed with memories. "We shared concerns about the Church, how out of touch it was, its tendency toward authoritarianism, the reluctance to share power with bishops, its willingness at times to do the bidding of dark forces...."

Still having trouble turning the globs of syllables that stuck in his throat into words, Larson raised his hand. He wanted to hear more about the dark forces, for the cardinal had trailed off.

O'Rourke nodded. "Yes, all in good time." He took a deep breath, which Larson envied and continued. "I had my suspicions about Innocent, that he might've had a role in the death of his predecessor, but I couldn't prove anything. I told Aleister my concerns." O'Rourke chuckled. "At first, he brushed them off as the ramblings of an old man, but later he said he believed me, asked me to keep a close eye on Innocent to see if I could find any proof for my claims. Your uncle"—he glanced at Zady— "was a good man, had that certain *je ne sais quoi* that made you trust him, want to confide in him."

A tear rolled down Zady's cheek. Larson reached out and clasped her hand, which she squeezed tightly.

"So," the cardinal resumed, "I kept a close eye on the pope, stayed on in my role as head of the household, as I'd been for years, tracked Innocent's every move. God only knows why he kept me on. Maybe he was afraid getting rid of me would've made him look guilty of something. I tried to trip him up, though. I'd say things like, 'For the wages of sin is death,' tried to serve as the voice of what I truly believed was his guilty conscience but there was nothing overt, nothing he said or did that was incriminating. But shortly before he died, he grew jumpy, startled easily. I'd catch him talking to himself or to his long-dead mother. And there was one behavior that bothered me more than if he'd threatened my life."

Larson's curiosity was so intense he almost didn't realize his breathing had eased. Because he still felt incapable of speech, he willed O'Rourke to continue.

"Every Sunday night, around ten, I'd follow him to the archives. At a certain place, he'd crank the shelves apart, revealing, to my amazement, a door set in the brick wall. There was a fingerprint scanner and a lock he opened by entering a code. He'd disappear behind the door, emerge a while later. I couldn't tell what he was doing. I never saw anything beyond the door. I didn't want to risk trying to open it when he wasn't there in case it set off an alarm. But when I told Aleister about it, he didn't seem surprised."

A slash of lightning lit the sky. O'Rourke ran his fingers through his long, thick beard. No longer looking at Larson or Zady, he was caught up in a reverie all his own. In the aftermath of thunder, he continued.

"He spoke only in broad terms, nothing specific. Said there was a force deep in the bowels of American politics that called the shots, directed events at home and abroad the way a conductor leads an orchestra. He believed the pope was in touch with this force, that behind the secret door in the archives, he communicated with it, and he told me to keep watching Innocent without giving myself away."

"And that's all he ever said about it?" Zady asked.

The cardinal nodded. "Things went on as usual for a while. I kept my suspicions about Innocent; he continued his trips to the archives. But a few days ago, right after the explosion at the Great Pyramid, things changed. Aleister contacted me and said the pope was no longer cooperating with this secret force, that instead of viewing Innocent as a threat, I should look out for him, try to make sure nothing happened, keep him safe if I could.

"I was flabbergasted. It didn't make any sense. But I did what he said and kept a close eye on the pope. And was Innocent frazzled! In the last two days of his life, it was as if he were being haunted. He didn't sleep, he didn't eat. He was at a breaking point. Last night, I had the chef prepare his favorite dish. Before it was brought to him, per Aleister's instructions, I added a sedative, so Innocent could get some rest—he looked terrible; I didn't think he'd be able to last another night without sleep. I checked on him a little later. He appeared to be sleeping, which I reported to Aleister. We figured the sedative had worked. But when I checked on him after that, he was dead. Someone had shot him in the chest. The Vatican issued an 'official' statement that he'd died from natural causes, but unless you consider a bullet through the heart a natural cause, it was a cover-up."

"And tell him about the text message," Zady said.

"Yes. Around three o'clock Wednesday morning, after I'd checked on the pope and went to bed, convinced he was finally asleep, I got a text from Aleister. I was sleeping at the time—it wasn't until an hour later that I woke up and read it. But it's what prompted me to check on Innocent and led to the discovery of his murder. The text said Aleister was looking for Brynn but that if anything happened to him before he found her, some of his people would pick me up at the Vatican and take me to Egypt, so I could find you. Aleister thought Long might be after you and that it would be easier to find him and his men than the two of you. We spotted his forces and followed them to you. We overpowered the soldiers at the tent and snatched you away without firing a shot. You were both unconscious. Unfortunately, as Zady told me, we didn't grab her tote bag that had your phones and other correspondence."

"The important thing is you saved us," Zady said. "But there's still one thing I don't know. Where we're going."

O'Rourke shook his head. "Young lady, if you thought what I just said was amazing, just you wait."

69

The woman hadn't stayed on the phone long enough to trace the call, but the number on Aleister Mabrey's phone registered and it didn't take too long for Sterling to determine the caller's identity. Once he did, he phoned Banner and told him Madge Roberts was trying to reach Mabrey. Banner said he'd take care of it and hung up.

Now Sterling stood at the foot of the bed, eyeing the damage he'd inflicted on his prey. He recalled an old joke, twisting it to suit his purposes: What's black and blue and red all over? The answer wasn't a newspaper, but this former nun, bleeding from her mouth and other facial cuts and bruised head to toe from the beating he'd given her. It felt so damn good. He picked up one of the burner phones on the floor and clicked photos of his work. Just in case Long hadn't killed the dumbass duo yet, he sent the pics of Brynn to Zady and Larson, to add to their torment. Then he tossed the phone on the floor and crushed it with his boot.

He popped a squat next to the bed and thought about his next move. There was no point in letting this bitch live any longer. She didn't serve any purpose and since Long was taking care of her sister and Larson, he could kill her whenever he wanted. But just killing her wasn't much fun. He was pretty sure she was unconscious, but he gave her a rough shove in the back just to be sure.

No response.

But he was sure she'd wake up. He hadn't beaten her *that* badly. He felt the corners of his lips rise at the thought of reviving her and doing it again. Only this time much worse.

His cell phone rang in his pocket.

Fuck! Who was calling now?

He fished out the phone and glanced at the little screen. Didn't immediately recognize the number, but knew he had to answer just the same.

"Hello?"

"You dumb fuck! What are you doing?!" Long screamed. "Why are you sending pictures?"

"I just thought, if Larson and his girlfriend were still alive, they might get a kick out of 'em. You got their phones? That's all that's left, huh?"

"Not quite," Long said icily.

It was scary how the man could go from one extreme to the next in a nanosecond. "What do you mean?" Sterling asked.

"They, um, got away," Long said quietly.

Sterling had all he could do not to gloat. He hated the way Long treated him, like a subhuman. "You better tell Banner. He's not gonna be happy."

"Don't tell me what to do, you piece of shit. I call the shots. Remember."

"But you're gonna have to—" Sterling stopped when he found himself talking to no one.

He pocketed his cell and sunk into the chair, arms across his chest. It was about time Long fucked up. And even though Larson and Zady had escaped, he was happy it was Long's head that was on the chopping block this time.

And come to think of it, given this turn of events, it might make sense to let the bed-lump live. He could use her as bait, after all, to lure her sister and that pain-in-the-ass priest here so he could do away with all of them, and finally secure control of DoveCo.... And the first thing he was going to do was change that stupid fucking name.

He looked at the motionless body on the bed. If they came for her—no—*when* they came for her, he'd be ready.

His cell phone rang again. He didn't recognize the number, so he didn't answer it. He'd already decided what to do and didn't need advice from whoever the fuck was trying to reach him. Zady would find him and Brynn. She was a resourceful bitch. Yes, he'd wait and in time, all good things would come to him.

70

They'd ridden north through the desert for hours. Somewhere near Cairo the truck stopped, and Larson hopped out of the back onto the gently sloping sand, stretched his back, and looked up. The morning canvas stretched over a huge sky the color of dirty dishwater. Zady's inability to reach Sterling to see if he'd found Brynn only added to the gloom, especially since the deadline was almost up. But O'Rourke assured them that the person they were about to meet was crucial not only to Brynn's fate but to countless others.

Larson turned to help Zady out of the truck, but she shook her head and jumped down. The convoy they'd been traveling in formed a circle around them. Between a gap in the vehicles a short, dark-skinned woman garbed in a long, sleeveless purple gallabiyah appeared. As she approached, Larson could only guess her age. Her unwrinkled face was round and unblemished, but her eyes seemed as old as the planet. She nodded, welcoming them with a smile. The effect was soothing, like a mother's hug. When she spoke, her words carried on a susurration of warm morning wind.

"I have much to tell you," she said in a mahogany voice.

"Who are you?" Zady asked.

The woman chuckled luxuriantly. "That is a good place to start. Ms. Jones, Doctor Larson, I am Masika, an old acquaintance of your uncle," she said, looking at Zady before dropping her eyes. "I am the source of the envelopes."

Zady shot Larson a look, and though she didn't speak, its meaning couldn't have been clearer: *I told you it wasn't me!*

"Let me explain," Masika proceeded. "Aleister and I met a lifetime ago when we were very young." She smiled at the memory. "He came to this country on business, so he said. We met at a lecture on Egypt's Eighteenth Dynasty."

"Which included Akhenaten," Larson said.

Masika nodded. "We became friends. We were intrigued by Akhenaten, his rejection of all Egyptian gods but one, the world's first monotheist. When his reforms proved unpopular, he fled to Amarna. But no one knows how he met his end. Originally, he was buried in the Valley of the Kings, near Amarna, but his body was removed at some point long ago. Who took it and why are questions that remain unanswered.

"Aleister and I talked of such things. Slowly, we pieced together a theory about Akhenaten, one that involved Moses. You see Moses' origins as told in the Old Testament, are like those of an ancient king who long preceded Moses. Sargon I, ruler of Babylon and Sumer, was found as a baby floating down the river in a basket. Similar foundling stories are told of Oedipus, Perseus, and Heracles. Is this simply a coincidence? Perhaps. But other ancient texts speak of other biblical events, like a great flood, hundreds of years before the Hebrew scriptures were written."

"So, you think some of the stories in the Old Testament are based on older texts, from different cultures?" Larson asked. "Like the Egyptian account of creation, which is similar to the one in Genesis and the Egyptian spell that sounds a lot like the Ten Commandments?"

"Yes," Masika said. "Some believe the River Gihon in the Garden of Eden is actually a branch of the Nile. And like the forbidden fruit from the tree of knowledge, gardens in Akhenaten's temple at Amarna contained a sacred tree, whose fruit was destined only for him. There are also cases where a word or phrase in the Bible represents something else. For example, the word 'ark.' In Genesis and Exodus there are two arks: Noah's ark, and the Ark of the Covenant. In Egypt, an ark was a boat-like vessel in which a god was carried in formal procession, like a coffin or sarcophagus. Perhaps the Ark of the Covenant was a reference, not to a box that held the commandments, but a coffin that held someone's remains. Someone like Moses.

"But who *was* Moses?" Masika continued. "Was he Hebrew? Or was he, as people like Sigmund Freud claimed, Egyptian? Did he really exist or was he just a mythological character, one who helped establish the Promised Land of Israel like Romulus did Rome? After all, no archaeological evidence has ever been found that he existed, that the Ark of the Covenant was real and held commandments, or that there was even an exodus of Hebrews out of Egypt. The ancient Egyptians were excellent record-keepers, yet there's no record of such a migration. Nor is there evidence of an encampment at the base of Mount Sinai, where the Hebrews awaited Moses' return after talking with God and receiving the commandments. Even identifying the time Moses lived is difficult because the pharaoh who persecuted him in Exodus isn't mentioned by name."

Larson felt many of his thoughts were being expressed beautifully by this mysterious woman and he listened raptly as she spoke.

"The more Aleister and I thought about it, the more we believed that just as real places and objects in the Bible were disguised as others, the same could be true of people. Perhaps characters in the Bible were only based on real historical figures, curious combinations of fact and fiction, used as an allegory, for moral instruction. If true, Moses could've been based on a real person, one who had some of the experiences attributed to Moses in the Old Testament. Putting this all together, we started to wonder if the character of Moses was based on the real life of Akhenaten."

The morning had become soundless, like the void of interstellar space. Not a single noise came from the trucks or the mercs. Larson noticed he'd been holding his breath for a long time. He coughed then gulped greedily at the warm still air.

"But why did you slip us the envelopes?" Zady asked.

"Because of Aleister," Masika said simply. "We lost touch for a very long time. I didn't hear from him in almost forty years, until the attack on the pyramid. But during all that time, I loved him."

"That's one hell of a hiatus," Zady said.

"Yes, but he insisted on it. A year after we met—we were in our late twenties—he left Egypt, and I didn't hear from him until four days ago. He was afraid the explosion in Giza was more than just another attack on a 'pagan' shine that predated Muhammed. He never said just what, but he was worried about the safety of everyone he loved, you"—she nodded at Zady and Larson— "Brynn, and me. He said it was imperative to get you out of the country because something big was happening. So, I sent you messages, texts about Moses' treasure, then, as you got closer, I had people slip you the envelopes."

When Zady just stared at her with a perplexed look, Masika went on.

"When Brynn was kidnapped, Aleister asked that I draw you away from Washington. But he made me promise I wouldn't reveal my identity or location because I would be placing myself in danger. The day before yesterday, he contacted me and said if anything happened to him, I must contact O'Rourke. Then when I didn't hear from him after that, I grew worried and contacted the cardinal. He said Aleister had been killed, but that he'd planned, in case he was killed, for some of his men to pick up O'Rourke, and to bring him here to help you. Aleister's death released me from my promise to keep my whereabouts secret, so I told O'Rourke who I was and where I was, and he picked me up."

So many things puzzled Larson that he almost didn't know where to begin. But he started with the first questions that popped into his mind. "How did you pass the envelopes to us? And how does Moses' true identity relate to what's been going on?"

"And do you know if Brynn is all right?" Zady asked.

Masika took a deep breath, raised her arms, and beseeched the sky. As her arms slowly returned to her sides, she said, "There's more I must tell you if we're going to save her." When she continued speaking under the limitless sky, Larson had never felt so small.

"In the Old Testament," Masika continued, "much is made of the rivalry between Egyptians and Hebrews; they despise each another—one physically oppresses the other. But what if this wasn't true? What if it wasn't a case of Hebrew monotheists throwing off the yoke of their Egyptian polytheistic oppressors? What if, in fact, monotheism didn't start with one man, Abraham, but was a product of two great peoples coming together? When is Egypt first mentioned in the Bible?" She continued without awaiting a response. "When Abraham and his wife Sara go there in search of food due to a famine in Canaan. But there's no proof Abraham or Sara really existed. The next time Egypt is mentioned might be a different matter."

"You mean with regard to Joseph and his family?" Larson said.

"Yes," said Masika. "Joseph's eleven brothers, out of jealousy for their father's doting on him, sold him into slavery. He ended up in Egypt and, after a difficult start, became pharaoh's second in command. When his family later came to Egypt, Joseph forgave his brothers, who went on to sire the twelve tribes of Israel. Joseph, for his part, married an Egyptian noblewoman and had a daughter named Tiye. Tiye grew up at Pharaoh's court, in the company of pharaoh's family, including his children. One of those children was Amenhotep III. Eventually, Tiye—Joseph's daughter—married Amenhotep III. That marriage produced offspring, one of whom was Amenhotep IV, who later took the name Akhenaten. Thus, the houses of two great peoples—the Egyptians and the Hebrews—were joined in royalty and blood. They have been linked ever since."

"But how can you be sure of all this?" Zady asked.

"We can't. Or at least we couldn't, until recently. In 1903 a tomb was found in the Valley of the Kings. It held the body of Yuya, a powerful Egyptian courtier during the Eighteenth Dynasty, and his wife. The contents of the tomb—a chariot, fine garments, a golden necklace, and a small funerary statue—led some to believe Yuya was the biblical Joseph. At the time, such assertions couldn't be proven. But over the years, the development of DNA testing made genetic tracing possible. In the past couple of decades, it's been shown that Jewish rabbis share a DNA marker that separates them from their secular counterparts, but it couldn't be traced back to a common source. But recent tests conducted outside the public eye have shown that Yuya's DNA matches that of Jewish rabbis, strengthening the case that the biblical Joseph is really Yuya."

"Who conducted these tests? And why don't more people know about them?" Larson asked.

"That goes back to how I was able to get you the envelopes. There have always been people committed to the truth, good people, like-minded individuals working to create a better world. Such people, friends of mine, have been giving you the envelopes, smoothing things out when you ran into trouble. Now, here is what I need you to do. I need you to find Akhenaten's final resting place."

A quick intake of breath set Larson on a coughing spree.

"You need us to do *what*?" Zady said, slapping him on the back.

"We need Akhenaten's DNA to see if there is a connection with Yuya and the haplotype in the blood of Jewish rabbis. If we can show a genetic link, it will strengthen the case for a connection. If my suspicion that Moses was really Akhenaten is correct, you will find what you need in his tomb."

"But how will we know if we've found it?" Zady said.

"The sarcophagus will be marked with his cartouche—an oval containing his hieroglyphs. Akhenaten's cartouche is two identical ovals with the same hieroglyphs. A cartouche can also mean a carved tablet, so the cartouches are like—"

"The two stone tablets on which the Ten Commandments were inscribed," Zady finished.

Masika nodded. "There should also be a royal staff, like the one Moses has in Exodus. And a canopic chest that holds the organs. If my assumption is correct, the chest should be the same size and shape as the Ark of the Covenant described in the Bible. Hopefully, Nefertiti, his wife, will be there as well."

Larson coughed then wiped the spittle from around his mouth with the back of his hand. "But even if we find all this, how is that going to help? If Akhenaten is the biblical Moses wouldn't that just make things worse for relations between Israel and Egypt?"

"I have given much thought to that," Masika said. "Perhaps at first zealots on both sides are bound to lash out. Ultimately, however, I believe it would make things better. Most people want peace, they want to live in harmony and make better lives for themselves and their children. People have more in common than what divides them. Political and religious leaders and arms dealers are the only ones who benefit from conflict. I think Jenkins' administration is caught up in all this and that spurring on religious conflict is a large part of his plan. Showing that monotheism was brought about by the intermingling of the Egyptian and Hebrew royal houses might help dampen religious conflict in the long run, at least it could be a start. And that is what Aleister always wanted. But I'm afraid you don't have much time. From what Aleister said, the deadline for saving Brynn is later today and so is—"

"The end of Jenkins' trial," Zady said. "At least that's what everyone hoped. But Sterling is in the States, and he says he's close to finding Brynn. He said Aleister was convinced we were receiving messages from the same source and that finding Moses' treasure was just as important as finding the nameplate. Except—"

"Except," Larson interrupted, "from what Masika just said, those messages were coming from different sources, which Aleister knew. Whoever had Brynn was texting us about the nameplate, while Masika was texting us about finding Moses' treasure and sending us the envelopes."

"There's something else," Masika said. "The last time I spoke with Aleister he said he was worried he might not make it through all this, that someone close to him might be a traitor. What if that person is Sterling?"

"Shit, Scott," Zady said. "If Sterling's the one looking for Brynn, there's no telling what he'll do if he finds her—if he doesn't have her already. That might be why I haven't been able to reach him."

"Here's what we're going to do," Larson said, relishing the words as they came out of his mouth, it felt so good to commit to a course of action. "You go back to the States with some of Aleister's men and try to find Brynn. I'll stay here with O'Rourke, if he agrees, and look for Akhenaten's tomb."

"But where will you—?" Zady began.

"I have an idea. Besides, it's better if we split up. That way it'll be harder to kill both of us."

"I think," Masika said, her voice thick with emotion, "Aleister would have been proud."

71

The hangar's high-pressure sodium lights were so violating Larson couldn't stop squinting. Breathing was easier, but his lungs still felt like a couple of punching bags. He knew he was somewhere near the Cairo airport, but after being tortured, and hearing Masika's shocking revelations, he wasn't sure if it was Friday or Cleveland.

The pair of shiny white Learjets before him were doppelgängers of the plane they'd flown in before. *How many aircraft did Aleister own?* Several armed mercs stood sentry around the planes; others worked busily preparing for take-off.

"I was going to say don't do anything stupid," Zady said beside him. "But you're a man, so..."

Larson smiled. "How about I'll try not to do anything *too* stupid?"

"That'll work," she said. "I feel like you're all grown-up and going off on your own."

"I'll have you know I was doing pretty good when I met you."

"You were a hot mess. Now you're...well, a little less of a hot mess."

"Don't worry about me. Just worry about finding Brynn. And take care of yourself. You sure you're going to be all right?"

"Aleister didn't raise me without teaching me how to take care of myself," Zady said. "But do you think she'll be all right?" She nodded at Masika who stood a few yards away, talking to O'Rourke. "Can we trust these guys to keep her safe? To keep *us* safe? How can we be sure they won't turn on us like Sterling might have?"

"We can't. But so far, they've proven themselves worthy. And I think at some point you have to trust people. The alternative is bleak."

"Okay, who are you? And what did you do with Scott?"

"Not everybody's bad." He looked at O'Rourke. "Even in the Vatican."

Zady pointed to the duffle bag at his feet. "You've got a burner so we can stay in touch, and it'll give you Internet. I know it's not your preferred method, but it'll have to do."

A soldier came over and told them it was time. Zady hugged Larson then he got on the plane without looking back.

72

Larson didn't know the exact location of the landing strip as they approached, but assumed it wasn't far from Jerusalem.

"I'm gonna hit the can before we go," he told O'Rourke as the plane coasted to a stop. Inside the tiny compartment he was caught midstream by the pilot's voice announcing it was time to disembark.

Then he heard two gunshots.

Somebody must've boarded the plane. But who? Long's men? Israeli soldiers? Rogue DoveCo.? Or was it O'Rourke? Had the cardinal just been playing them?

He risked a quick peak through the cracked bathroom door. One thing was certain: the shots hadn't come from O'Rourke: the cardinal was crouched behind his seat, having somehow managed to jam his absurd bulk between the back of his seat and the side table bolted to the plane's panel. When he looked in Larson's direction, the unmitigated terror in his face was all too genuine.

Larson shut the bathroom door. He didn't have much time. Any second now the person or people who'd shot the pilot and copilot—assuming those were the two shots—would discover his whereabouts and tear down the door or shoot through it, and the tiny space yielded no hiding place or any way to shield himself from bullets.

God, he missed Zady. But this was exactly the type of thing he'd hoped to spare her from when he told her to go back to the States. Hopefully, she'd find Brynn before Sterling killed her—if, in fact, he had turned. At least the sisters could go on, have normal lives, and—

Men's voices, not far away.

"Where is he?" one said.

"Quick, toward the back," another urged.

Sounded American—most likely Long's men, or rogue DoveCo. But they were coming his way. And they were certain to see O'Rourke when they got closer.

As his mind slashed and burned, Larson instinctively gazed upward for whatever assistance might come his way.

Then he got an idea.

With one foot on the toilet and the other on the sink, he pushed up one of the ceiling panels. Yes! Just as he'd hoped, it gave way to an air duct. He shoved the panel to the side and hoisted himself up, then replaced the panel. Carefully balancing his weight on the metal strips framing the bottom of the narrow passage, he crawled forward on hands and knees.

He froze when he heard voices directly below. They'd found O'Rourke, demanded Larson's whereabouts. To his credit, the cardinal maintained his silence.

Larson listened, heart ready to explode, as a soldier ransacked the plane, and discovered Larson was nowhere to be found. Then he heard a soldier crash through the bathroom door, shooting as he went. When the soldier discovered that the bathroom was unoccupied, Larson heard him race back to his comrade and relay the news.

"I think he's right over us," the soldier said.

Larson started to panic. What if they started shooting through the—?

A bullet ripped through the bottom of the air duct, missing him by inches.

"Shit!" he gasped then cupped his mouth with his hand. *Way to go, dumbass, why don't you just text them your coordinates?*

The next shot went through the empty space between the thumb and forefinger of his left hand and tore through the top of the vent.

A third shot grazed his left side. He lost his balance, teetered on the air duct's metal frame then crashed through the roof, landing on top of the soldier nearest O'Rourke. The soldier lost his grip on his pistol. Larson grabbed it, shot the soldier in the head then fired at the other one just a few feet away. The bullet lodged in the center of his chest, and he dropped to the floor. Larson got to his feet and offered O'Rourke a hand.

"Like manna from heaven," the cardinal said, disentangling himself from the dead soldier, and trying to coordinate the parts of his large body to stand. "That was fine shooting."

"Beginner's luck," Larson said. He couldn't believe what he'd just done—killed two people. Definitely not part of his Jesuit training, though given the turn his life had taken, maybe it should've been. But he didn't have time to think right now. And something had scratched his side. Must've banged himself up in the fall. He touched the sore spot and when he took his hand away saw blood. Not a lot, but enough. That's when he remembered the bullets—one of them had grazed him.

"We've got to get out of here," he told O'Rourke. "I don't know if that's all of them or not."

"I thought I heard something before the engines cut off. There might be more of them out there."

"Get behind me," Larson said.

Larson crept forward, aiming his pistol in front of him. When he reached the plane's open door, he ran past it then grabbed O'Rourke by the elbow and swung him around it as fast as he could. When they reached the cockpit, he nodded one, two, three, then threw open the door. The pilot and copilot were slumped forward in their seats, gunshots to the backs of their heads.

"Now we get to see if anyone else is out there," Larson said, nodding toward the open door.

"You first," O'Rourke said.

"That's kind of you, Cardinal."

Larson raised his weapon and stepped cautiously through the door onto the loading stairs. In the ghoulish glow of the fluorescent lights, the bodies of a dozen mercs lay scattered on the hangar floor. Larson surmised that the men waiting for the arrival of the plane—Aleister's men—had been ambushed by Long's forces. But who knew for sure? It could've just as easily been a battle between two rival DoveCo. factions. Larson felt like he was plummeting head over heels to the bottom of an abyss. He, too, had participated in the carnage, and wondered how many more would die before this was all over.

"Doctor Larson! This way!"

The voice came from below on his right. He twisted his upper body to face it, pointing the gun in that direction. The pain in his side made him wince. The source of the voice was...a head coming from the ground? It wasn't until the lid was fully raised that he saw the opening in the floor. He motioned O'Rourke to join him, and both men scrambled toward the young soldier whose upper half was now visible.

"This way!" he called. "We don't have much time!"

73

What fresh hell is this? Zady wondered. Uncle Aleister is dead. Brynn is God knows where and in what shape. Akhenaten might be the biblical Moses, and Israeli rabbis the descendants of Egyptian pharaohs. Yeah, so this was turning out to be a banner week, a real red-letter fuck-fest of thrills, chills, and excitement.

At least she'd been right about one thing: her parents hadn't died in a car accident. That meant they were caught up in all this...whatever *this* was.

And here she was, flying back to the States, with no more than the broad goal of "rescuing Brynn" as her agenda. By the time she got home, the seventy-two-hour deadline would be over, but she couldn't think about that now. Regardless of who was holding her captive, she had to believe Brynn was still alive. She was glad Scott had suggested she go home alone, while he transformed into Lara Kroft with man parts, charged with the thankless task of finding Akhenaten's mummy, and getting a DNA sample.

She blew a raspberry. It was all too much to think about. She had to focus on saving Brynn. She stared out the window. The unrelenting gloom enveloping the jet felt poised to swallow her whole. Her head hurt where Long had clubbed her with his rifle; at some point she should probably get it checked out. Actually, her whole body hurt. What she wouldn't give for a long hot bath and a change of clothes. At least there was some food on the plane, and she could rest too, for the first time in a long while. She unzipped her boots, tugged off her socks, and wriggled her toes on the piled carpeting. Heavenly.

She felt guilty about Aleister and Brynn...

And angry.

The hum of the engine threatened to lull her to sleep, but she wouldn't let it. Not now. Even though she was exhausted, bone tired as Uncle Al would say, there was too much shit to think about.

Thinking of Scott was the only pleasure she allowed herself. He was cute, in a Hugh-Jackman-if-Hugh-Jackman-was-a-dork sort of way.

But he was also...well, a disaster. He was a genius, in some ways, but at the same time, he was so...so...

"Clueless, is the word you're groping for, Zee," she said in the stillness of the cabin.

He didn't have the sense God gave geese. She worried if he knew enough to close his mouth in the rain. Of course, it wasn't his fault. He was born that way; he was a man, so it came with the territory. Her pull to him was based partly on a belief that he couldn't navigate through life without her by his side. The fact that he'd made it this long was kind of a miracle.

Not that she pitied him, exactly, but...

Yeah, okay, she pitied him. But she found herself useful around him—even though she was probably ten years younger than him—and drawn to him in a way she didn't fully understand.

She found it cute the way he struggled with his attraction to her. He wasn't even sure he knew he was attracted to her. The Church could really fuck a guy up. He'd probably never even been with a woman. If it came to that, he'd probably want to study up on different positions before they slept together, critically analyzing the benefits and drawbacks of each. Yeah, getting intimate would definitely be an uphill battle.

It also infuriated her that he hadn't fully trusted her, thought she'd been the source of the envelopes. Though when she thought about it, she saw where he was coming from. His own order *had* tried to kill him, so trusting people wasn't high on his list.

She worried what might happen to him as he tomb-hunted. They'd keep in touch via burner phone, but only when necessary. After he found the tomb, he'd join her at home. It wasn't a great plan, but it was better than nothing.

"Onward and upward," she said gazing out of the window of the plane. She was ready for whatever was coming. Since getting back from Afghanistan, she'd honed the skills she needed to take care of herself—skills she hadn't had the chance to put into practice yet. Long had taken them by surprise in the desert. But when it came to saving Brynn, the only person left of her family, she was willing to do whatever it took, even if it meant killing someone—or more than one—to do it. And right then and there she made a decision, one she knew was right, but one that troubled her nonetheless. She would have to rescue Brynn on her own, because at this point there was no one she trusted to go along with her, especially now that Scott had stayed behind. Yes, the DoveCo. mercs that had rescued them in Egypt had been helpful so far, but she didn't know if one or more of them might turn on her if and when she got close to finding Brynn.

A shiver went up her spine and she hugged herself in the cold that suddenly surrounded her.

74

Larson strained his eyes wide as his surroundings slowly emerged from the shadows. The tunnel was about eight feet high and wide. Bare bulbs fastened with wire were strung on the earthen walls like a sparsely decorated Christmas tree. It smelled damp and musty. In all the excitement, he'd almost forgotten about his wound. He lifted his shirt and touched his side gingerly. The blood was mostly dried, a little sticky but dried, so that was good.

After fastening the trap door closed the young merc scrambled down the ladder and stood before Larson and O'Rourke, who'd descended first.

"Name's Reddy," he said thrusting out a meaty hand. "You okay?" he asked, pointing to Larson's side.

"Glad to see you," Larson said, as the merc pumped his arm. "And yes, I'm all right, thanks." He was in pain, but so many things had happened that getting grazed by a bullet barely registered.

Reddy nodded and turned to the cardinal.

"Jim O'Rourke," he said, caught in Reddy's vigorous grip.

"I'm the only one left," Reddy told them, casting his eyes to the ground. "A bunch of us were ready to meet you, but we got ambushed."

"Long's men?" Larson asked.

Reddy nodded.

"We're sorry for your loss," O'Rourke said.

"Where does this go?" Larson asked. From what he could see, the tunnel went straight ahead for several yards then snaked left.

"After a few miles it'll spit us out just south of the Old City, in Silwan," Reddy said.

"Lead the way," Larson told him.

Larson and O'Rourke lagged a few yards behind Reddy as they made their way through the tunnel.

"It has to be under the Temple Mount," Larson told the cardinal quietly. At this point, he wasn't ruling anything out: that Reddy had lied about being ambushed by Long's mercs and was leading them to their deaths, or that the tunnel was bugged. That's why he'd tucked the pistol into the back of his pants.

"But digging there is prohibited," O'Rourke said. "Plus, I'm not sure why an Egyptian pharaoh would be buried in Jerusalem. It just doesn't make sense."

"Hear me out," Larson said. "In the middle of the second millennium B.C., Canaan—what's now Israel—was part of the Egyptian Empire. Sometime in the fifteenth century B.C. the King of Qadesh, a strong unified kingdom in northern Syria, led a Syrian-Canaanite confederacy in a rebellion against Egypt. The pharaoh suppressed the rebellion. The clashing sides met at Megiddo, northwest of Jerusalem."

"The battle of Armageddon," the cardinal said quietly.

"Yes, in a sense. The pharaoh at the time, Tuthmosis III, attacked Megiddo then laid siege to it. During the siege, he stayed in a fortress to the east—by most accounts, in Jerusalem. Now, wherever pharaoh went, he took the ark of his god, Amun-Ra, with him. The ark, as Masika said, was a boat where the deity resided. It was carried by priests in ceremonies. An altar was built to house the ark of Amun-Ra, and it's likely that Tuthmosis chose Mount Moriah—a.k.a. the Temple Mount—for the altar, because it's an elevated spot. Such sites were used as threshing floors at the approaches to a city and often served as local cultic spots."

"So, you're saying Tuthmosis III built an altar to his god on the same spot where the Jewish temple later stood?"

"And here's where things get really interesting," Larson said. "Tuthmosis III was Amenhotep III's great-grandfather. And Amenhotep III was, of course, Akhenaten's father. Amenhotep III built many temples during his reign, not just in Egypt. Archaeological evidence at places like Hazor, Beth-shean, Lachish, Megiddo, and Gezer indicates he built temples in almost all Canaanite cities with Egyptian garrisons. These temples were built north to south, with the doorways on a single axis leading to three sections: a porch, a hall, and a holy of holies, where the ark was kept, like Solomon's temple in the Bible. Since temples were built at each military garrison, there's little doubt one existed on the Temple Mount, where the Dome of the Rock stands now."

O'Rourke halted mid-stride. Larson stopped beside him. Several yards ahead, Reddy waited. "Wait a minute," the cardinal said. "You think Amenhotep III, Akhenaten's father, and not Solomon, built the temple that used to stand on the Temple Mount?"

"I'm saying the evidence of temple building on the Mount dates to Amenhotep III's reign, in the fourteenth century B.C. There's nothing that dates to the tenth century B.C., in the time Solomon allegedly reigned. In fact, there's no historical evidence to support anything in the Old Testament before 900 B.C.—some say before 300 B.C."

The cardinal muttered something and started walking.

Larson followed. "There are references in some religious texts to secret scrolls of Moses, some believe they were plans for a temple. Well, what if the temple Akhenaten built at Amarna was based on his father's temples, including the one in Jerusalem?"

O'Rourke shook his head. "I'm still not sure how this leads to the conclusion that Akhenaten's body is under the Temple Mount."

"When Akhenaten was forced to flee Egypt because of his monotheistic beliefs, I think he led his wife and followers through the desert a la Moses and made his way to the temple in Jerusalem built by his father."

"And what makes you so sure of that?"

Now it was Larson's turn to stop. "Because in his diplomatic correspondence," he said, "Akhenaten refers to Jerusalem as 'his holy city forever'. Of course, we won't know if I'm right until we find his tomb."

"But even if it's there, how in the world are we going to get to it? You said it yourself, excavation on the Temple Mount is prohibited."

"That's a good question," Larson said.

"Do you have a good answer?"

"I'm working on it." But before he could say more, a wave of exhaustion crashed through him, bringing him to his knees.

"Are you alright?" O'Rourke said, his hand on Larson's shoulder.

"I think...I'm going...to pass out," he managed before darkness overcame him.

75

In D.C., darkness had overcome Madge Roberts as well: not the oblivion of unconsciousness, but the turmoil that shrouded her since she'd discovered the Easter egg in the photo of Yuya's tomb. She'd lain awake in bed for hours, the back of her hand covering her eyes, unable to accept what she'd come across when she'd rolled the cursor over the doorway to the tomb, two incredibly damning pieces of evidence.

How could you process something like that?

There had to be an explanation, one that would let her resume her normal, albeit hectic life, to go about her business as an elected official, whose job right now, as best she saw it, was to remove Jenkins from office.

Her mind groped for an alternative explanation for what she'd discovered.

Had the contents of the thumb drive been fabricated? It wouldn't have been hard, especially the transcript. But then there was the audio file. And if that was authenticated...

She was sure Aleister had sent it. And now that he was dead, there was a very real possibility he'd been killed because of the drive.

She didn't know Lance Sterling personally, but Aleister had

mentioned him in the past as someone he trusted, relied on. And yet...

She got up, wrapped herself in her terrycloth bathrobe, and padded barefoot down the hall to her office. She plopped in her chair then jiggled the mouse and opened the picture of the tomb—she'd left the thumb drive in the computer. Running the cursor over the entrance, she brought up the PDF document, reread it for the hundredth time, and listened again to the audio file. If they were genuine, then everything changed—her most cherished ideals, her belief in the goodness of people, the commitment she'd made to public service.

What in the world should she do?

If she raised this at the trial, or at any time, really, she could be charged with treason. Unless, of course, she could confirm it. But how? And even if she could, what would be the consequences? If it were true, who else was complicit? The president? His cabinet? Members of Congress?

She picked up the silver-framed picture of her niece.

"Oh, Corinne," she said aloud, her voice thick with emotion. "What kind of world are we leaving your generation?"

76

When Larson came to, he was stretched out on the tunnel floor, head pillowed on a flak jacket. O'Rourke sat against the wall with his legs stretched out in front of him. Reddy stood guard. Oddly, Larson felt better than he had in a while. When he went to touch his wound, he discovered that a bandage had been applied with some skill. It was sore but no longer throbbed like a tom-tom.

"Welcome back to the land of the living," the cardinal said as Larson raised himself on his elbows.

"Holy crap. What time is it?" he asked.

"A little after two in the afternoon," O'Rourke replied. "You've been out for a while."

"Feelin' better?" Reddy asked.

"Much. Thank you...for everything."

"No problem, sir. You all right to keep going?"

"Yeah, I'll be fine now." Larson got to his feet with the men's help.

Reddy reached into his pocket and pulled out a protein bar. "It's not much," he said apologetically.

O'Rourke smiled. "Breakfast of champions."

Larson nodded and ripped open the wrapper, gnawed off a

chunk of what tasted like cardboard. They walked in silence for several yards, until they came to a ladder.

"You said this comes out in Silwan?" Larson asked Reddy.

"Yeah, near the Pool of Siloam." He set his rifle on the floor, took out a pistol, then climbed the ladder. When he reached the top, he removed a metal cover from the ceiling and peeked out. "All clear," he called down. "You guys need any help?"

"We're good," Larson said. He passed the rifle up to Reddy and watched him climb out then turned to O'Rourke. "You're next."

"No, you go. You're still weak."

Larson climbed the ladder slowly. When he got near the top, Reddy reached his hand down and pulled him up into the open. The cardinal followed closely behind. It took a moment to adjust to the daylight, but it was still overcast. They were near a small ravine thicketed with oaks. Up ahead, on a hill, white square tenement buildings were packed closely together. Beyond lay the southern wall of the Old City of Jerusalem. Larson breathed deeply of the fresh air.

They proceeded in silence to the walled city and paused outside the Dung Gate, just west of the Temple Mount.

"Mr. Reddy," Larson said, "we part company here." He stuck out his hand and the merc pumped it vigorously.

"You gonna be okay?"

Larson nodded. "Here, you better take this." He handed Reddy the 9mm pistol from his waistband. "We don't need to be stopped for any reason." He had grown to trust the young merc since he could've easily led them into a trap but instead had brought them to their desired location.

"And you take these." Reddy reached into his jacket and pulled out two small flashlights and a bunch of protein bars and distributed them to Larson and O'Rourke. "I'll hang around the tunnel. Call if you need me." He rattled off his number and Larson committed it to memory.

"I appreciate it," Larson told him.

He and O'Rourke entered the Old City and headed north, toward the Western Wall. There weren't many people, which made Larson glad; it'd make it easier to identify possible threats. Long was out there somewhere and there was probably a host of others who wanted to keep him from finding Akhenaten's tomb. As they passed Jerusalem Archaeological Park on the right, the cardinal asked how he was planning to get beneath the Dome of the Rock.

"There're four possibilities," Larson said, feeling like a professor again. "One is from above. But going through the front door, making our way to the Foundation Stone in the center, then crawling through the small hole that leads to the Cave of Souls seems a little farfetched."

"Agreed," O'Rourke said.

"Then there's a legend that the Templars dug a tunnel, in the southeast corner of the Mount. But there's no guarantee the tunnel exists and can be accessed. And if it could, there's an underground mosque there now. It'd be impossible to search for an access point without raising suspicions."

"Strike two," the cardinal said.

"Exactly. Some say the area under the Temple Mount can be reached through the Western Wall tunnels, which you can access near the Warren Gate, up ahead on the right." He pointed to the small section of the Western Wall that remained above ground, the Wailing Wall, as they passed. Several Jews were gathered there, davening.

"Story goes," he continued, "that in 1981 a rabbi working for the Religious Affairs Ministry was excavating underneath the Temple Mount when he discovered a chamber. He showed it to some colleagues, other rabbis, who claimed to have seen the Ark of the Covenant in the chamber. It led to a massive brawl between Jews and Arabs, so the tunnel was sealed by the Israeli police. You can see the sealed entrance from the Western Wall Tunnel that opened to the public in the mid-90s."

"I'm guessing that's not a viable option either," O'Rourke said.

"That leaves one choice," Larson said, as they passed under a stone arch that stretched over the paved road of the Old City. "This."

They stood in front of an open black iron gate. Beyond it a bronze double door was set into a white stone building connected to a basilica.

"The Convent of the Sisters of Zion?" O'Rourke said, incredulously.

"We need to get to a pool underneath the building. Just follow my lead," Larson told him. "I can be awfully persuasive when I have to be."

77

"Absolutely, positively not," the elderly nun said from just inside the door. The young sister who'd answered the bell had summoned her superior, who now refused Larson's request without a moment's hesitation. She pursed her lips. "In fact, you should leave."

Larson had been hesitant to reveal his identity, or the cardinal's. But this left him no choice. "Mother Superior, please. You may not recognize me, I look a little rough at the moment, but—"

"I most certainly do recognize you, Doctor Larson. You've already caused enough trouble for the Church, what with your controversial publications. To imply like you did in your book on the Dead Sea Scrolls that Mother Church might be holding something back. I don't know why they put up with you for so long. As far as I'm concerned, you're a heretic, just one step removed from the anti-Christ. It's as if Satan himself stood at my door asking to—"

"Forgive this bold and inexcusable intrusion, Mother Superior," the cardinal said, stepping in front of Larson. "You may not recognize me, dressed in civilian clothes, but I'm James O'Rourke."

"Oh, I beg your pardon, Your Eminence," the old nun replied, blessing herself quickly. "Please excuse my rudeness. Please, please, come in. We've all been so saddened by the Holy Father's death."

O'Rourke turned to a chastened Larson. "And that's how it's done."

Mother Superior led them down a series of stone steps to a large cuboid cistern beneath a barrel-vaulted ceiling. The dank musty atmosphere caused Larson to shudder.

"Now, if you'll excuse us, Mother," O'Rourke said. "Doctor Larson and I would like a little time for prayer and meditation."

"What are you going to do down here?" the Mother Superior asked suspiciously.

Without a moment's pause the words flowed from the cardinal's mouth. "You see, Mother, this pool was one of the many places Pope Innocent hoped to visit. Unfortunately, he never had the chance."

Larson almost laughed at the thought of a Holy bucket list, especially one that included this dismal place. The nun looked from O'Rourke to Larson and back to O'Rourke with narrowed eyes.

"Who can claim to know the ways of the Almighty?" Larson said, clasping his hands in prayer.

"Hmm," she said. "Well, the Lord does work in mysterious ways."

"The most mysterious," O'Rourke said. "Ways we can't begin to understand."

Larson added an enthusiastic "Amen!"

"Well, I'll leave you in peace," Mother Superior said. "We must start preparing for vespers anyway. Your Eminence...and company." With a slight nod she turned and headed upstairs.

"See, I told you," Larson said, once she was gone. "I've got this."

"Yes, it was a joy watching you work your magic. So, General, what is the plan?"

"This pool runs northwest to southeast and is bisected by that wall," Larson said, pointing to the wall on the left, "which cuts the pool into two rectangles. There's another wall, from west to east, that breaks the pool into four quadrants. We're standing in the northwest quadrant. See that blocked archway straight ahead, at the end of the pool?"

O'Rourke nodded.

"That leads to the southwest quadrant. Its tip connects to an aqueduct. These days you can tour the aqueduct; it runs parallel to the underground Western Wall. In *The Jewish Wars*, Josephus says that at one time, the aqueduct brought water to the Temple Mount. But the aqueduct that's visible today doesn't run into the Temple Mount. It skirts around the outside of the wall and runs south for about three hundred feet then stops. There must be a tunnel or a passage connecting the aqueduct to a water source inside the Mount."

"But how would we go about finding it, especially with a tour going on? Besides, there're probably security cameras all over the place."

"Agreed."

"Is there any place else it could be?"

Larson thought for a moment. "This is called the Struthion Pool, but it has another name, the Twin Pool. That's because the wall on the left cuts the pool into two long rectangles, like I said, that run north to south. If we can get beyond that wall, we can access the other half of the pool, the half that's closed to the public. Once we get on the other side, we might be able to gain access to the southeastern quadrant—especially if the archway on the other side of the wall is open."

"Supposing it isn't?" the cardinal asked.

"Let's cross that bridge, or arch, if and when we get to it," Larson said. "Right now, we've got to see if we can get through that wall."

He removed the flak jacket Reddy had given him, making sure his burner phone and the flashlights were inside, zipped snugly in plastic bags he'd brought with him to collect samples from the tomb, assuming he found it. He crouched on the side of the pool. The thought of what he was contemplating filled his stomach with lead. From what he'd read, it was a fourteen-foot drop, but there was only a foot of water at the bottom. If he could dangle from the edge and extend his arms as far as possible, he could drop the rest of the way, and he could stand in a foot of water—not exactly a drowning risk. Hopefully, the water would be shallow in the other quadrants of the pool, assuming they could gain access to them.

"You stay here," he told O'Rourke. "There's no point in both of us going down until I'm sure we can get through the wall."

"Break a leg," the cardinal replied.

"Not what I'm aiming for," Larson said. Dangling from the edge of the pool, he extended his arms fully, then dropped. When he landed safely in the shin-high water, he sloshed to the opposite wall, and pressed on it, checking for loose stones. A splash behind him caused him to stop and turn around suddenly, causing pain in his side.

"It'll be faster if we both look," O'Rourke said. He made his way over, carrying the flak jacket Larson had left poolside.

"You're right," Larson said. "This could take a while."

78

Brynn, or what was left of her, felt like she'd been ripped open, organs exposed to the foul air, emotions, mind, love, all that made up who she was, gnashed between the razor-sharp teeth of an abominable creature that had no name, but one that had devoured all that was human in her.

Shards of memories came to her, each more jagged than the last, snapshots of excruciating pain taken by a sinister camera that used her anguish for film. This was a place beyond good and evil, before the Fall, after Armageddon, the collapse of space and time into a vortex. There was no entry point, no egress, only this tortured moment for all eternity.

The only thing keeping her tethered to this world, the only object she could touch and feel that provided the barest sense of connection to what was left of the person she'd once been, was the key Aleister had slipped from around his neck and pressed into her hand the moment before he was killed, the key she'd clutched then instinctively slipped between the mattress and the box spring. She didn't know what it was, what it opened. But whenever she felt like yielding the last remnant of herself, she'd reach down and touch it.

She willed herself to do so now, if only for the last time.

79

Never was the phrase "going through the motions" more accurate.

Madge Roberts felt one screw short of becoming an automaton as she'd gotten out of bed, then showered, dressed, and dragged herself to the Senate chamber to hear the rest of President Jenkins' defense by the oily Larry Miller. But she hadn't been able to take in a word he'd said for—she glanced furtively at her watch—the last ninety minutes. The counsel's words were like trombone slides whenever adults spoke in Peanuts.

She was still at a total loss over what to do with the transcript and audio file, but knew she had to have the file verified for authenticity before bringing it to bear. She glanced at her colleagues on both sides of the aisle. It was impossible to think that any of them had taken part in such an inhuman plan. She was so much in her own head that she didn't notice Carl at her side until he touched her hand.

She jumped and stared at him, incomprehensibly.

"You need to come with me. There's been an accident. I'm afraid it's your niece..."

The world receded into nothingness.

80

"This one's loose," Larson said from a corner of the pool underneath the Convent of the Sisters of Zion. Hunched over, his hands below the shallow water, he shoved as hard as he could. But the stone barely moved.

"Hold on," O'Rourke said. "Let me try." He reached under the water, and with a tremendous grunt, pushed against the stone. There was a grating sound, of stone against stone, but the water stayed at the same level.

"I think the one next to it's loose, too," O'Rourke said. "If we can move a few of them, there should be enough space to crawl through."

"Great," Larson said, trying to swallow his fear. The thought of wiggling through a small wet space, even in shallow water, terrified him. It didn't really matter how deep it was—you could drown in a bowl of soup. But if the water stayed at the same level, it probably wouldn't be any deeper on the other side of the wall.

Combining their efforts, they managed to shift six stones near the bottom of the pool, creating a space big enough to get through, one at a time. The only comfort Larson took in all this was that the water they stood in didn't rise.

O'Rourke volunteered to go first, but Larson wouldn't allow it. Acting with more bravado than he felt—much more—he sat in the water and stretched his legs through the opening, felt his feet come out on the other side of the wall.

That was the easy part. And now, for my next trick...

"After I go, push the jacket through," he told O'Rourke. "We're gonna need the flashlights. Here goes nothing."

After a deep breath, he lay flat until the water nearly touched his nose then pushed himself forward and squirmed on his back through the narrow opening. Submerged in wet darkness, he wriggled through as quickly as he could and was on the other side of the wall before he counted to twenty.

Once through, he rolled over and shot up, taking a deep breath as he stood. The water was the same level, only about a foot deep. He rubbed his eyes dry, blinked, but couldn't see much. It was only a little brighter than when he'd visited Howe Caverns, and the guide turned off the lights to simulate the cave's natural blackness. The wan glow from the other side of the pool was the only light.

"Okay, give me the jacket," he told O'Rourke, in a shaky voice. Who knew what lurked in this chamber? Shuddering, he crouched to pull the jacket from the hole as O'Rourke pushed it through.

"What can you see?" O'Rourke asked.

"Not much," Larson replied. "Give me a second." He unzipped the pocket, pulled the flashlight out of the plastic bag, and shined it around. This pool was the same size as the one on the other side, with walls on three sides.

"Coming through," O'Rourke said, and before Larson knew it the old guy had thrust through the opening and stood beside him.

"Pretty spry for—" Larson began.

"Go ahead and say it," O'Rourke said, rubbing his eyes. "Pretty spry for an old fart."

Larson and O'Rourke sloshed to the wall behind which the southeast quadrant of the pool should lie.

"Should we look for loose stones again?" O'Rourke asked.

"We can start with that," Larson said.

For the next half-hour they ran their hands over the rough ancient stones but were unable to shift any of them; the old rocks just wouldn't budge.

"This is ridiculous!" Larson cried and stomped his foot in frustration. When he did, the spot where his foot came down moved slightly.

"What?" O'Rourke asked when Larson started pressing the ground beneath the water.

"I thought I felt something shift. There's something here... wait."

His index finger found a small depression. He sought another hold along the floor's rough surface and detected a slightly raised round stone disc. "Here! Give me a hand."

O'Rourke leaned down and Larson guided his finger to a shallow trough under the lip of the disc.

"One, two, three!" Larson cried. The men lifted as hard as they could and watched in silent fascination as the water drained into the opening made by raising the disc.

"Holy——" the cardinal began.

"Shit!" Larson finished. "It's like an ancient manhole cover!"

Once they got a better grip on the cover, they pulled it out and placed it to the side of the hole. It was big enough for them to fit through one at a time.

Larson peered into the opening with the aid of his flashlight. "It looks like it drops about eight feet, probably into a tunnel, otherwise the water wouldn't have drained; there's barely any at the bottom. Hopefully, it goes right under this wall."

He tied the jacket around his waist and lowered himself in, flashlight between his teeth. After extending his arms, he dropped to the floor then shined the light around. A tunnel ran straight ahead for several meters before winding left.

O'Rourke lowered himself with ease, begging off assistance. Silently, they trudged ahead. The tunnel was wide enough to stand abreast with a few feet to spare. The water that had poured down from the pool was only ankle high. When they rounded the corner, the tunnel dead-ended in a water-filled trench that ran the width of the tunnel. The wall on the other side was about twenty feet away.

"Thoughts?" O'Rourke said.

"The tunnel might stop here, or it could connect to the aqueduct on the other side of the wall. Best case scenario, it continues southeast and goes under the Temple Mount."

"How deep do you think the trench is?"

"Your guess is as good as mine," Larson said.

He *so* did not want to do this, everything in his body and mind screamed against it, but he'd come too far and there was too much at stake. He sat on the edge of the trench and dangled his legs in the water. When his feet didn't touch bottom, he turned around and slowly lowered himself into the water, his arms in a push-up position on the stone lip. He pointed his feet down as far as he could, toes desperately searching for the bottom. Nothing. Straining, he lowered himself slowly till his elbows broke the plane. Now he'd have to pull himself out of the trench instead of pushing himself out of the water. Lower. Lower. Just before his mouth submerged, his feet hit bottom. He smiled nervously up at O'Rourke.

"Touch down," Larson said. "Assuming it doesn't drop off."

Inch-by-inch he made his way to the far wall, terrified his foot would touch nothing and he'd be pulled under. To his utter relief he reached the wall, head still mostly above the water. His relief screeched to a halt when, tapping his foot against the wall, he felt a small open space.

"What've you got?" O'Rourke asked.

"An opening," Larson said.

"How big?"

"That's what I'm about to find out."

He took a deep breath and crouched below the water, felt the width of the space with his hands, held them in that position, then stood. A couple of inches shy of two feet. Son of a bitch. He repeated the procedure to measure the gap's height: about the same.

"I've got some bad news and some...other bad news," he said. "I might be able to squeeze through. But you won't. And even if I can get myself into the opening, I've got no idea how long it is, or if it opens up anywhere. It could just dead-end." His own words chilled him.

"What now?" O'Rourke asked.

What now, indeed?

81

Staring at the world, a world that was something apart, something other.

In the Middle Ages people with depression said they felt as if they were made of glass, about to fracture, shatter—yup, just like that.

I'm looking through glass, I'm looking through...the windshield.

Things outside have no substance, ephemeral, ghosts, spirits of trees, buildings, pedestrians, other cars, amid a convoy of security vehicles, and I think I'm moving, I think Carl—is that his name?—is driving, what a weird concept, driving a car, as if being in control of a four-thousand-pound vehicle meant you were in control, in the driver's seat, but she wasn't in the driver's seat, she was just a passenger and why was it so cold? The heat is on, Corinne, I'm coming... I can hear it, I can smell it, and I'm not even there yet, Corinne, light of my life, candle in the darkness—

Accident...

There's been an accident...

Your niece, my niece, has been...has been what, you fool? Has been what?

Killed.

The ugliest of ugly words. Killed.

And it felt exactly like it sounded. Like you didn't feel anything that was said after the word was pronounced because everything that followed didn't exist either—everything had been killed, and killed was final, there was nothing that existed beyond it, it was the coda to an unfinished symphony, the end of words mid-sentence and why are you dead, goddamn it! Goddamn you, God! or god....

Accident...

There was an accident...

She was killed at the parking garage.

And heeeeerrrrrreeee's the parking garage! Everything started to go downhill when Johnny Carson left *The Tonight Show*.

The impossible bulk of fire engines, police cars, ambulances, people, awkward-looking, Feds, security all surrounded the entrance to the garage where she'd parked her car that morning.

Should she get out now that the car had stopped?

At least she thought it stopped, maybe it was still moving, something about her was still moving, her stomach, the hum in her head, but could she get out? That was the question—whether to be or not to be had already been answered in the negative, there was no being after this.

And now she saw it, in the dimly-lit parking garage, punctuated by the flashing lights of official vehicles: a cordon of pain, a ringworm of suffering, twisted metal hunks, and the smell of... even through the window—of gas, fire, smoke, burning metal... charred flesh.

This was an accident?

I suppose you could accidentally plant a car bomb, like on the wrong car.

Four words penetrated her closed window because she tried to get out but discovered she'd gained 250 pounds on the ride here and hadn't yet learned how to maneuver the extra bulk, to hoist it up, to carry it, she'd have to practice before she could pull it off successfully, and she'd have time to do that now because there wasn't anything left to do since Corinne was... wasn't.

And the four words from the lips of a man, a Fed: "ISIS has claimed responsibility."

And that's when she started laughing, laughing so hard she thought she'd pee herself, but she couldn't get it together because to say that ISIS had done this was like saying the crowing of the rooster brought the sun up and now she just could not, not for the life of her, not for the life of Corinne – wait, Corinne no longer had a life – could she stop, could she stop laughing and laughing and laughing...

82

L arson had to decide.

And he had to do it now.

Either he was going to shove himself into the narrow gap below the water and hope it opened somewhere or he was going to have to stop here, task unfinished. But one thing was certain: there was no time to turn back, form a new plan, try again later. And, really, what other option was there? Even if he had scuba diving equipment—assuming he knew how to use it, which he didn't—the opening wasn't big enough for a person strapped with an oxygen tank. Just do it, he told himself. *Thanks for the catchy slogan, Nike.* Sometimes you just had to suck it up and do the thing you least wanted to do. That's what Zady would say, Zady for whom he suddenly realized he had very strong feelings. Had he had them all along? Of course, he had—he must've. But that's what the Church could do to a guy, make him deny the inevitable, suppress thoughts and feelings, logic even, so much so that you didn't know which end was up. He would do what he was about to do for Brynn, on the off chance it would help save her, so that Zady wouldn't lose the last surviving member of her family.

"Keep your flashlight on," he told O'Rourke. "I've got mine

and the burner sealed in a bag in my pocket. When I make it to the other side, (*if there* is *an other side*) I'll let you know. I'll yell, or something."

"Be careful," the cardinal said.

"Um, yeah." Larson hesitated for a moment, took a deep breath, then with an image of Zady in his mind, submerged.

Laying on his stomach, he stretched his arms in front of him and pushed himself into the gap like some blind, primordial creature. Quickly as he could, he pulled-pushed himself, arms extended, hands and fingers probing every inch, hoping, praying to whatever god or goddess that might exist, that he'd find an opening.

Nothing.

Stretch, reach...

Can't hold my breath much longer.

Any longer.

I should've told Zady I loved her.

One last reach for her sake...

Edge!

With the last vestige of strength, Larson gripped the edge of an opening and pulled himself through. He stood in darkness, face just above water, hack-coughing in deep breaths, not knowing what surrounded him. Arms raised above water, he unzipped the jacket, took out the flashlight, and shined it around.

He was in a pool about ten feet in diameter. A stone tunnel continued straight ahead as far as he could see. He shouted to let O'Rourke know he was through. It risked drawing attention to himself, but he doubted anyone had been in this tunnel in a very long time. Cocking his head, he listened for a response. Just when he thought the old man hadn't heard, a faint "good job" reached his ears. Stepping slowly, deliberately, as if relearning how to walk, unwilling to assume the floor of the pool was flat, he reached the edge, set the flashlight and jacket on the dry floor, and hoisted himself out of the water. He stood and shook himself off like a dog.

A cold wet Larson navigated the narrow passage he found himself in. At several points along the way, the stone tunnel had collapsed, and he had to spend huge chunks of time removing rocks and debris before continuing. When his phone showed it was eleven o'clock, he turned a corner and hit a wall.

"So, this is how it ends," he said. "Not with a bang, but with a wall." They were the first words he'd said in a long time and the sound of his own voice, deep below the earth, frightened him. He was exhausted, and despite his best efforts, he'd failed. Frustrated, he sank to the ground, back against the wall, and took a protein bar out of his jacket. He'd need nourishment for the return trip because this path wasn't getting him anywhere.

83

Zady's trip home had been uneventful, and she'd been able to eat and rest a little on the plane. It was just after business hours when she punched a code on the back-door keypad then climbed the stairs to her uncle's office at DoveCo. H.Q. in Reston, Virginia in a building all jutting angles and glass, as if its architect had conjured up the ghost of Picasso. There shouldn't be too many people here now—just a security guard or two—but her heart raced just the same. If Sterling had turned, it pointed to the possibility of a coup in the upper ranks, and there would be no telling how far down it went.

She tried to focus on the only good news she'd had in a while: a text from Scott she'd gotten when she pulled up. He was safe. But he still had to find Akhenaten's tomb.

And she still had to find Brynn.

She reached the third floor, cracked the stairwell door, and peeked into the hall. Empty. So far, so good. She tip-toed down the hall, trying not to let her boot heels resound on the polished floor. When she reached the second door on the right, she punched the code on the keypad. As slowly and quietly as she could, she opened the door.

From what she could tell nothing had been disturbed. Of course, it would've been hard to tell if somebody had ransacked the office, so sparse were the furnishings. An oak desk, a computer, and a bookshelf with a fern on a low shelf so Aleister could water it.

She crossed to the desk and leaned over the computer. The picture of her, Aleister, and Brynn in Santorini hurt her heart. But there was no time for that, so she turned it over and laid it on the desk. She had to find what she needed. Fast.

She called up the computer's search history. Nothing. He must have deleted it the last time he'd used it. But she knew how to retrieve it. Soon she was staring at different locations on half a dozen Google maps.

She yanked at the desk drawer, looking for paper and pen. Locked.

She tugged open the drawer on the right, found what she needed, jotted down six pairs of coordinates, starting with the last and ending with the first—she assumed Aleister had visited some of them and come up empty.

After deleting what she'd done, she turned to go and found herself face-to-face with a security guard pointing a gun at her.

84

As Larson chewed the last bite of his protein bar, he knocked the back of his head against the wall in frustration. It was harder than he'd intended, and it caused him to rub the spot. When he did, he felt something chalky. He looked at his hand. It was covered with a powdery substance, almost like talc.

He stood up, wrapped his jacket around his elbow, and banged it against the wall, grimacing a little at the pain from his wounded side. Soon he was engulfed in a cloud of dust.

He untied his shoe and pounded it wildly on the soft, crumbling rock, venting his anger and frustration, until there was a hole big enough to stick his arm through. Holding the flashlight, he peered through the hole:

A flight of stairs led down into the darkness.

"Today's lesson boys and girls: sometimes it pays to be frustrated. Maybe there's something to the whole celibacy thing after all."

85

"Oh, put down the damn gun and listen," Zady told the guard, sounding more confident than she felt.

"Keep your hands up," he said.

"Look at the picture next to the computer." She pointed to the photo on the desk that she'd laid face-down.

The guard kept his pistol trained on her but inched to the desk, picked up the photo, and looked at it.

"See anyone familiar?" she said, hoping desperately he wasn't part of the coup.

He looked from Zady to the photo and back again. "That's you."

"I'm Zady Jones, Aleister Mabrey's niece. And you must be... well, new."

The guard lowered his gun then holstered it. "Yes, ma'am. Started a week ago. Sorry. Name's Johnson." The look in his eyes told Zady he was too embarrassed to do anything so bold as to offer a handshake. She immediately pitied him. *Every guy really is a mess.*

"It's all right, Johnson. You were just doing your job."

"Thank you, ma'am," he replied, sheepishly.

"Oh, and Johnson? Drop the ma'am. From the looks of it we're about the same age."

"Yes, ma—"

"Zady, just Zady."

Johnson nodded. "I'm sorry about Mr. Mabrey. He was a good guy."

"Thanks," Zady said.

"Is there anything I can do?" he asked.

"Yes. Don't tell anyone I was here."

86

Larson counted the steps as he descended deeper into the earth. His breath quickened with anticipation. His hands started to sweat. As he stepped from the final, twelfth, step to the floor of a long, narrow tunnel, words from the eighty-fifth psalm echoed in his mind: *Truth shall spring out of the earth.*

He'd gone about twenty yards when his flashlight hit on a shiny reflective surface straight ahead. Looked like a door set into the wall. He walked closer. Odd that someone had put a reflective door so deep underground. Was it wet? Or glass. Or...

Wait.

Could it be?

It was...

Gold.

Larson ran the last few feet to the shiny gold door—

But it wasn't a door; it was an opening. Stepping across the threshold he shined his flashlight around a vast circular gold chamber. He was so awestruck it took him a moment to catch his breath. The walls, ceiling, and floor were covered with gold so shiny that everywhere his light hit dazzled his eyes, like sun on snow. Casting the beam around, he tried to take in everything at once, trying hard to convince himself that what he saw was real, and not some weird effect of being underground for so long. Paintings applied directly to the gold surface, decorated the walls. His heart nearly stopped when his light rested on two large stone sarcophagi in the center of the chamber, surrounded by furnishings, many made of gold and encrusted with precious jewels. Chariots, fine vestments, a throne, weapons, chalices, vases, magnificent jewelry, all neatly arranged.

Larson gulped air taking in the surroundings, unsure which treasure to examine first. But then he remembered why he was there and stepped reverently to the coffins. Holding the flashlight in one hand, he ran his other hand along the stone surface of the larger sarcophagus. Apart from the carved hieroglyphs, it was incredibly smooth. The day before, Masika had sketched Akhenaten's double cartouche—a half-loaf, waves, reeds, and full circle, representing the sun. He easily identified the markings on the lid of the larger coffin as a match. Shaking with excitement, he turned to the smaller sarcophagus, convinced he already knew its occupant. The cartouche on the lid—five crosses, two half-loaves, waves, sun, and bowed figure—confirmed his suspicions: it was Nefertiti, Akhenaten's wife.

To fulfill his mission, to get DNA, he might have to lift the lids of the sarcophagi, an unpleasant prospect to say the least. Then it occurred to him: he might find what he needed among the myriad objects surrounding him. He shined the light on the floor, toward the feet of the coffins, where he saw part of an object that looked like—

At first, he couldn't believe his eyes and blinked a few times just to make sure what he thought he saw was real. He stepped gingerly, as if on broken glass, until he stood directly over the ornate golden chest then dropped to his knees. Without a ruler, it was impossible to know the exact measurements, but the chest was about fifty inches long, thirty inches wide and deep, the same measurements as the Ark of the Covenant in the Book of Exodus. The golden lid atop the chest had a bust on either end, one male and the other female, adorned in royal headwear: presumably Akhenaten and Nefertiti. Larson had always found it curious that the detailed description of the ark in Exodus said little about the cherubim on the lid; now he knew why. Everything fit: the dimensions, the gold molding, the four rings of gold attached to the corners of the chest, through which wooden gold-plated staves were inserted.

He set the flashlight on the floor, pointing up, and went about removing the lid. As he did, a sentence from Paul's Letter to the Hebrews rang in his mind: *The Ark of the Covenant was covered on all sides with gold, in which was a golden jar holding the manna, and Aaron's rod which budded, and the tables of the covenant.*

He gasped when he removed the lid. A small golden jar inlaid with precious stones inscribed with Akhenaten and Nefertiti's cartouches lay on the bottom. Next to it was a bronze rod topped with a serpent. The two stone tablets were inscribed with the cartouche of Aten, the royal couple's one true god. Larson gently removed the rod and jar then delicately lifted the stone tablets. A chill went up his spine when he noticed cracks in the stones and remembered the passage in Exodus: *And Moses' anger flared up. He threw from his hands the tablets and broke them at the foot of the mountain.*

Setting the gold jar next to the rod, he paused, then picked up the jar and took off the ornate lid. It was filled with a gummy resin the color of hoarfrost, made up of little pellets the size of coriander seeds. A dark ball of string was stuck to it. Thread, maybe? No. It wasn't strong enough. He picked up the flashlight and shined it on the ball. It was twisted strands of hair. Two types, one coarser and thicker. He remembered how a similar item had been discovered in the tomb of King Tut, who was mostly likely Akhenaten and Nefertiti's son. A small alabaster chest bearing the cartouches of Tut and his queen held two balls of hair wrapped in linen, like an ancient contract, a covenant. He took strands from each ball and placed them in separate plastic bags, then placed both balls in another bag and zipped all the bags into one of the small pockets of his flak jacket. For the first time in a very long time, luck, fate, a higher power of some sort, was on his side.

After a quick look at the rest of the items in the tomb, including the wall-friezes, he clicked some pics with his phone then headed back to O'Rourke.

87

This was it. Finally. It'd all come down to the last set of coordinates. In a small clearing in a West Virginia forest, two mercs stood smoking near the front door of a cabin.

Zady let her binoculars dangle from her neck as she patted herself, making sure everything she'd brought was exactly where it needed to be. This was no place for gunfire—she had no idea how many men were inside—so she'd brought knives and throwing stars. She watched the mercs finish their coffin nails then duck inside.

Sunshine had given way to clouds.

Dusk was coming.

Time to put her plan into action.

Okay, maybe calling it a plan was a bit of a stretch. The goal was simple enough: find out how many mercs there were, take them out one-by-one, and rescue Brynn—if she were still alive. But exactly how to do this was about as clear and straightforward as one of Scott's ramblings on ancient history. And it wasn't like she could call for backup. She had no clue how far any coup that might've occurred had spread among the rank and file of DoveCo. and, as far as the law was concerned...well, who knew whose side they'd be on? Things were murky these days, to say the least. But she felt certain Lance Sterling had turned, killed Aleister, and held Brynn, exactly why she couldn't be sure—maybe just to take over DoveCo. and the rest of Aleister's vast resources, maybe for larger reasons that played into whatever the hell was going on at the top of the political food chain.

She crept silently, from one tree to the next, till she was within fifty feet of the cabin. She heard the cabin door open then bang shut and risked a peek around the tree. A different merc came out, probably for a smoke. He stepped off the porch and leaned against a tall skinny pine tree. She watched smoke from his cigarette curl upwards, connecting the earth to the sky with a blue-gray string.

She took a deep breath and crept toward her prey. Despite the care she took, each step seemed to ricochet off the trees and echo in the forest. Slowly, she closed the distance.

Twenty feet...

Ten...

Five...

The merc kept smoking. The only real movement was his right arm, as he drew the cigarette to his lips, sucked, then dropped it.

Now she was on the other side of the tree where he leaned. She'd been holding her rainbow-colored dagger as she approached and now, in a smooth, quick, motion, she reached around the trunk. Sound stopped. Time froze. With one quick motion, she slit his throat. He clutched his neck, gurgling, and fell to the ground. Somewhere a bird cried. Then silence.

Zady stepped from behind the tree. "Surgeon General's warning, dumbass: Smoking is hazardous to your health."

She bent down and wiped the gore from her knife on some leaves. She grabbed the dead merc under his arms and, straining, pulled him behind the closest, biggest tree.

"One down, at least three to go," she whispered, assuming Sterling was in the cabin.

Exhilarated, she crouched behind a tree, let the feelings course through her, rode high on the river of adrenaline. She'd just killed someone. All that training she'd done had paid off. But she didn't allow herself time to gloat. If she were to survive, she'd have to kill again. And next time might not be so easy.

Now, to roust the other foxes from the henhouse. She picked up a handful of stones and one-by-one chucked them at the cabin, aiming at the door. Three times she threw, and three times hit her target. After the last one, a merc she'd seen before threw open the door, gun drawn, and whipped his body from left to right, checking for danger.

"That you, Jayce?" he called. "Where you at?" When he got no response, he ducked inside for a second then emerged with his smoke buddy. With any luck, only Sterling and Brynn remained inside.

Zady knew she must act quickly, had to lead the two men away from the body behind the tree. She pulled out two Chinese dragon rainbow throwing stars from an inside pocket of her jacket, gripped one in each hand, and launched them in opposite directions into the woods on either side of the cabin.

"What the fuck?" Merc 1 said.

"You take that side, I'll take this," Merc 2 replied.

Zady watched the men head in opposite directions, away from where she crouched. She followed cautiously behind Merc 1, keeping at least twenty feet between them.

Suddenly, he stopped, swung around in her direction.

She dove headfirst behind a pile of brush, her heart throbbing in her throat so loudly she knew he could hear it. Unable to tell if he'd seen her, and unwilling to peek, she lay on her back, hugging herself.

Where's the fucking cloak of invisibility when you need it?

She reached for her knife and clasped it tightly against her stomach with both hands, straining her ears for the slightest sound.

But there was nothing: no voices, no snapping of branches. Even the birds were mute.

Then with the quickness of an apparition, a face appeared over her. Whether it was a reflex, an instinctual act of self-preservation, or because the merc had scared the shit out of her, blinding her with fury, she rose and drove the blade of the knife directly into his right eye. She heard and felt a sickening squish as she did.

The soldier screamed, clutching his eye, blood pouring between his fingers. She plunged the knife into his throat, bringing his cries to a halt, then drew the blade across his jugular. As he slumped to the ground, she heard a noise.

Someone was coming. Merc 2. Drawn by his comrade's scream. Making no attempt to hide his approach.

Zady stepped around the pile of brush and crouched next to the fallen body. As the rustling grew closer, she risked a peek over the top of the brush.

Merc 2 was racing toward her.

"I'm coming, Ty!" There was something desperate in the voice, almost a lover's plaint. Maybe "Don't Ask, Don't Tell" had reached private security companies. It was the only way to make sense of such reckless behavior. At least this time she wouldn't be taken by surprise.

She stood up, hoisted the corpse in front of her face-to-face to use as cover against the charging man, who by now, must've seen saw Ty standing erect, back facing him. Hopefully he was too blinded by emotion to see her behind the dead soldier holding him up.

"You alright? Answer me, Ty!" the merc shouted, exasperated his buddy wasn't responding. When he was within fifteen feet, Zady dropped the body and flung the star in her right hand.

"What the f—?!"

The star struck his throat. He fired his gun instinctively, straight up in the air, before he dropped it and fell to his knees. Zady ran toward him to finish him off. One of the points had embedded itself up to the circle in the middle of the weapon. Before she yanked out the star, she twisted it, then used it to cut a deep gash across his throat.

"Who said you can't hit a moving target?" she said, wiping the gore off the star with some leaves.

But now she was worried. Whoever was left in the cabin would've heard the gun. It wasn't all bad: at least she'd get a better idea of how many mercs were left. She grabbed the rifle from the ground and settled behind a tree, waiting to see who'd come. After a few minutes passed without anyone coming, she pulled out her phone to watch the time.

Ten minutes passed.

Twenty.

Still no one.

Maybe Sterling was the sole survivor, and he was inside the cabin guarding Brynn, lying in wait for Zady to come. If there were any mercs left, they were in the cabin too. As more minutes passed, and nothing happened, she came to a conclusion, which led to a decision, the only decision, for that matter: if she wanted to find Brynn, she'd have to breach the building.

She crept from tree to tree till she reached the one where she'd dragged the body of the first merc she'd killed.

"There's no good way to do this," she whispered.

She heard Uncle Aleister's voice, telling her to "keep a stiff upper lip," saw Larson smiling at some snarky comment of hers. But it was the thought of Brynn, hurt or worse, finally within her reach, that ultimately propelled her into action.

She came out slowly from behind the tree, pointing the rifle in front of her. She couldn't see into the windows on either side of the door. It was only when she got within ten feet that she saw why: they were covered with dark fabric.

She took a deep breath, ran the last few feet as quietly as she could, drew up to the side of the door. Tried the handle.

Unlocked.

This was another situation where there was no way to prepare yourself. The action she needed to take was against the law of self-preservation, it was hurtling toward death, rather than away from it. The only thing to do was force her body through the door and meet whatever was on the other side.

The dark fabric over the windows kept out natural light so she reached into her jacket, pulled out a flashlight, and tucked it underneath her left arm. It might be dark inside, especially after being outside for so long; she might have to shine the light and shoot at the same time. She counted backward from three. After one, she threw open the door, hit the floor on her stomach, pointed her rifle up and shined the light.

The room was empty. It was dark, but she could still see.

She stood, shined the flashlight in the corners, just to be sure. Sleeping bags scattered around. Some kind of food on paper plates. Camo fatigues. A ratty couch. It stunk of body odor and feet. In the far corner a partially open door led to another room. As she neared it, there was movement beyond the doorway. Something or someone lying horizontally. It looked like—

It was.

Brynn lay on a bed, hands tied in front of her, mouth stuffed with a rag. Her blackened, unseeing eyes rolled in her head.

Zady rushed toward her, desperate to end her sister's pain and suffering, to soothe her, restore her to the sweet, innocent, naïve person she'd always been. Zady reached out to touch the bruised body. But just before she did, a tremendous force hit the back of her head.

SATURDAY

88

Having cleared the rubble and debris on the way to the tomb, Larson's return trip was much quicker, though he worried if the cardinal would still be waiting for him and if Reddy would've stuck around the opening of the tunnel outside the walls of the Old City. Wiggling through the narrow passage at the bottom of the circular pool wasn't quite as awful the second time. He was extremely relieved when he stuck his head above the water-filled trench to see O'Rourke, who looked as if he'd just roused himself from dozing. Rubbing his eyes, the cardinal peppered him with questions.

"Did you find it?"

Larson sat on the edge of the trench, gulping air. He waved O'Rourke off but managed a nod. The wound in his side ached, but it was more a dull throb than a steady, sharp pain.

"Two coffins," Larson said between pants, making a V with his fingers.

"Akhenaten and his wife?"

"Yup. And I got a hair sample."

"What else?" O'Rourke asked.

"Many wonderful things," Larson replied. "Come on. I'll fill you in."

When they reached the Struthion Pool, Larson worried Mother Superior would be on the other side, arms crossed, foot tapping, waiting to box their ears. He was relieved to find the basement unoccupied. The old nun must've given up long ago and gone to bed. They crept up the stairs to the first floor of the convent and escaped into the night.

Larson tried to reach Zady several times as he and O'Rourke walked through the Old City and exited the Dung Gate in the southern wall. He only stopped trying long enough to call Reddy. The merc said to meet him by the tunnel in Silwan.

"Is he coming?" the cardinal asked when Larson ended the call then tried to reach Zady again, but she still didn't answer.

"He's at the tunnel," Larson said distractedly.

A cool night breeze blew as they walked south to the Palestinian neighborhood. Larson tried hard not to concoct worst-case scenarios involving Zady and her attempt to rescue Brynn as O'Rourke pestered him about the tomb. When they reached the entrance to the tunnel, Larson kept his eyes on the hole, expecting Reddy to stick his head out at any moment. He jumped when the young merc approached them silently from behind.

Larson quickly filled him in on what he'd found.

"But here's the problem. I can't get hold of Zady. I have no idea where she is, or if she's all right." He hesitated, wondering if the course of action he was about to propose was the best one. "I'm going to need you to take this hair sample to Egypt," he told Reddy. He wasn't sure he could completely trust the soldier (which is why he kept some of the hair he'd found in a separate bag) but his concern for Zady and Brynn was paramount. He had to get to them. He gave Reddy the address in Egypt Masika had said to take the DNA sample and handed him the two bags of hair strands.

"You can count on me, sir," Reddy said, zipping the sample in his jacket pocket. "Now let's get you guys outta here."

Instead of taking the tunnel to the airstrip, as Larson expected, Reddy led them to the outskirts of the neighborhood, to a small run-down house that looked as if someone had started bulldozing but lost enthusiasm before finishing the job. They entered through what was left of the doorway; the inside was a miniature junkyard: fragments of furniture, outdated appliances, car parts, and machinery piled high on the floor. Reddy hustled to a corner and started clearing a space. Just as Larson was about to ask what he was doing, the merc bent at the waist and raised a portion of the plywood floor.

"This leads to another strip," Reddy said. "By the time you get there, there'll be a plane waiting."

Larson's mind ran to familiar ground: suspicion, made worse by the fact that Reddy was armed. He doubted he could overpower the muscular soldier if it came to it. But he'd try if he had to.

"I don't think it's a good idea to fly out of the same strip," Reddy continued. "They nailed our location when we landed. What's to say they won't again? I'm gonna go back the way we came then head to Egypt. And if we split up, at least one of us will reach our destination—you know, alive and all. Speaking of which." He reached into his jacket and pulled out the pistol Larson had given him.

"Take it," he said, handing it to Larson.

Reddy gave him directions—this tunnel wasn't one-way— and told them not to be too alarmed if they bumped into someone, as the tunnel was used to get from place to place in the Occupied Territories that were surrounded by high fences and concertina wire, but to be prepared—he nodded at the gun— just in case. They were to follow the passage east for two miles, making the turns he specified.

Larson nodded at O'Rourke to descend first, then followed closely behind. The tunnel was a lot like the other one: big enough to stand, sparsely lit by bulbs casting wan shadows on the earthen walls. They didn't encounter anyone along the way. When they exited the tunnel, they boarded the jet that awaited them without incident. Larson took his seat and tried to reach Zady for the umpteenth time as the plane took off but to no avail.

89

Sleeping next to Brynn was wonderful, Zady thought, as she snuggled against her sister's shoulder. If she could only get rid of her headache. But getting up and taking ibuprofen took too much energy. If she just laid here and counted backwards from a hundred, it would go away, and she could fall back to sleep. Then when they got up, they'd join Aleister for breakfast. It was nice having the first meal of the day with her little family. She missed her parents, but Brynn and Uncle Al loved her very much. And that was a lot more than some people had. It wasn't perfect, but—

It was as if a calm, soothing record had been playing, and someone yanked the arm and ripped the needle across the vinyl.

She wasn't sleeping next to Brynn. She'd been unconscious from a blow that caused noisy vibrating pain in the back of her head, which, when coupled with the spot of her forehead that still occasionally screamed—like now—from getting rifle-butted by Garner Long, created a discordant symphony of anguish.

And Brynn wasn't resting by her side: she was unconscious and trussed, her body beaten and bruised.

When Zady tried to move, she found herself constrained as well, hands tied behind her back, feet bound. Though clothed, she'd been stripped of her jacket, which held her throwing stars and phone, the only link to Scott. She couldn't touch it with her hands, but she knew the knife she'd strapped to her right calf was also gone, felt its absence like a recently pulled tooth.

And the person sitting at the foot of the bed wasn't Aleister.

It was Lance Sterling.

She had no idea what time it was, what day. The windows in the little room were covered with dark fabric. The only light came from a lamp on the bedside table.

Sterling stood up and stepped to Zady's side. He leaned over and yelled into her ear, "Good morning, sunshine! Wakey, wakey, bend and shaky!"

The words scratched her brain, echoed in her head, like a person running their nails on a chalkboard in the middle of the Grand Canyon.

"It's time to commence the festivities," Sterling said. "And you won't want to miss out on any of the fun."

"Why are you doing this?" Zady exclaimed, trying to ignore the screaming pain that shot through her head when she spoke. "What the fuck's wrong with you?"

Sterling stood with his arms behind his back, head cocked, seemingly taking the question quite seriously. "Do you know what it is to covet? Have you ever wanted something so badly it consumed you? A desire that sharpens all your attention, all your energy, to a fine, excruciating point, like a bad tooth? But I suppose you can't imagine that. Everything you've ever wanted has been handed to you. People like you will never understand what it's like to want what you can't have."

"Hurry up with the soliloquy, Hamlet, and get to the fucking point," Zady spat.

"With Aleister gone, there're only two obstacles in the way of getting what I want. Obstacle number one"—he nodded at Brynn—"and obstacle number two"—he nodded at Zady.

"You couldn't have done this alone," Zady said. "You must've had help. And I'm not talking about those junior flunkies out there."

"I suppose it doesn't make any difference now. It was the Council."

"What the fuck are you talking about?" Zady said. But it was moot. Sterling was hell-bent on killing her and Brynn. Unless she could get loose and outmaneuver him, nothing else mattered.

"Never mind," Sterling said. He took his pistol out of his waistband and aimed it at Brynn. "First her, then you. I want you to watch. She got to see me kill your uncle. It's only fair you should see the last member of your family die."

Zady screamed.

The scream mixed with a gunshot.

Sterling slumped to the floor. Blood spurted from a hole in the back of his skull.

Zady couldn't figure out what had happened. Then she looked in the doorframe. The young man she'd encountered at DoveCo. stood holding an assault rifle. She tried to remember his name but couldn't, just stared at him.

"Johnson, ma'am. I followed you here. Had a bad feeling. Can't explain it. Just did. Sorry, it took me a while to find an opening." He stepped to the bed and undid Zady's restraints. She checked Brynn's neck.

"She's got a pulse," Zady said. She stroked Brynn's cheek and watched as her sister slowly opened her eyes.

"Hey, Zee," she said weakly. "Thank you."

"Shh," Zady soothed. "Don't talk. I'm going to get you fixed up."

"There's a key," Brynn said. "Under the mattress."

Zady felt under the mattress and pulled out a key on a chain. She knew immediately what it opened.

"How close are you parked?" she asked Johnson.

"Closer than you, ma'am."

"Cut the ma'am crap. You just saved our fucking lives."

"Yes, ma—okay."

"Carry her," she said, nodding at Brynn. "But first give me your gun."

Johnson handed Zady his rifle then scooped Brynn off the bed and headed out the door.

Zady pointed the gun at Sterling's dead body and emptied the magazine. She grabbed her crumpled jacket off the floor then ran to catch up.

90

Larson hadn't been able to reach Zady, and his anxiety rocketed with each passing hour the jet sped through the sky on the way to D.C. He tried distracting himself by thinking about the contents of the tomb, and what Masika had said, trying to figure out how everything fit together. But his mind kept returning to Zady.

Please, God, let her be all right.

It was early morning when the pilot announced that they'd reached the States. Not long after—or so it seemed—the plane approached the capital. Larson had been awake the whole flight, but O'Rourke had fallen asleep a couple hours ago and hadn't budged since.

Larson watched the sleeping cardinal on the port side. He felt guilty for having doubted him. The man had saved his life. Of course, his doubts were understandable; not all that long ago the Church had tried to kill him. Still—

The jet swerved to the left, jolting O'Rourke awake. "What's going on?" he said groggily.

"I don't know, but—"

Larson watched through the portside windows as a plane approached. The jet banked to the right, then sharply increased its altitude. Something sped past Larson's window. Then it registered: the pilot was taking evasive maneuvers against missiles launched by a fighter plane, what looked like an F-15.

Gunfire strafed the port side. O'Rourke was riddled with bullets before he could get out of his seat. Larson hit the floor, crawled on his belly across the aisle, and felt the cardinal's wrist. No pulse.

The jet plunged then leveled. Larson scrambled to his feet. He grabbed a parachute from the overhead compartment and strapped it on just as a missile tore off the starboard wing. The death spiral caused him to ricochet around the cabin. Struggling to right himself, he threw his body at the emergency exit, yanked open the door, and fell through.

91

Zady and Johnson brought Brynn to the nearest hospital. The thought of leaving her sister sickened her, especially as she was still drifting in and out of consciousness, but she was safe for now, and that's what mattered. Zady knew she should get herself checked out as well—a CT scan of her head was definitely in order, but not feeling any of the effects associated with a concussion, she decided to put it off and settled for eight hundred milligrams of ibuprofen. Right now, she had a strong feeling the key Aleister had given Brynn right before he was killed fit the lock in his office desk drawer. She hoped with all her might something inside would shed light on what was going on.

On the way to DoveCo. H.Q., Johnson drove while Zady tried to reach Larson on the burner, but he didn't answer, giving her two people to worry about. Since it was a little before 8:00 a.m., only a couple of cars dotted the parking lot when they arrived. Johnson swung the car behind the building, turned off the ignition, and looked at Zady.

"We shouldn't run into any trouble," she told him. "I don't think the rebellion was too widespread. First thing Monday, I'll hold a meeting, fire some people, then lay out where we go from here."

"Sounds like a plan, ma—Zady," Johnson said.

She smiled. "You're trying. Let's go."

She punched the code into the keypad on the back door. They climbed the stairs and made it to Aleister's office without running into anyone. The cars in the lot were probably house-keeping, their owners elsewhere in the building. After entering the code to her uncle's office, Zady headed straight to the desk. The key Brynn had given her fit the lock perfectly. She opened the drawer to find a sealed envelope with her and Brynn's names on it. Swallowing hard, she tore it open, yanked out two sheets of paper covered on both sides in neat handwriting, and started to read.

> My dear Zady and Brynn,
> If you're reading this, I'm no longer alive. There are so many things I need to tell you, things I should have told you many years ago but was kept from doing so partly by cowardice, but more so, by my love for you and the fear that what I had to say would cause you more pain than you've already suffered.
> I believe it is best to start with the most diffi-cult piece of information I must convey, and it concerns the deaths of your parents. At the time you were both little, and I said they'd died in a motor vehicle accident. It was the least painful way I could think of to explain their deaths, but it wasn't true. To this day, I don't know the identity

of the person who killed them—though I have my suspicions. However, and this pains me more than I can say, I must tell you the role I played in their demise.

I was once associated with a group that I believe was ultimately responsible for your parents' murders. To help you understand, I must delve a little into British history. It's the only way you'll understand why your parents were killed and the threats that have surrounded you your whole lives—threats I've tried desperately to keep at bay, and which have accounted for my silence until now.

During the reign of Henry VIII, a coterie of advisors formed a company that would become the primary means of extracting resources from England's far-flung colonies. The British East India Company was officially chartered in 1600, but its roots go back to Henry, and it lasted into the latter half of the nineteenth century. Originally a means of generating wealth separate from the Roman Catholic Church, it grew enormously powerful after Henry broke with the Church in 1534, after the pope refused to annul his marriage to Catherine of Aragon.

The company was created and run by a board of twelve men. The members, of course, changed over the years, but the mission remained steadfast: to lead Britain to global dominance, and help her to become the greatest empire the world has ever seen. Britain was, of course, the first country to industrialise and as the global capitalist market came into being, she was quick to recognise the valuable role this economic system played in oppressing the masses at home and the native populations in the colonies, ensuring the dominance of a tiny elite whose interests were furthered by what became known as The Council of Twelve.

But capitalism was only one component of this system of oppression. Christianity was the other. The Council recognised the Romans' brilliance in making Christianity the official religion of their empire. It was the first religion to hold out the prospects for immortality in a blissful afterlife, and to put forth the belief that the more one suffered in this world, the greater the reward in the afterlife. No greater justification for exploitation has ever been devised. One can see the coming together of these two forces—capitalism and Christianity—by noting that the King James Bible was issued in 1611, just a decade after the formation of the British East India Company.

By the dawn of the twentieth century, Britain's

supremacy was ending—the Boer War was her swansong. Early in the first decade of that century, Britain's status was eclipsed by the United States. As Britain decolonised and retrenched, the U.S. expanded, gaining colonies, building a powerful deep-water navy, and negotiating an end to the Russo-Japanese War. This expansion was undergirded by unfettered capitalism as epitomised in the development of Henry Ford's mechanised assembly line.

Considering these developments, the British Council of Twelve urged the creation of a similar institution in the United States. A secret meeting of the British Council with elite Americans from the country's most influential families took place in 1903 at St. Ermin's Hotel in London. The British and American Councils served as the basis of the oft-touted "special relationship" between the two nations, one that continues to this day.

Christianity's part in America's flourishing is well-known. It animated its founding documents, provided the pretext for Manifest Destiny, and served as the source of its spiritual power that emanated from the nation's capital like a shining beacon on a hill. After the Second World War, faith in Jesus fueled the country's battle against the godless communism of the Soviet Union and China, and as it currently does in the case of Islamic terrorism.

The story of Moses is at the heart of this American historical-religious experience. One need to look no further than the displays of the Ten Commandments throughout the nation's capital to see how deeply Moses shaped the United States and became America's prophet, if you will, used by pilgrims and politicians alike to found the American "promised land" and to help transform the country into the "New Jerusalem."

But archaeological discoveries in the early twentieth century threatened the Judeo-Christian narrative crucial to the American experience. The discovery of Yuya's tomb in 1905 was especially detrimental. This was because Yuya, a powerful Egyptian courtier who held several important titles, was none other than the biblical Joseph, as verified by items in the tomb identified in the Bible as belonging to the Hebrew patriarch.

This discovery, along with the development of genetics around the same time (not a coincidence), threatened the credibility of events in the Old Testament, especially the alleged rivalry between the Egyptians and Hebrews, that culminated in Moses' exodus. This is because Yuya's (that is, Joseph's) daughter, Tiye, married King Amenhotep III and produced Akhenaten. As a result, Hebrew and Egyptian royal lines have been united for centuries.

But after WWI something even more detrimental to the Judeo-Christian tradition occurred—namely, Howard Carter's discovery of King Tut's tomb in 1922. For the British and American Councils, this discovery was much more dangerous than Yuya's tomb. For the contents of the boy-king's burial chamber—not least of which was a crown of thorns and a treasured drinking cup—bore a striking resemblance to elements of the Christ story in the gospels. And if people were to suspect that Jesus Christ was the historical King Tut, then they might piece together the identity of Jesus' father: not God, but Pharaoh Akhenaten, history's first recorded monotheist.

The Council of Twelve is committed to maintaining the twin pillars of its power—capitalism and Judeo-Christianity—at all costs. Anything that threatens either of them must be eliminated. Your parents, my dears, were very much involved in uncovering the truth, so close, in fact, that the American and British Councils felt they must be eliminated. I was a member of the British Council at the time and tried to persuade the rest of the members that their deaths were unnecessary. When they refused to listen, I broke with the Council, left England, and formed DoveCo. The Councils in England and America agreed to leave me alone if I didn't disclose their existence or the truth they insisted on covering up. They threatened to kill you both if I didn't comply with their demands.

Most recently, I believe the Council instigated the terrorist attack by ISIS at the Great Pyramid. In the past, radical Islamists have threatened to destroy the pyramids as pagan monuments predating Mohammed, so it certainly looks like their work. Such an attack serves two purposes. First, it protects the traditional Judeo-Christian interpretation of historical events because something might have been discovered in the Great Pyramid that threatened this interpretation. Second, it creates a rally 'round the flag effect which reinforces the idea that radical Islam is the primary threat to American security, and that President Jenkins, the most Christian president to date, must remain in office.

There are three people who might be able to help you, people who I'm sure will reveal themselves now that I'm dead. The first is Cardinal O'Rourke. He is a friend of longstanding and has been my eyes and ears in the Vatican for decades. He is a good man, and someone you can trust. The second is a woman I met and fell in love with many years ago, but parted company with when I joined the British Council because I worried my involvement might jeopardise her life. She's had her suspicions about some type of cover-up all along. I won't disclose her identity here, but I am certain she will seek you out if something happens to me. Finally, there's Senator Madge Roberts. I had one of my men slip a USB drive in her mailbox that alludes to much of what I've said. I suggest you contact her immediately.

While these three people are beyond reproach, I'm having doubts about the fidelity of some of my employees at DoveCo. For reasons I can't fully explain, even my erstwhile closest colleagues are raising my hackles. In any event, be extremely cautious of trusting anyone.

Please know above all that I love you both with all my heart, however un-English that sounds. You were truly the pride and joy of my life. Of course, I'll never forgive myself for the part I played in the deaths of your parents, and there is nothing I could ever say or do to remedy that.

Love,

Aleister

Zady finished reading and tried, unsuccessfully, to swallow, and say something to Johnson, who'd been standing nearby, silent and still, as she read. Just then her cell phone rang. It was Scott.

"Where the hell have you been? I've been worried sick about you," she blurted.

"Up a tree."

"I know. I'm at a loss, too. Especially after what I just read."

"No, I mean literally up a tree. I got tangled in the branches of an oak when I jumped out of the plane. Lost my phone in the commotion. O'Rourke's dead. Did you find Brynn?"

"Oh my god. Um, yes. She's in the hospital. Tell me where you are. There's so much I have to tell you I don't even know where to start."

92

After picking up Larson in Leesburg, less than twenty miles from DoveCo. H.Q., Zady introduced him quickly to Johnson then called Madge Roberts. She offered her condolences—her niece's death was all over the news—and learned the senator was at home. From what Roberts said, she was finished with politics. Zady told her she completely understood but asked if she could come by and share news she hoped would shed insight into everything that was going on. Roberts agreed very reluctantly.

En route Zady filled Larson in on the details of Brynn's rescue and Aleister's letter. Larson absorbed everything as best he could then told her about finding Akhenaten's tomb and how he'd handed over the hair sample to Reddy, but had kept some strands, just in case. He shared his concern that he hadn't heard from him since parting company.

When they reached Roberts' house it was surrounded by security. Roberts came out to meet them and ushered them into the living room. Zady sat next to her on the couch. Larson and Johnson sat on comfortable chairs on either side of the sofa.

"Can I get you anything?" Roberts asked sullenly.

After everyone politely declined, Zady relayed the gist of Aleister's letter. All the while, Roberts listened, quietly composed.

"I knew Aleister was responsible for the thumb drive in my mailbox," she said, staring into the distance.

"What thumb drive?" Larson asked.

Roberts told them about the drive and its mysterious contents, which, she said, were much more understandable now.

"But that leaves so many unanswered questions," Zady said.

"Such as?" Larson asked.

"For starters, who sits on the American Council? How is it structured and who does its bidding?"

"Those are good questions," Larson said.

"But still," Zady continued, "if the DNA sample shows a genetic link between Akhenaten-slash-Moses and Yuya-slash-Joseph, and between Akhenaten and Tut, then the Egyptian and Hebrew houses have been linked for centuries and Akhenaten was the world's first monotheist, the product of a Hebrew mother—Queen Tiye, Joseph's daughter—and an Egyptian father, Amenhotep III. And if Tut is the historical person Jesus was based on, then the whole Judeo-Christian tradition has a huge Egyptian component. People need to know all this, Senator. Please help us."

"But what can I do?" Roberts asked.

"You can put me on the stand before the trial ends," Larson said. "The Jenkins administration is connected to all this, with or without the consent of the president. Even if there's not enough votes to convict him, what we've discovered must be revealed."

Roberts looked as if she were in pain as she considered Larson's words. But it was the first time he'd seen any emotion on her face, and he was grateful to witness this battle between her debilitating grief and her commitment to public service.

"I just wish I could get the audio file verified for accuracy. I'm sure it's genuine, but I need proof."

"I can do that," Zady said. "It won't take long."

"Yeah," Larson said. "She's a tech wiz."

"Well," Roberts said, looking at Zady then at Larson. "What the hell are we waiting for?"

93

"Since there are no questions from the floor, we'll move to a vote on the articles of impeachment," Chief Justice Buckner said from the Senate dais. "Let me remind you that—"

"Hold up just a minute," Roberts said, striding down the center aisle to her seat, dragging Larson by the hand.

"I want to call a witness," she said, still in motion.

Buckner's mouth formed an O. "The agreement was for no witnesses," he said.

"Wrong!" Roberts shouted. "The agreement was to postpone the decision on whether there'd be witnesses. We postponed it; now it's time to decide."

"As I'm the one presiding over the trial," Buckner said, "I declare the time to vote on witnesses has come and gone."

"Wrong again!" Roberts cried. "You're in my house and we're gonna vote with or without you."

Buckner looked at the parliamentarian for guidance, but he just shrugged. Neither man was eager to butt heads with the grief-stricken, unstoppable force from Virginia. Buckner thought for a moment. "Very well. We'll take a vote."

"Damn right we'll take a vote," Roberts said. She whispered

to Larson as the votes were being cast that a simple majority was all that was needed. The outcome was perfectly partisan: the fifty-one Democratic senators voted to allow witnesses, while the forty-nine Republicans opposed.

Larson was on. He stepped to the dais and Buckner swore him in. A chair was placed for him in front of the platform, and he sat.

"Please state your name and credentials," Roberts said, standing before him.

"Stop," Buckner said. "You don't think for one minute that you're going to question the witness? It must be a House manager."

Roberts glared up at the chief justice, feeling like she was on the brink of murder. "Oh, I'm as sure as hell gonna question this witness. You see, my niece is dead, and I have every reason to suspect the administration is behind it. Now either I go ahead and question this witness, or I start administering my own brand of justice. Anybody got a problem with that?"

No one did, so she proceeded. "Please state your name and credentials."

Larson's mouth was so dry he didn't know if he could speak. "Scott Larson. Ph.D. in religious history. I've taught courses in Rome and in the States, and I've written several books and articles, mostly on early Christianity. I'm a former Jesuit."

"A former Jesuit? Why did you leave the order, Doctor Larson?"

Roberts' eyes bore into him. He looked around the chamber until he spotted Zady, seated in the gallery next to Johnson. She nodded slightly when she caught his gaze. "Because they tried to kill me."

Murmurs rent the air.

"Order!" Buckner exclaimed, pounding his gavel.

"Would you mind explaining?"

Larson related the events from the time of Senator Walker's death in the confessional, when his old friend had gotten him involved in the murder investigation to the discovery of the testimony gospels in the Afghan cave, and the attempt that had been made on his life by his Jesuit roommate and others along the way.

"What are the testimony gospels?" Roberts asked.

"Contemporary eyewitness accounts of events in first-century Judea."

"And whose accounts were they?"

"Most of them were written by Jesus and his brothers, James, Peter, Joseph, and Judas."

A collective gasp came from the crowd.

"Are we to believe Jesus Christ, the Son of God had siblings?"

"Yes and no," Larson said. "There was a man called Jesus who had brothers named James, Peter, Joseph, and Judas, but they were all human. They familiarized themselves with the events of the Old Testament then set about making it look as if the prophecy of a messiah had been fulfilled, what the early Church used as the basis for the gospels in the New Testament. The resurrection of Jesus was a fabrication."

"Order, order!" Buckner shouted, pounding his gavel as the crowd erupted.

When things quieted, Roberts resumed her questioning. "Are you saying the early Church Fathers knowingly misled people into believing a man called Jesus was actually the Son of God?"

"Correct. The testimony gospels are what many came to believe was the Cathar Treasure, a treasure secreted off Montségur in southern France in the mid-thirteenth century the night before the Cathars were massacred. But those gospels weren't the real treasure. I've come to believe that the real treasure, possessed by the Cathars and other gnostic groups throughout the ages, as well as the earlier Essenes, was knowledge of a secret concerning the identity of a father and son, real people who existed centuries earlier, who were used as the basis for two of the most important characters in the Bible."

"Which biblical characters are you talking about?"

"Moses and Jesus."

"And who were the real people on which these biblical characters were based?"

"The Egyptian Pharaoh Akhenaten and his son King Tut."

The roar of the crowd was impervious to Buckner's gavel. People were on their feet. Larson feared a riot. Then something strange happened. The sergeant at arms, buttressed by a group of armed guards, began ordering people out of the chamber. No one was exempt: the news media, who left their equipment behind, the spectators in the gallery, even the senators themselves. Larson stood and looked at Roberts for guidance and she thrust a hand in front of her, motioning him to stay put, so he sat back down. The chamber was nearly emptied when the sergeant at arms approached Roberts.

"Senator, you need to leave now," he told her.

Hands on hips, Roberts eyed him up and down. "Excuse me?" she said.

"There's been a bomb threat."

"Let me guess: ISIS."

The sergeant nodded as more armed guards approached closely followed by Zady, who was carrying a camera a news station had left behind, filming everything as it unfolded.

"Yeah, right. If you want me to leave, you're gonna have to shoot me," Roberts said.

Zady pulled to the senator's side. "Me, too."

"Same here," Johnson said.

Larson stood. "And me."

94

"Make sure you keep filming," Roberts told Zady with the sergeant at arms and the guards watching from a close distance as the stand-off continued.

"Oh, I will. I sent Johnson to tell the senators to turn on their cell phones—he texted me that they're being kept just down the block. Some bomb threat."

"You ready to continue, Dr. Larson?" Roberts asked.

Larson nodded.

"So, as you were saying," Roberts said, "Moses and Jesus of the Bible are really the ancient Egyptian pharaoh Akhenaten and his son, King Tut? What makes you say that?"

"First, there's no evidence of a mass exodus of Hebrew slaves from Egypt. The ancient Egyptians were excellent record keepers; if something like that happened, there'd be some account of it. The exodus in the Old Testament better describes Akhenaten's flight from Amarna to Sinai when he was forced out by the priests opposed to the religious changes he made. He was history's first monotheist; he abolished the worship of all gods but one, Aten, and disbanded the established priesthood. Also, the Ten Commandments are based on the ancient Egyptian Book of the Dead, written centuries before the time

Moses allegedly lived. But what really convinced me is Akhenaten's tomb, which I discovered under the Temple Mount in Jerusalem."

"Go on," Roberts said.

"People have been looking for his tomb for centuries," Larson said. "And its contents demonstrated to me that Akhenaten was the biblical Moses. In addition to two sarcophagi, which bore the hieroglyphs of the pharaoh and his wife, Queen Nefertiti, I found a canopic chest that perfectly matches the description of the Ark of the Covenant in the Bible. Inside was a stone tablet, a double cartouche of Aten's name, which had been broken, exactly like the Ten Commandments described in Exodus."

"What else?" Roberts asked.

Larson's cell phone vibrated in his pocket. He pulled it out, read the text, then stuffed it back in his pants. "In the New Testament, in Paul's Letter to the Hebrews, he describes the contents of the ark. He says that in addition to the stone tablets, the ark held a staff, and a gold jar filled with manna. These were the objects I found in the chest in Akhenaten's tomb."

"I wasn't aware of a reference to the Ark of the Covenant in the New Testament," Roberts said.

"Many people aren't. And Moses is mentioned in the gospels, which sheds light on Jesus' true identity. The historical Jesus—that is, King Tut—was the Son of God: The Egyptian Pharaoh Akhenaten. According to the ancient Egyptians all pharaohs were gods. The fact that Akhenaten worshipped only one god, Aten, represented in the form of a solar disc, gave the term "Son of God" a double meaning. And items found in King Tut's tomb in 1922, including a chalice made of alabaster—a Holy Grail, if you will—and a crown of thorns, fit the story of Jesus. The contents of Tut's tomb were passed down over the ages and became part of the legend of Jesus Christ."

"But this is speculative, right?"

"Well, something else I found in Akhenaten's tomb provides

scientific evidence that lends credence to this view. Inside a gold jar was a ball of hair. The hair has been analyzed and I just got the results. The DNA shows a familial relationship between Akhenaten and Tut, whose DNA we've had for some time, proving their father-son relationship. What's more, it matches the results taken from a tomb found in 1905, from a person who appears to be the biblical patriarch, Joseph."

"Could you please elaborate?" Roberts said.

"The results show that Akhenaten was related to Joseph. Joseph's daughter, Tiye, married Amenhotep III, Akhenaten's father, and the couple produced Akhenaten. What this means is that Akhenaten, the first monotheist for whom there's historical proof, was a product of two great peoples: the Hebrews and the Egyptians. Both played an important role in creating monotheism, and one should not be privileged over the other. And there's more."

"Go on," Roberts said.

"To this day, there's a unique genetic configuration of male priests in Israel, the existence of a heretofore unidentified haplotype that separates them from the rest of the male population. The DNA evidence I mentioned shows that this haplotype is consistent with the DNA from Akhenaten, which means that rabbis are descended from the ancient pharaoh—a man who shared the blood of Egyptian and Hebrew houses. When Akhenaten and his followers were forced to flee Amarna, they journeyed through the Sinai, into Canaan, which was an Egyptian province at the time. This is most likely the exodus of biblical fame. Akhenaten's followers mixed with the Hebrew inhabitants and their descendants began the line of what became Jewish priests."

"So, you're saying the Egyptians and Hebrews haven't always been sworn enemies, as depicted in the Bible?"

"Exactly. Over the centuries, the connections between the Egyptians and the Hebrews have been lost or obscured. But if you go back, you can see them. For example, if you compare the

Hebrew alphabet with ancient Egyptian hieroglyphs, you can see the two are closely related. Also, the vestments worn by rabbis are almost carbon copies of the vestments worn by Egyptian pharaohs."

"You say this connection has been lost or obscured over the ages. Obscured by whom?"

"By religious and political leaders whose dominance rests on the traditional version of religious history. Each religion wants to be different, unique, the only possessor of the Truth, with a capital T. There's money and power to be had in stressing the differences among groups of people, despite all the things they have in common. This goes a long way to understanding the so-called 'secret' knowledge possessed by gnostic groups over the centuries. The Essenes, the Cathars, the Templars, and the Mandaeans most likely knew the truth, at least in part, about the origins of monotheism, especially the enormous debt owed to Egypt."

"So, in your view, Egypt played an important role in the creation of monotheism," Roberts said.

"Yes, but it's much more than that. A lot of what's deemed western civilization started in Africa. Greek philosophers like Pythagoras, Archimedes, and Plato traveled to Egypt to learn and brought their ideas back to Greece. And homo sapiens emerged in Africa. Why should it come as a surprise that civilization started there, too? To try to hide the African origins of so-called western civilization is another attempt to marginalize Blacks."

"But who do you think is behind this attempt?"

"A privileged, white elite. History isn't a series of accidents. Major events are often designed by a small group of people who benefit disproportionately from the existing distribution of resources."

"Tell me what you know about the Council of Twelve," Roberts pressed.

Larson recounted what Aleister had relayed in the letter to his nieces, without disclosing names.

"You have to admit, Dr. Larson," Roberts said when he'd finished, "that what you say sounds like the wildest conspiracy theory ever."

Larson considered for a moment. "I'm not sure that what we're talking about is a conspiracy theory. Plato wrote about something he called the noble lie. This was the falsehood at the core of every society, often political and religious in nature, that was necessary for its very creation. Every country has one. But no society can continue to exist based on a lie. Ultimately, the truth will out. If not, society will collapse, as we've seen throughout history. Ignoble lies can only be perpetuated for so long. The elite whose interests these lies serve suck the resources out of society until it can no longer sustain itself. Then it collapses from internal and external strife. The challenge we face is to construct a society based on truths—ones that can be measured in this world, like the number of people living in poverty, the homeless, the malnourished. We need to base our political decisions on what we know in this world, not on what might or might not exist in the next, and certainly not upon fables or delusions about what happened in the past."

"And if what Dr. Larson just said seems questionable," Roberts said, pulling a few sheets of paper from the pocket of her jacket, "may I present this: a transcript of a conversation between White House Chief of Staff Waverley Banner and a top ISIS official, where Banner gives the green light to an attack on the Great Pyramid of Giza. This is evidence of a force in American politics acting behind the scenes to sow strife at home and abroad. For those in doubt, I have an audio file of the conversation that has been authenticated."

Roberts read the transcript into the record, and with no further questions, Larson stepped down.

95

J ohnson had been busy ever since the Senate was evacuated. His first stop was Aleister's townhome down the street. Zady had given him instructions on how to upload her streaming footage of Larson's testimony so it could be broadcast to everyone with a cell phone, part and parcel of a project she'd been working on for months.

His other task was to make a copy of the articles of impeachment for every senator to mark their votes on, so the results could be tallied by hand. By the time he returned to where the senators were being held just down the block from the Capitol, they were watching Larson's testimony with reactions that ran the gamut of emotions: from shock to anger to enthusiastic agreement.

Copies of the articles had just finished circulating when Roberts, Zady, and Larson emerged from the Capitol and made their way to the group of heavily guarded elected officials. The deep spring sky was powder blue, without a cloud in sight. The fresh spring air was invigorating.

No one seemed to know what to do until Roberts stood before her colleagues and asked if any felt the need for more witnesses. Whether because of the bomb threat or the perceived certainty of their cause, all of them were eager for a vote on the articles. The next few minutes were spent in silence as the senators marked their sheets. The parliamentarian collected them. Roberts watched over his shoulder as he tallied the votes.

"How do you think it's going to go?" Zady asked Larson, as she continued filming.

"I hope it's a conviction, but I'm not optimistic. The other question is, how are people going to react to what I said in there?"

"Can I have your attention everyone?" Chief Justice Buckner said. "The votes have been tallied. The results are fifty-one in favor of conviction, forty-nine for acquittal. Without a two-thirds majority, President Jenkins remains in office."

A sullen, chastened Roberts was walking over to Zady and Larson when a shot rang out. The senators scrambled for cover.

Larson clutched his chest and dropped to the ground. Johnson ran off in the direction of the shot. Despite the danger, Zady and Roberts rushed to Larson's side. Zady's face was the last thing he saw before he closed his eyes.

96

At dusk in a clearing in the woods, Zady practiced her target shooting with Johnson's Glock. She could see the old farmhouse from where she stood. It had been in her father's family for generations.

"You're as good with that as you are with pointy things," Johnson said.

Soon it would be too dark to shoot. Zady finished unloading the pistol then policed her spent ammo. She looked around as if for something she'd never find then headed to the house with Johnson at her side.

Roberts had insisted on fixing dinner, and by the time Zady and Johnson entered the kitchen, she was slicing the ham. She'd already set the table, so there was nothing to do but take their places. Three pairs of eyes looked at the empty chair at the head.

Zady rolled her eyes and screamed, "Scott!"

Larson came in, slowly. The bulletproof vest had blunted the impact of the shot, but a black and blue welt the size of a lemon rendered the slightest movement painful. He lowered himself carefully in the chair. Isabelle rubbed against his legs.

Plates of ham, mashed potatoes, asparagus, and biscuits started circulating. It was cozy, like a home should be.

"Did you see the news, about the protests outside the White House?" Zady asked.

"I did," Larson said.

"We did everything we could," Roberts said. "The genie's out of the bottle. It's up to the people now. Maybe Jenkins will be forced to resign."

"What about the Council?" Zady said.

"That's a bigger problem," Roberts replied.

Larson nodded. "We don't even know who sits on it, or anything else. You think Masika knows more than she said? She talked about her friends, the people who helped us when we ran into trouble at the Israeli airport, and in jail in Egypt. Maybe they're better organized than she let on."

"Maybe," Zady said. "But one thing's for sure: people are going to look at the next big bad thing that happens in the world in a different way. They'll be more aware of the forces at work behind the scenes, less willing to accept bad outcomes."

"There's one more thing that's certain," Roberts said. "We don't have long to wait before the next big bad thing happens."

"Amen," Zady and Larson said at the same time then looked at each and smiled.